ALONE AT THE END OF THE WORLD

SYMPATICO SYNDROME WORLD: BOOK ONE

M. P. MCDONALD

MPMCD PUBLISHING

Copyright © 2020 by M. P. McDonald

All rights reserved.

No part of this book may be reproduced in any form or by any electronic or mechanical means, including information storage and retrieval systems, without written permission from the author, except for the use of brief quotations in a book review.

❦ Created with Vellum

ALSO BY M. P. MCDONALD

The Mark Taylor Series:

Mark Taylor: Genesis
No Good Deed: Book One
March Into Hell: Book Two
Deeds of Mercy: Book Three
March Into Madness: Book Four

CJ Sheridan Thrillers:
Shoot: Book One
Capture: Book Two

Suspense:
Seeking Vengeance

Sympatico Syndrome Series:
Infection: A Post-Apocalyptic Survival Novel (Book One)
Isolation: A Post-Apocalyptic Survival Novel (Book Two)
Invasion: A Post-Apocalyptic Survival Novel (Book Three)

Dedicated to frontline workers everywhere, but especially to all of my fellow respiratory therapists. If you can't breathe, nothing else matters.

ONE

Noah Boyle whistled along to the music on his playlist as he loaded his fishing gear into the back of his truck. He tucked the poles into a corner then angled them over the back seat, pausing

his whistling for a moment to curse under his breath as he jammed the wide end of his fishing net against the back seat, trying different angles until the pole end braced against the corner near the tailgate. He tested it. Perfect. It created a barrier and protected his reels from damage by the other items in the back. The tent, tackle box, and a box filled with his lanterns, flashlights, and first aid kit took up half of the bed, but he still had room—barely—for a cooler, his bear box, and his folded camp table. Fitting everything in the back was like playing real-life Tetris, and he continued to curse until he managed to fill every nook and cranny. He frowned as he looked at the second folding camp chair but then grinned when he found a spot to wedge it in.

He tried to figure out when he had come to need so many creature comforts. It had only been five years since he got out of the army, and back then, he'd managed to fit everything he needed into one pack. Now, he had lanterns, propane, a stove, and even a special pan just for popcorn.

No wonder Miguel had skipped out this time. He liked to poke fun at all of Noah's cooking gear. He teased that MREs were all he needed, not fancy sauces and spice rubs.

Noah sighed. He'd really missed Miguel this year, but his buddy had texted to say that he had a family emergency and to go without him—maybe he would join him later. But he'd never arrived, even though Noah had sent a text saying exactly where he'd set up camp.

The lack of reply left Noah unsettled. It wasn't like his buddy to ignore him unless he was having one of his bad times when the post-traumatic stress hit him. The family emergency could have triggered him. Noah paused, his hand on the bear box, wondering whether he should have pushed harder to know what was going on.

Since boot camp, Miguel had been more of a brother than Noah's real brother, Dave, had ever been. Noah shook his head, trying to push the last time he'd seen his brother from his mind. Dave had been found guilty of aggravated assault after he pulled a knife on a guy while in a drunken rage. Dave had been lucky that the other guy had recovered—otherwise, his sentence would have been a lot longer. Noah sighed and made sure the box wouldn't slide around, tucking a few towels in the gap between it and the cooler.

They'd made a pact. In order to get past everything they'd been through, they had vowed to always be there for each other. Unfortunately, even though Miguel had married and had his first child, the depression and nightmares didn't seem to be getting better. His buddy sure had picked a good one to marry, though. Noah smiled, thinking back to his friend's wedding. He'd been the best man and had given a silly, sappy toast, but it had earned him a hearty hug from Miguel and a warm hug and tears from his bride, Alexa.

The memory reassured him. Miguel was in good hands. Maybe the text never went through. Cell service was spotty in the Northwoods and had been even worse than usual for a few days. He checked his cell and was surprised to see that he had a new text. Smiling in relief, he opened his messages.

As he finished packing, he'd checked the cell every few minutes, but every time, it said "no service." He didn't even have the "emergency call only" message anymore. He worried about Miguel and his family emergency. Fear niggled at the back of his mind, but he wasn't sure why.

Miguel would surely have messaged him if something horrible had happened. They'd both been in high school during 9/11, and it had been their reason for joining the service after high school. If something of that magnitude had happened, Miguel would have texted him about it. Probably. Unless he didn't want him to learn about it via text. Noah sighed. No, even if Miguel just wanted to talk, he would have sent a text if he couldn't reach him by phone. At some point over the last two weeks, a text should have made it through. He adjusted his packing, tucking a box in tighter and making sure everything was as secure as possible. Soon, he'd be able to reach Miguel to find out what was going on.

He stood back, satisfied that he'd worked everything in the best that he could. He made sure that his gun rack held his rifle and shotgun. It wasn't deer season, but he didn't trust leaving them home—a rash of break-ins in his neighborhood had him worried his guns would be stolen. He really should have moved already, but he'd been promoted to executive chef and was hardly ever home, anyway. If he wasn't working, he was hiking, biking, or fishing.

The one weapon he always carried fishing was his nine-millimeter. He'd splurged on a chest holster so he could wear it comfortably even while casting. Luckily, he'd never needed to use it, but he saw unsavory types in the woods more and more often. Illegal marijuana growers liked the cover of the forest, and he'd stumbled upon an abandoned growing operation a few years before. The trash and damage they had left behind had sickened him. He'd reported it to the rangers, who had told him to be careful out there.

Noah shut the tailgate, opened the door to the back seat, grabbed his duffel bag from beside the truck, and tossed it into the back seat. He gave his campsite a visual sweep. He had disposed of what little was left of his trash.

The lake receded in his rearview mirror as he drove onto the service road. He loved his annual spring getaway—it restored his sanity. It was just warm enough during the days not to have to worry about snow, and mosquitoes had yet to breed. Another plus was that it was too early in the season for the summer crowd. He still had a little more time. It would take four hours to make the drive home, and he didn't plan on rushing it.

Once off the service road and onto the two-lane highway, his mind was still back at the camp. He relived his biggest catch, marveling that he'd landed such a large northern pike. After a quick photo of it beside a tape measure and with a scale attached, he'd released it back into the lake. He cooked the smaller fish for dinners, but there was no way he could eat such a huge fish all by himself. Damn, that had been fun. He grinned, tapping out the beat of the song playing from his playlist on the steering wheel.

A car far in front of him suddenly veered across the center line, and reflexively, Noah hit the brakes. The car swung back onto the right side but then drifted again before making a fast right turn down a side road.

Noah blasted his horn as he passed the road, shooting an angry glare at the back of the car as it weaved away from him on the narrow road and wondering what was wrong with some people. It wasn't as if another car had caused the other driver to veer. In fact, there were no other cars, which was weird. But it was only Monday, unless he had his days mixed up. Most people who didn't live in the area had probably left to go back to their jobs already, and a new group of outdoor enthusiasts wouldn't make the trek north until later in the week. Maybe it was just how traffic was up there.

He'd only gone another mile or so when he spotted a different car, which had gone off the road and was wrapped around an oak tree like a horseshoe around a spike. He slammed on the brakes and eased onto the shoulder, checking his rearview mirror, but no other cars were in sight.

He grabbed his cellphone and punched in 911, but the call didn't go through. *What the hell?* While he was still pretty deep in the woods, he was on a highway, and he was pretty sure he'd had service on the way up.

Well, shit. He had to do something. It crossed his mind to drive to the nearest town and summon help that way, but a quick calculation of the distance told him it would have been about a forty-minute drive.

There was no movement in the crashed vehicle and no sound at all. Noah paused, wondering when the accident had happened. The ditch went down at about a sixty-degree angle, and he took it sideways with his arms spread to keep his balance.

The driver's side door had slammed into the trunk of the oak, making it appear as if the tree had grown through the vehicle. Noah cringed at the sight. From the road, he hadn't been able to see the side of the car. The driver's seat had been obliterated—the tree had cleaved right through the metal of the door and roof. His heart hammered, wondering if anyone could have survived and afraid of what he'd find. He wasn't going to get into the car on this side. He stepped over the deep tire tracks in the ground and circled to the passenger side.

The few times he'd been in an accident, there were sounds. Radiators hissed, glass tinkled against the hood or dashboard, and hot, twisted metal groaned, but today, all was silent. There were no sounds of movement from within the vehicle—no moans, no whimpers, no cries for help.

As he moved closer, he gagged and covered his nose. He hadn't ever thought about how a car accident smelled before, but it definitely wasn't like this. He supposed he could recall various aromas from leaking fluids such as gasoline, oil, and antifreeze, but they didn't compare to this foul odor of rot. The stench filled his head despite his attempt to block it. He dry heaved and blocked his face with the back of his forearm, recoiling from the wreck as he identified the odor —*death*. It wasn't that he knew it firsthand, at least not from people. When he was a kid, a raccoon had died in his grandma's attic, and the stench had nearly made the house unlivable. She'd stayed with them while his dad and uncle had removed the carcass and cleaned it up. Even months later, on a hot day, there were still traces of the odor. This was a hundred times worse.

Despite his aversion, he crept closer, wondering what would happen if there was a kid in the back seat. The window had popped, but the frame was so mangled that the front passenger seat had been pushed up, the headrest half out of the window. If anyone had been sitting there, they would have been crushed. Dried blood coated the spider-webbed remains of the windshield, and a tree limb skewered the back seat, embedded in the cushion. At least there was no child's car seat in sight.

He squinted and took a closer look, wondering what was with all the packs of toilet paper. Had they been going to a summer home and planning to stock it for the season?

Noah retreated to the side of the road, drawing a deep breath as he scanned the highway and wondered where everyone was. Granted, it was midweek, but there should have been some cars through there by then. He had to report the accident, but his feet remained planted on the gravel. He guessed he could drive farther and check to see if he had a signal and report the accident then. It seemed cruel just to leave, though, as if the life behind the wheel didn't matter.

He stared at the destroyed car and hoped the occupant had died quickly. The thought of someone suffering for hours or days made him swallow hard. Switching to analytical mode, he wondered what had caused the accident. Possibly, the driver had fallen asleep at the wheel, or a deer could have crossed the road. The lack of skid marks didn't mean anything, as the gravel along the shoulder had deep gouges. He followed the gouges back, finding where one of the tires must have hit a drainpipe exiting beneath the road. A deep black mark scarred the pipe. He touched the mark, rubbing his thumb over it as he thought of the driver of the vehicle. Sighing, he returned to his car.

With his hand on the door handle, he glanced down the road the way he'd come, relieved to finally see another car moving toward him. He waved his arms over his head, crossing them in the universal signal to stop. At the very least, maybe they had a cell signal and could call the police.

The car came closer, slowing for an instant before swerving around him. Someone in the back seat leaned out the open window and chucked a bottle at him. Ducking behind his raised arms, Noah turned away, flinching as the bottle crashed in a spray of glass and beer a few feet away from him. Manic laughter faded away as the car sped up.

More shocked than angry, Noah watched until it disappeared over a rise. Shaking his head, he started to turn back to his car when a minivan heading in the opposite direction crested the rise. Noah crossed the grassy median, waving his arms again. "Stop! Please!"

The van slowed and swerved away from him, its horn blasting. Noah clenched his hands in front of his face in a "please" gesture, and the van slowed, stopping twenty feet to his left. He jogged up to the van as the window cracked open. "Thank you! Do you have a cellphone?" He didn't wait for them to answer because everyone had a cellphone. Instead, he gestured to the crash site. "There's been an accident, and my phone isn't getting a signal. Could you call the police and notify them?"

As he spoke, he moved closer to the minivan.

"Stop! Don't come any closer, man!"

Noah halted immediately. He should have known better. Being out in the wilds fishing for ten days meant his appearance was rough, to say the least. He hadn't shaved the whole time, and he still wore his stained fishing clothes. "I'm sorry, sir. I didn't mean to scare anyone. I just don't know what to do. I came upon this wreck, and I'm pretty sure the driver is deceased. It needs to be reported."

"There's nobody to report to. Where've you been? Living in a cave?"

A woman's voice floated out to him. "He'd be lucky if he had been."

Noah squinted, shading his eyes from the midmorning sun slanting off the top of their van. "Excuse me?"

"Dude, there's nobody to call. If I were you, I'd go back to wherever you came from. You don't look like you got the virus, so whatever you did to stay away from it, keep doin' it."

"Virus? What are you talking about?"

"Back up a few steps."

Noah complied, holding his hands out for the other man to see. "I'm not looking for trouble." He didn't want a confrontation and worried that's what the man was after, given the harsh tone of his voice. The weight of his gun still strapped to his chest gave him a smidgen of comfort, although his coat was zipped. If he had to reach for it, there would be a bit of an impediment. Part of his mind worked on a way to ease his zipper down without being obvious. He wore the gun around the campsite and while fishing. He'd never had to actually use it.

The driver's window slid down another couple inches, just enough for Noah to see the driver from the bridge of his nose to the top of the forehead before the window frame cut off the rest of the man's head from view. *He must be tall.* That was Noah's first thought.

The man eyed Noah as if he was about to address an idiot. "The *virus*! You know… *Sympatico Syndrome*?"

Noah looked around, almost expecting a hidden camera crew to pop out. It was too weird. "Sympatico… *what?* I have no clue what you're talking about."

"It's been on the news for more than a week!" The man rolled his eyes and looked at Noah like he was dense, which he was, at the moment.

"I'm sorry, I'm totally confused here."

The man searched Noah's face with his eyes narrowed as if he was trying to decide if Noah was smart enough to understand him. That didn't make sense to Noah because *he* wasn't the one rambling on about some virus. "How could you have missed it? Everyone on the planet knows about it." His eyes glazed for a moment before he added, "Or, they did. Until they all died."

Noah shrugged. Clearly, the guy was exaggerating. There was no way he could have missed seven billion people dying. "Well, it may have been on the news, but I've been camping and fishing for a couple of weeks. I'm on my way home now, so I'm a bit out of the loop."

The man's eyes widened. "You mean, for real, you don't know?"

"Dexter, *close the window!* He could infect us all!"

Noah ducked his head, searching for the speaker, intending to try to assure her he was free of whatever disease she thought he had. The narrow opening allowed him to see only a flash of pink pants. He shifted his focus to Dexter, if that was his name. "No, sir. I, *for real*, have no idea what you're talking about. What's going on?"

Hushed and angry conversation took place between Dexter and the woman, but after a few seconds, the man turned back. "Dude, you need to find a newspaper or something. The last one I saw was the day before yesterday, and it was a day old. The world is dying. There's a virus that hit about ten or so days ago. The world's gone crazy, and pretty much everyone is dying." Dexter jutted his chin toward the wreck. "That driver probably was dead before he hit the tree. That's how it happens. We only got through here by detouring as far east as we could on a service road, around a pile-up on both sides of the highway about a mile south of here."

"That's why there aren't any cars." Noah spoke aloud, but the observation was for himself.

"No cars and no people. Not alive or uninfected, anyway. You're the first person we saw in three days who seemed normal."

"Three days?"

Dexter nodded. "Yep. Three days ago, pretty much all hell broke loose. Stores were looted, and people died in the streets. Some died right on TV while giving the news. We stayed in the house as soon as we heard about the virus. I'm kind of a germaphobe. Didn't go to the store, didn't stock up. Nothing. Just hunkered down. But when the power went out, we packed up everything we could. We're headed to the state park."

"Camping?"

"Don't tell him more, Dexter."

"Hush, baby. He's not sick. I can tell." As if to prove his intuition, he rolled the window down all the way. Noah still couldn't see much of the woman, as she'd turned her head away and crossed her arms.

Noah met Dexter's eyes. "I haven't seen a soul for two weeks. Swear to God. Not until you drove up. Well... except, just before you came by, some kids drove by, but I didn't technically see them. Just saw an arm and heard their voices."

"Red sports car?"

"Yeah." He hadn't paid any attention to the make or model, but now that it had been mentioned, he saw it in his mind's eye. "A Charger, I think. Looked like some kids partying. Horsing around and stuff. They threw a bottle of beer at me."

Fear rose in Dexter's eyes. "Did any of it get on you?"

Noah looked down at his legs. There were no stains that he could see. He shrugged. "No. No harm done."

"You're lucky. Those kids probably had the virus. They could even be dead by now. It's the apocalypse, man."

"No way. They were full of life." Noah chuckled.

"No! You don't *get it*. The virus, that's what it *does*. People go crazy, laughing, partying, and having a great time until they just die." He brought one hand down on the window ledge of his car. "And *blam!* They're dead. Just like that."

Noah didn't know whether to believe the man or not. He shook his head. "That's... That's insane." But Cassie's message and Miguel's family emergency flew into his mind. No, they couldn't be related.

Dexter raised a finger to Noah but turned away from him. "Hold on a second."

His voice was quiet, but there was a note of urgency. Noah couldn't make out what they were saying, but their voices shot back and forth like a heated volley on the tennis court.

Noah scanned the highway again, hoping another car would come by so he could reassure himself that this guy was nuts. He had to be. The apocalypse wasn't real. It couldn't be.

"You really haven't seen anyone for ten days?"

Noah pulled his focus from the far distance and pinned it on Dexter. "Yeah. Every year I take a long fishing trip. Usually, my friend meets me, but he couldn't make it this year, so I went alone."

"This friend... did he say why he couldn't make it?"

Noah shrugged. "He had a death in the family. Someone on his mother's side..." A shiver rippled down his body as he recalled the voicemail from Miguel. It had sounded crazy. Well, not crazy, exactly, but panicked. He'd said his wife's family had died. Noah had thought he'd misunderstood or that there had been a car accident. He'd expressed his shock and condolences and asked what he could do to help, but Miguel had told him to go to the campsite, saying it was important that Noah go. Noah had taken that to mean Miguel would eventually meet him there, but Noah's attempts to contact Miguel resulted in messages that his phone wasn't available.

The door opened, and Noah moved back. Dexter stepped out. He left several feet between them, unsure what the man's intentions were. "Listen, my name's Dexter."

"I know."

Dexter raised an eyebrow.

Noah waved a hand towards the minivan. "I heard your wife say it." He guessed on the wife part.

"Oh, okay. But yeah, we haven't stopped for anyone. This apocalypse... it's for *real*." He raised his arms, rubbing his hands on his head, clearly spooked. "I know it sounds crazy. I mean, a week ago, I showed up to work at the warehouse and found it locked. *Locked!* Can you believe that? I was locked out of my own job! There was a sign saying that it was closed until further notice because of the virus."

"What did you do?" Noah wondered about his job. Why would a warehouse close because of an illness? A school, sure, but a warehouse?

"I went and got the kids from school—which was also about to close too—and got my wife from her job. We've been hiding in the house ever since. We didn't open the door for *nobody*. I even boarded the windows and doors. We watched it all on TV until the electricity went out yesterday."

"The electricity?" Noah was dumbfounded.

"Yeah. There's no more electricity. *Gone.*" Dexter's eyes welled, and he bit his lip. "*Everybody* died. Or enough of them that the plants can't run, anyway."

Noah's brother and niece and nephew flew through his mind. "What about the government? Aren't they doing anything?"

Dexter laughed then clapped a hand over his mouth, his eyes wide. "I'm so sorry. I'm not sick. That wasn't a real laugh. That was sarcastic."

"Um... okay."

"The government told everyone to 'shelter in place' so we wouldn't spread the virus. But they all got it too. And the way this sickness makes people act. *Whew.* It was like a freaking nightmare. Like *Dawn of the Dead* for real!"

Noah didn't know if the guy was exaggerating, but as his gaze swept the road, he had to admit the silence was eerie. A sudden urgency to reach his brother's house ignited in him. Dave might not have been the best brother in the world, but he and his kids were Noah's only living family. "Do you know of a road I can take downstate that isn't blocked? I need to get—"

"Haven't you heard a word I said?" Dexter cut him off. "The roads are mostly blocked by accidents, and unless you have a stockpile of food and weapons in your home and you live in a bunker in the middle of pasture hidden by woods, I wouldn't bother."

"As a matter of fact, I do."

Dexter stared at Noah and recoiled. "No shit?"

Noah chuckled but swallowed a full-blown laugh. "Whoa. I'm kidding. I live in an apartment in the middle of Madison."

Dexter's eyes narrowed. "You can't joke about things anymore. Somebody's liable to shoot you. I've seen it happen. Everyone is worried that someone else has the virus and shoots them down, and the police are dying just like the rest of them. It's kill or be killed in the cities."

The last traces of humor dropped from Noah's voice. "I'm sorry. Can you blame me for being a bit skeptical, though? I mean, I flagged you down just to see if you could call the authorities for that car crash, and you basically told me that the world has died. That's a bit much to swallow."

"At least you haven't been living it like we have. Now, best bet, take yourself back to your campsite if nobody saw you. Hide as long as you can."

"I wish I could, but I can't. I got a message the other day but only just saw it now. My sister-in-law needs some kind of help. If what you say is true, I need to get to her. My niece and nephew... they're just little kids." He couldn't remember their ages. He was a terrible uncle.

The look in Dexter's eyes turned to pity. "I'm sorry, man. I hate to be the one to tell you, but they're probably dead. Most everybody is, or they're gonna be soon. Especially if they're in Madison."

Anger surged through Noah, his fists balling. "You're full of shit, you know that? You're sick!" It couldn't be true. None of what this man said could be true. There's no way all of this could have happened in the mere two weeks Noah had been fishing in the woods.

"Hey, I get it!" Dexter raised his hands as if to push Noah away, but Noah hadn't moved any closer.

If what the man said was true, he wondered if he was going to get it just from talking to him.

Dexter continued, "You don't believe me. Whatever. I got no reason to lie. And my own family is at risk every moment I stay here talking to you." He motioned toward the car.

Noah drew a deep breath. Dexter hadn't given any indication that he was making up any of it. It was just such a fantastical story that it was hard to swallow. If he wasn't making it up, then it had to be true. "My sister-in-law doesn't live in Madison. They live in a small town. Probably about ten thousand people at the most."

"I'm sorry I'm the one to bring you the bad news, but"—Dexter's shoulders slumped—"chances are even if you make it through on the highways, your brother and his family have died."

Noah closed his eyes and bent forward, his ears buzzing, his chest aching. His brother was dead? And his niece and nephew? They were just little kids. He cursed himself for not taking the time to get to know them—he'd thought he'd had all the time in the world, but now, their time was gone. He groaned, clutching his middle. The buzzing receded, but his chest still felt like a dagger protruded from the center of it. He wondered why it hurt so much.

As if from a distance, he heard Dexter's footsteps recede then the slam of the minivan door. They were leaving.

That was fine by Noah. He wished he'd never met them.

Dexter called to him a few moments later. "You got camping gear?"

Opening his eyes, he straightened, feeling as though he'd aged ten years in the minute or so since the terrible news had been delivered. "Well, yeah. Of course." He drew in a ragged breath, turning away slightly and trying to bring to mind his niece's face from the last picture Cassie had sent him. She had always been good about sending pictures the old-fashioned way. She knew Noah rarely used social media so always sent him real copies. He'd looked at them, smiled at the cute kids, wondered how Dave could have fathered such adorable children, then piled them on a shelf. For years, he'd kept meaning to put them into frames but had never gotten around to it.

The other man shot a look at his wife before turning back to Noah. "Um... enough for two more adults and a couple of kids?"

Noah squinted in confusion. "Enough what?" He'd totally lost the thread of the conversation.

Dexter slid his window almost all the way down and jabbed a thumb over his shoulder. "We're clean. Haven't had contact with anyone except you since a week ago. From what they said on the news, before they stopped broadcasting, it spreads fast and quickly, but incubation is just a few days, so we should be all clear. And if you're telling the truth, you should be clear."

"I have a tent. It sleeps six. Eight in a pinch. But I only have one sleeping bag." He had a spare tent, too, but decided to keep that information to himself for the time being.

"Oh, we all got sleeping bags." Dexter shrugged, his expression pained. "Sort of, anyway. The kids used them for sleepovers at their cousins, not camping out, but they're all we have. No tent, either. I have a tarp and was going to create a makeshift tent if I couldn't get lucky and find an abandoned hunting cabin."

Noah waved a hand toward the surrounding forest. "Yeah, well, we're pretty much in a national park here, so you won't find abandoned hunting cabins. Those would have to be on private property."

Dexter's face fell. "Oh."

The woman leaned into view. "We didn't want to risk going

anywhere and getting supplies, so we only have what we had in our house. It wasn't much."

Noah rubbed his jaw, the prickle of beard reminding him that he must look like a wild man. Wanting to risk going into the forest with him must have meant they were pretty damn desperate, especially if they had kids. Nobody wanted to share a tent with an unknown man when they had children. Noah wasn't a threat, but they didn't know that.

He wasn't afraid of them, either, but he knew he was armed and could take care of himself. "Okay, listen. I gotta have more proof of this so-called apocalypse than just your guys' say so." It was a last-ditch effort on his part. In the time they had been in the middle of the road, no other cars had come from either direction. Even if there was a detour farther south, there should have been at least one other car coming from the north in the middle of a beautiful spring morning.

Dexter turned to the woman. "Did you bring the newspapers?" He turned back to Noah. "We thought we could use them to light a campfire."

A rattle of newsprint preceded the presentation of a wrinkled wad of newspaper. Dexter extended his arm, showing a measure of trust just in that gesture. Noah took it and saw the paper was from a midsize town he'd heard of farther downstate, near the Illinois border. The headline screamed, *"Worldwide Fear!"*

The article talked about how millions were dying around the globe. Noah raced through that article and on to the next one, which had photos of bodies piling up in the streets of Chicago, New York, London, and other major cities. His hands tightened, balling the edge of the paper into his fists. He fought the urge to throw it away. It was a lie. A hoax. It had to be.

But even as his hands clenched, he skimmed it, keeping one eye on Dexter. He wanted to say something and question him, but he felt as if every drop of moisture had evaporated from his mouth. He stared at him, willing the man to tell him it was all a joke or a horrible mistake. But Dexter's eyes brimmed, and Noah heard the wife blowing her nose.

Still not convinced, Noah turned to the inside of the paper, which featured more stories of the virus and how fast it had hit. There was none of the usual politics, general news, or even a weather report. It was all about the virus. Noah's knees buckled, striking the hot asphalt. The newspaper rattled in his hands as he struggled to make sense of it all. *Who is left? Is there anyone that he knew left alive? Dave, Cassie, Bella, and little Milo.* While he hadn't seen his brother and his family in a few years, it was only because… dammit, it was because he couldn't stand what his brother had become. Every time he looked at his niece and nephew, he felt guilty that he couldn't fix his brother's problems. That pain was too fresh and unprocessed. He pushed it into a corner to deal with later. It was how he'd handled losing good friends during combat. There was no time to mourn when the battle was still raging. And right now, there was a battle at hand. A battle for survival.

At least he didn't have a family of his own to worry about. For the first time, he realized why Dexter was desperate enough to trust a total stranger. He handed the paper back. "Follow me."

TWO

CASSIE BOYLE FLUNG BLOUSES AND SHOES BEHIND HER AS SHE DUG through the back of the closet to reach the gun safe. She hadn't been to the range in almost a year, and it had been about the same length of time that she had gone without cleaning the closet. She swore once, and as she swept aside a pair of hiking boots, she swore again, wondering why she hadn't kept the gun safe accessible.

Tossing hoodies, sweaters, and jeans out of her way, she hissed when her knuckles scraped metal. With no time to waste, she shoved aside the pile of blankets she'd stacked on top of the gun safe last spring. At the time, she hadn't given it a thought. The guns only ever came out when she was in the mood to practice. Lately, she hadn't been in the mood, nor had she had the time. She sucked a sore knuckle on her left hand as she stabbed the buttons on the safe with her right, punching in the code, her grandma's birthday.

The pounding on the door grew louder along with the yelling. He was drunk, which wasn't surprising. What *was* surprising was that he was pounding on her back door at all. He was supposed to be in prison, and she wondered what he was doing out already.

She pulled the Beretta from the safe, shoved a magazine in, then grabbed two more magazines, stuffing them in the front pocket of her hoodie. She burst from the closet, raced through her room to the hallway, and practically flew down the stairs. With her breath coming in great heaving gasps, she raced into the kitchen just as the back door shuddered under what must have been her ex-husband's shoulder.

"Damn, it, Dave! I told you to stay away!" Her voice shook—not much, but she knew Dave would hear it and revel in any sign of fear from her. He always had. The last thing she wanted was to give him any way to get under her skin.

"Why did you change the locks? I live here too!" Despite the onslaught, the bolt still held, and he hadn't yet managed to break in.

"No, you don't. You signed the divorce papers."

"That doesn't mean shit. I didn't have a choice. I was in jail, remember?"

"I'm not discussing it while you're drunk. Go away. I've called the police. They'll be here any minute." Sirens wailed in the distance, but she didn't know if they were coming her way. She'd been hearing sirens all day but had been baking for the big order that had come in last week. She vaguely wondered whether the cakes had survived the pounding on the door. The smell of vanilla and strawberry were incongruent with the violence taking place.

"Nobody's coming, bitch. They're all either sick or trying to keep sick people from spreading the virus."

The virus? She'd heard about some virus a few days ago on the news, but with all the work she had to do, she hadn't had time to focus on it. "The stomach bug?" She didn't believe a word he said. Since when did the police stop responding to emergency calls? Even a virus wouldn't stop them.

Even if they had the nasty stomach bug that had kept Bella and Milo home from school this week, the bug was more of an annoyance than something that would have kept a whole police department from responding.

Judging from the way her children had devoured the pancakes she'd made them this morning, they were back to normal and probably could have gone to school, so there was no way the police wouldn't respond. Besides, she could hear the sirens, which had to mean something.

"Dave, you have to go. You're going to scare the kids." She kept an ear peeled, listening for any sounds from upstairs. Thank god they slept like rocks. Both had somehow napped through their dad's assault of the door, and she prayed they'd stay that way. She had closed the door to their rooms on her way to get the gun.

Dave laughed, and a note of hysteria in his laughter raised the hairs on the back of her neck. Before she could process why the note scared her, the thick glass in the small window in the middle of the door shattered. She jumped back as glass tumbled onto her clean kitchen floor. Recovering, she leaped forward, snatched a small cast-iron skillet on the stove, and brought it down on his fingers as they poked through the window. It wasn't as if he could reach the bolt, but she didn't stop to consider that. If he broke this window, there was nothing to stop him from breaking the large front window and just climbing in.

After a scream and a string of cursing, he snarled through the gaping hole. "You're gonna pay for that. And the kids too!"

Any shakiness she felt vanished at his threat to the kids. Her voice steady, she called out, "I've got the gun, Dave. Now get the hell out of here!"

"You won't shoot me."

"I will, and with the way you broke the window, I'd be justified. *Now leave!* On the count of five, I'm going to start firing through that nice hole you made for me!"

He slammed against the door once more and then, from the sound of it, punched the heavy wood. "*Bitch!* I'll be back."

It sounded like he was moving away, but she didn't relax her guard yet. She'd learned the hard way that Dave didn't give up easily.

Fifteen minutes went by before Cassie peeked out of the hole that used to be a window. He was gone from sight. That he hadn't stuck around surprised her, but he no doubt took off to score some drugs. In the back of her mind, she'd thought maybe, *just maybe*, he would have used his time in jail to reflect on the mistakes he'd made.

Sighing, she shook her head. Of course, he didn't. She was convinced the drugs had permanently altered his personality. He'd overdosed more times than she could count and, if nothing else, he'd probably suffered effects from those episodes. She found it difficult not to feel sorry for him, even after all he'd put her through. He'd had a hard childhood, but his brother had survived the same abuse and hadn't turned into a monster. At least, he hadn't seemed to the last time she'd seen Noah, but that had been years ago. Back then, Dave had been doing okay and fighting his demons without drugs. If only —she shook her head. No. No more letting Dave off the hook because of his upbringing. It's what had always drawn her back before, but never again. The kids deserved better.

Straightening, she repaired her mental defenses. She had closed the door on him when she'd signed the divorce papers last year, and even if he showed up clean, sober, and repentant, she wouldn't take him back.

Only when she confirmed he wasn't at the front door either did her hands start shaking. Damn him and damn the drugs that had changed him. Tears trickled from her eyes as she set the gun down on the kitchen counter before she shot herself in the foot. Cassie scrubbed her eyes with the heels of her hands, swiping away the tears. Her reaction was a byproduct of her fear for the kids, not because she had felt anything for him. With the threat gone, she drew a deep breath, exhaling slowly.

It was hard to believe he was the same man who had been so excited when the twins had been born. She wondered where that man had gone. She'd stood by him for four years, waiting for him to return, but he was gone for good, swallowed up by anger brought on by the vicious hold drugs and alcohol had on him.

She put the gun on top of the refrigerator to keep it out of reach of the children, making a mental note to secure it in the gun safe again when she was absolutely sure Dave was gone for good.

The interruption had put her behind. Her dining room table overflowed with a dozen small cakes, each one nearly identical with their intricate decorating. The next day was delivery day, and she was just going to make it, if she could get the last four made and everything boxed in time. She'd lived, breathed, and slept those cakes. The payment on them would carry her through the next two months and give her enough capital to move to a commercial kitchen, if all went well.

Cassie entered the living room. Before she got back to work, she had to make certain Dave wasn't lurking anywhere near the house. He'd only done that once before, when he'd cornered her when she'd gone to take out the trash. Good thing her neighbor had looked out his back door when he'd heard Cassie's exclamation of surprise. That time, he hadn't ever come to the door and had claimed he'd just arrived and had heard the back door shut. He'd claimed he wasn't waiting to ambush her. She hadn't been sure whether to believe that or not but had let it go. That could have been a mistake.

Today, when she'd heard the first sounds of Dave at the back door, she hadn't known it was him and had looked out the front window and had spotted an unfamiliar older-model car with one panel the dull gray of primer. Confused, she'd wondered about it, but before she'd had time to run through possibilities, she'd heard her ex-husband's voice. It had to be his old junker. No way was it a coincidence.

Cassie froze as she peered between the curtains to the street. *The car is still there.* She instinctively turned towards the back door, just visible through the kitchen doorway, idly hoping that she hadn't somehow unlocked it. She let out a giant breath when she noted that the dead bolt was still engaged.

However, if the car was there, that meant Dave hadn't left and was around somewhere. That freaked her out more than seeing his face in the window had earlier. Racing back to the kitchen, she grabbed the gun and fought to keep her hands from shaking as she gripped it. The bastard. She should have realized he wouldn't have given up so easily.

Sirens still howled all around, but none were close. *Why haven't the cops shown up yet?* It had been almost a half hour since she'd dialed 911 on her mad dash up the stairs to get the gun. Maybe there had been some major catastrophe she didn't know about—a plane crash, a huge fire. The weather was too clear for it to be a tornado.

Cassie crossed the kitchen and move into the den, ducking below the windowsills as she crept up to the side window. The den bordered the driveway, and she could get a good view of the junker and the portion of the driveway that led to the backyard. Peeling back a corner of the drapes, she peeked out. Nothing. *Is he sitting in the car? Is he waiting for me to lower my guard?* He was mean and violent, but his style was to break a door, not hide behind it—most of the time, anyway.

She flinched at a sudden thump overhead, her heart lodging in her throat. In the next instant, she realized it was coming from Bella's room. Taking the steps two at a time, Cassie burst into her daughter's room—maybe Dave somehow slipped in through a window. It would have been just like him to use the children to get at her.

She found Bella perched on a miniature chair with a book in her hand and the large volume of bedtime stories on the floor at her feet. Cassie panted in the doorway, searching for the threat.

"Sorry, Mommy. I wanted to read."

"It's okay, hon." Willing her hands to stop their trembling, lest her observant daughter notice, Cassie crossed the room and crouched, pressing a hand against Bella's sweet cheek, caressing it with her thumb as she tried to paste on a smile. "Can you do Mommy a favor and stay in your room for a bit longer? I'm in the middle of making the cakes." She held the hand with the gun behind her back, praying Milo wouldn't emerge from his room, cross the hall into Bella's, and see it.

Keeping the gun hidden behind her, she sidled over to Bella's window. From the second floor, she knew she should have an even better view of the front yard, the street, Dave's car, and the driveway. She swept the neighborhood. Nothing. His car still hadn't moved. As she studied the street, searching for Dave, she noticed something was off. She'd been looking for movement, from her husband—ex-husband—skulking around the bushes or possibly trying to charm the older couple next door with some tale about locking himself out. Good thing she had told Alice the whole story. No way would she give Dave the spare key she kept with them.

While not a main thoroughfare, the street was a busy secondary street and had regular traffic. At least a few cars traveled on it every minute, but not that day. There wasn't a single person out and about. No cars rolled by, no moms pushed strollers to the park, and no one mowed their lawns or trimmed hedges. It was a beautiful day. Bikers used the side street to get to the bike trails. It was safer than the main road, but the only biker she saw was sitting against a tree halfway down the block, apparently resting with his bike lying beside him. *Is he resting? Or did he crash? Is he hurt?* Before she could decide, she noticed splotches of color dotting the lawns and driveways. The splotches looked like piles of laundry dumped from baskets.

Her mind tried to make sense of what she was seeing, but none of the pieces of the puzzle fit. Her gut twisted, and the hairs on her arms rose. A wave of fear like she'd never known swept through her, coiling in her belly and slithering up her throat, almost choking her.

Deep down, she recognized the shapes but tried to deny what they were. Her gaze leapt from yard to yard, sidewalk to sidewalk, front stoop to front stoop, bundle to bundle.

Her frantic scan of the neighborhood screeched to a halt on Alice's front walk. Only part of it was visible from where she stood, but it was more than she could have seen from downstairs. There was one more bundle on her neighbor's front walk that contained the same blue plaid that she'd seen on Dave's arm when he'd reached through the window.

Blinking hard, she rubbed the window where her breath had fogged it and flinched. *Dave.* The sidewalk ran red with his blood. She gasped. *So much blood! Is he dead? How can that be?*

She cast about for a source of the violence, wondering whether all those bundles were other people. None of it made sense. Other than the sirens she'd noticed that morning, she had heard nothing unusual. She'd had her music on as she baked. She always did.

Far down at the intersection at the end of the street, a car had crashed into two parked vehicles, but nobody was near the wreck. In the distance, a black column of smoke spiraled toward the sky. Beyond that, another column rose. Both were near the airport, and she stifled a scream. *Has there really been a plane crash? Is that why the cops haven't responded? But what of the other bundles? Are they all like Dave? How is it possible?*

"Mommy, what's wrong?"

Cassie spun from the window, pressing the Beretta against the small of her back, out of sight. "Nothing, honey." She smoothed her daughter's silky dark hair back, letting the strands flow through her fingers as she came up with an excuse for her behavior that wouldn't alarm Bella.

"I think there's a car accident at the end of the street. Nothing serious, but will you do me a favor and stay here and read your books until I come back? And if you hear Milo wake up, call him in here with you. I'm going to see if anyone needs help. Sit tight, okay, hon?"

Bella nodded, already opening her book again. "Okay, Mommy."

Cassie dropped a kiss onto the top of her head, thankful that her daughter was calm and could usually be counted on to listen. Milo, on the other hand, was a rambunctious little boy and pushed limits. She prayed he would sleep for the next few minutes. A quick peek in his door confirmed he was still sound asleep, his blanket clenched in his teeth—a habit from when he was a baby.

Less than five minutes later, Cassie locked the door behind her. She'd taken the time to shove ammunition in her jacket pocket and had strapped on the shoulder holster she'd received as a gift years ago but had never used. She even had her concealed carry license, but when the children were born, she'd had so much to juggle to get out of the house that remembering to strap on her gun had dropped to the bottom of her list. Today, it was at the very top. At the last second, she'd remembered to grab her cellphone too. An attempt at calling 911 failed. Earlier, her call had been answered, but now, it went to an automated message telling her that her call would be answered in the order in which it was received. She stared at the screen. *What the hell? Since when does 911 have voicemail?*

She crept as close as she dared to Dave. Her stomach churned, threatening to heave at the sight of the amount of blood pooled around his head. The edges of the pool were already congealing, and a fly landed on his nose and crawled toward one of his unblinking eyes. He was dead. There was no mistaking it.

She turned away and vomited into the neighbor's azaleas. A distant part of her mind tried to stay focused as she wondered what to do. Cassie bit her lip. Her feelings for her ex-husband had faded a long time ago, but she hadn't wanted him dead. *How am I going to tell the kids?* Hands shaking, she swiped the back of her mouth and tried again to call 911. Then she tried the non-emergency number.

"*Goddamit!* Why isn't anyone answering?" Swearing in fear and frustration, she knocked on the neighbor's front door, harder than she'd intended. "Alice?"

THREE

"Mom!" Ethan O'Connor rushed to the kitchen at the sound of dishes and something heavier crashing to the floor. He skidded to a halt, but one sneaker-clad foot slid in the puddle of blood already spreading from his mom's mouth. "Oh no... oh, *Mom!*" Ignoring the blood, he grabbed a dish towel from the oven door handle and knelt, pressing the cloth against her lips as if that could save her. He'd done something similar with his dad and his baby sister, Amber, only the day before. He didn't bother to call 911. They hadn't come for his sister. They hadn't come for his father. They wouldn't come for his mom.

His eyes burned, and he blinked as his mother's face swam in and out of focus. Three days ago, when the news was still on, they said it was bad, that it was the deadliest pandemic the world had ever seen.

Letting the towel drop into the puddle of blood, Ethan backed away from his mom's body. He had taken his dad's and sister's bodies out to the front of the yard, by the street, just that morning. That's where his mom had told him to take them. She'd heard it on the news earlier in the week. There were too many bodies for the coroner's office to handle, so a truck would be by at some point, and the bodies would be picked up, but nobody had come yet.

Woodenly, he grabbed his mom beneath her arms and dragged her through the back door and around to the front, carefully placing her beside Amber, satisfied that his parents seemed to be protecting her.

Flies circled the toddler's head, and Ethan swatted them away. "Get the fuck away from her!" He choked on the last word. It wasn't right to leave them at the mercy of the insects and animals. The day before, he'd seen a couple of ravens pecking at the body of a neighbor across the street. He couldn't let them do that to his family.

He dashed back into the house and returned with a soft, pink blanket for Amber—her favorite. She had left it on the floor of her room, which was the only reason it wasn't covered in blood like the sleeper she'd been wearing. He buried his nose in the blanket, a sob stretching his chest as he fought to hold it back. It smelled like her, a sweet mixture of shampoo, milk, oatmeal, and her baby skin. He couldn't describe it and hadn't even known the smell existed until he knew he would never smell it again. His eyes welled, and he swiped the tears with his shoulder as he gently settled the blanket over his baby sister where she lay, between his parents. It's what they would have wanted. A moment later, he spread his mother's favorite plush blanket over all three. *There.*

Ethan stared at the lumpy blanket. Maybe he should just lie down beside them and await his turn. He had no doubt he would succumb sooner or later. Everybody else had. Nobody had been outside on the block since the big party his dad had gone to see about a few days ago. There were some bodies lying by the curb, but not enough to account for everyone. The rest of his neighbors had probably died in their houses, and there was nobody left to take their bodies to the street.

He went to swipe at his eyes, but the dried blood on his hands made him freeze. He wasn't worried about catching the disease. In fact, he expected it and just wished it would hurry—he couldn't figure out why he had been left for last. He flung a stick at a black bird getting too close to the blanket. "Get out of here, you nasty bird!"

If he had been the first to die, then he wouldn't have to feel all this pain. It wasn't fair. The only consolation was that Amber hadn't been last. His already tattered heart nearly dissolved at the thought of her all alone. Yeah, maybe it was better that he was last. He'd been able to take care of them all. He only wished he wasn't alone at the end of the world.

He bent and tried to wipe the blood off on the grass, but some had dried between his fingers. He gagged, dry heaving as he furiously scrubbed his hands on tree leaves. He wasn't supposed to be cleaning his mom's blood from his hands. It had always been the other way around. She had always been the one to take care of him, to bandage his cuts and scrapes, to give him popsicles when he had a stomach bug and chicken soup when he had a cold. And now her blood stained his hands. She would never care for him again.

The dam broke, and Ethan sank to the ground, curled into a tight ball, and sobbed until there was nothing left. With puffy, burning eyes, he waited. Death would come. He hoped it would be as painless as it appeared. One minute, he could be alive and feeling wonderful, or so it had looked, and the next, he could keel over, dead.

It hadn't been an hour before that his mom had come into his room, a glass of wine in her hand. His mom rarely drank, so the wine glass had startled him, but she had just lost her daughter and husband. If anyone deserved to drown their sorrows, it was his mom. She'd offered him a glass, but he'd said no. He hadn't had the energy nor inclination to drink. Plus, he was only fourteen. Plenty of kids he knew drank, but he'd never tried it. He didn't associate drinking with drowning his sorrows, but he could finally understand why some people did.

He sat for hours, moving only to swat at flies and a few brave birds. Up and down the street, the only sound came from the cackles of crows and car alarms and sirens in the distance, although where the sirens were going was a mystery. They sure hadn't come his way.

His neighborhood was quiet. A few days before, it had sounded loud and boisterous, like a carnival. He'd wanted to go out and see what was going on, but his mom refused to let him. Instead, she had sent Dad to see what was going on. *Is that when he caught it? What about little Amber? How could she have caught the virus before any of them?* His mom had said maybe it was because she was so young, she didn't have a chance. She was probably right, but Ethan didn't think any of them had a chance, young or old.

Mr. Berkley across the street had been the first one on the block who had died, and he had been old. At least sixty. That was when life was still normal. Ethan had been mowing the lawn, earbuds in, when an ambulance had rushed to Mr. Berkley's house. Half the neighborhood had gathered to see what was going on, and Ethan had been as curious as the others. *Could it be that it had been only a bit over a week ago?* At first, everyone had thought the older man had died of a stroke or heart attack, but his widow told Ethan's mom that the doctors said it was some new disease that they had no clue how to treat, let alone cure.

Ethan's legs grew stiff, and he shivered as the sun lowered behind the trees, considering what the first symptom might be. The waiting was killing him. He almost chuckled in morbid humor. Every growl of his stomach or twinge in a muscle caused him to freeze and hold his breath. *Is it starting? Am I minutes from death?*

Is the headache I now have the first symptom? Or is it from crying? He hadn't cried in a long time before today, probably not since he'd flown over his handlebars and skinned his knees and elbows along with banging his head, which left a huge lump on his forehead. But even then, he'd only cried for a few minutes, and any headache was probably from smacking his head on the street. Still, maybe *this* headache was a symptom. And maybe the shivering was part of it, too, except he just felt cold. It wasn't like the time he'd had the flu. The cold he felt was no different from what he had experienced hundreds of times, standing out on his front porch, talking to his best friend, Colin. His mom used to scold him to wear a jacket, but he'd reply that he was only going to talk for just a minute.

The corners of his mouth turned up reluctantly at the memories of his mom finally opening the door and handing him his jacket but also admonishing him to keep the conversation short because he had studying to do.

His dad hadn't seemed cold or shivery when he'd shown signs of the virus. Instead, he'd become almost giddy, blasting old music from the seventies for hours right after Amber had died. Ethan yelled at his dad, asking him how he could be so happy with the baby dead in her crib. She hadn't yet been moved to the curb, and Ethan didn't yet know what the signs of the illness were. He'd thought his dad was being cold and heartless. Ethan had stormed past his dad and turned the stereo off—they couldn't waste generator fuel.

His dad had stared at him as if unable to place how he knew him. Then he'd opened his mouth, and blood gushed out an instant before his dad collapsed on the living room floor. That was the part that scared Ethan the most. *Will it hurt when the blood comes? Will I drown? Or will I die quickly, like Mom and Dad did?* Amber had choked a little, crying and gurgling for a few seconds before going silent. Ethan didn't think he would get that sound out of his head if he lived to be a hundred. That was a big if. He doubted he would live to see the sunrise.

Ethan guessed the sun had set over an hour ago. The birds and flies were gone for the time being, although snarling from down the block made him wonder what animal was down there. It sounded too harsh for stray dogs. *Coyotes?* He shivered again. It was just the cold. He shrugged. Okay, and a little bit of fear. He wasn't sure he could guard against coyotes if they wanted his family's bodies.

He dragged the back of his hand across his eyes, smearing tears across his cheek. *How much longer do I have? If I fall asleep, will I ever wake up? And if I do, will I be sick?* The train of thought was too scary to follow to the final destination, so he hopped off and let his mind wander to happier times. Just the month before, he'd been thrilled to make the traveling baseball team. It was his first time making the team after three prior attempts. He'd finally had a growth spurt and wasn't the smallest one trying out anymore. His mom always complained that she was going broke keeping him fed and clothed. Ethan sniffed, wiping his nose with the same hand he'd swiped across his eyes as he corrected the thought to past tense. She *had* always complained.

A soft breeze whispered through the treetops, and he craned his head back, peering up at the patch of sky visible between the trees in neighboring yards. He'd never seen so many stars before. Under other circumstances, he would have marveled at the sight of the Milky Way stretching across the sky, but it barely registered, and he turned as a snarl sounded closer than before. The lights were mostly out as far down the street as he could see except for a few small solar-powered ones along walkways. It was just enough light for Ethan to detect shadows scurrying from curb to curb, nosing the bodies, sometimes tearing into them. He vowed to remain on guard all night, and he did his best, standing a few times and jumping around. He hollered at the animals growling down the street and was rewarded as they moved in the other direction, but despite his best intentions, he fell asleep at some point, curled into a tight ball for warmth.

FOUR

Noah turned his truck around and drove back to his campsite. He turned on the radio. With the headlines still scrolling in his mind, he scanned for confirmation that what he'd read was true. Even so far north, he usually picked up a few local radio stations. Pressing the scan button, he willed something to come in. Anything. He wasn't picky. Sports scores, weather, farm reports. *Anything*.

The radio spun through all of the bandwidths on FM with nothing but static. Noah tried to tune in a station manually with the same results. *Damn it!* He slammed the heel of his hand against the steering wheel. *Think*. FM didn't carry well. That had to be it. He was well over a hundred miles from the nearest big FM station. He changed to the AM dial and mashed the scan button. For a moment, the static became louder, and he held his breath, but when he tried to fine-tune it, he lost whatever it was. He tried again and again.

As he reached to turn the radio off, a roaring started in his ears. A buzzing, really, as if a thousand angry bees had taken up residence in his skull. At first, he thought it was something from the radio, but when he turned the knob and the light dimmed on the console, he realized the roaring was inside of his own head.

How can this be happening? Or rather, how could it have happened? He screeched to a halt. He couldn't drive and process at the same time. Dexter's car slowed to a stop behind him, but the other man made no move to exit his car. He simply stared at Noah's bumper.

Noah rested his forehead against the steering wheel, clutching it so tightly that his fists ached, but he continued to cling to it as if by doing so, he could hang onto the past by sheer will. Letting go would allow the horrific reality in, and he wasn't ready for that. Not yet. Not until he was absolutely sure that Dexter spoke the truth.

His stomach churned as he processed all of the evidence. There was the newspaper, the lack of cars, and the decomposing body in the crash, his fishing buddy's messages at the very beginning, and now, no radio stations.

He raised his head from the steering wheel and glanced at his phone. There was still no signal, but that could be because of his location. There weren't even many farms up so far, let alone towns or cell towers. The soil was thin and sandy. It was good enough for vegetable gardens and grazing animals where it was cleared, but the towns were small—hamlets or villages, really. A bar, a church, and a gas station were all that made up most of them. He just wasn't in range of any radio signals, and his cell carrier always sucked up there. He'd planned on switching carriers when his contract expired just for that reason.

Noah glanced in his rearview mirror. Dexter and his family still waited behind him. *Why would the guy lie? And then why follow me if it all was a lie anyway? Just to see my face when I realize I've been pranked? Okay, maybe a good friend would do that, but a stranger?*

His heart thudded so hard it felt like only his shoulder belt was holding it inside his chest.

But if Dexter is lying, how does that explain the lack of other cars? Or the car accident just left for a day or more? Who pulls over when waved down at the scene of an accident and concocts a crazy prank? Nobody. That's who. Nobody in his right mind, anyway. He put the vehicle in gear and resumed driving.

He darted a look at the mirror again, contemplating why he was leading this man and his family to the only safe place he knew. For ten days, he'd been blissfully unaware that the world was ending. Not a soul had wandered into his campsite. Nobody else had fished his portion of the river. He had assumed there were other campers and fishermen but that they were farther up the river. It wasn't unheard of for him to go days without seeing another person at this time of year—the summer crowds had yet to arrive, and the winter snowmobile enthusiasts had left when the snow melted a month before. That's why he made his annual trip in mid-May.

If this is the apocalypse, where are all the preppers? While not one himself, a few guys in his unit had talked about preparations they were taking. That had been several years before, but one thing they had mentioned was having a bug-out location. Usually, it was someplace like a forest. He hadn't seen any preppers during his fishing trip, but he surely would have noticed an influx of military-type folks. *Could the virus have hit so hard and so fast that most didn't make it out of their towns and cities? Or are they hiding in their homes like Dexter's family had?*

The world is ending. The phrase crashed into his mind like a semi-truck through a barn, scattering his thoughts like straw.

The road narrowed, the edges of the forest encroaching on the pavement. He had always loved when he reached that point—it meant solitude. But the trees seemed thicker, darker, almost menacing in their appearance.

Noah slowed to find the turnoff, his thoughts so unfocused that he almost passed it when it appeared on his right. The road was hardly more than a muddy, rocky track winding through thick forest. He liked that because it kept the fancy travel trailers out. Only serious campers chose those spots.

A deep puddle forced him to slow almost to a stop as he went through it, his right front tire dipping down as if there was no bottom. It triggered déjà vu—he'd left the camp less than two hours before. Then, it had been the tire on the other side sinking deep into the puddle. His mood had been happy and content. He'd even looked forward to getting back to work. Noah missed the fast pace of the kitchen and the chaos that always managed to come together to produce fantastic food. And when a patron sent compliments to the chef, it made Noah's day.

But just like the truck going through the puddle, his whole mood had reversed. Instead of contentment, there was anxiety. Instead of eagerness to get back, dread filled him. If Dexter was wrong, Noah would be fired from his job for not returning to work, but if Dexter was right, the few people he loved in the world were dead. His friends at work, his buddies in the service—and this realization hit the hardest—even his family, such as it was, were gone. Every last one of them.

His eyes burned, and he drew in a deep, ragged breath. Reaching into the glove box, he found an old fast-food napkin and blew his nose. *Dammit.* He wasn't close to his brother, but damn, the pain of knowing he'd never see him again ripped through his gut, leaving him gasping. In the back of his mind, he'd always harbored the dream that someday, when they were old and gray, they would reconnect. His brother had been his only family.

Noah remembered the last time he'd seen his brother happy. It had been at the twins' first birthday party. They had laughed at how the babies smeared cake and frosting all over their faces, each other, and anyone who came close. *Are those precious children, my niece and nephew, also dead?* Bile rose in his throat, and he fought to keep it down. Cassie had flitted around, and Noah had complimented her on the beautiful cakes. As a savory chef, he'd always marveled at the creations the pastry chefs in his restaurant whipped up. He'd always wondered what she had seen in his brother, but that day, when Dave had been happy and loving to everyone, he'd finally understood. But now, they were gone, or in all likelihood they were.

It was too much for Noah to absorb at once, and he closed his eyes, pushing all the thoughts away. Later, when they were safe and camp was set up, he could unpack his emotions and deal with them then. Compartmentalizing was a skill that had allowed him to get through two tours in Afghanistan. It would get him through this too. It had to.

Taking another minute to collect himself, he finally stuck his hand out the window and gave a small wave to let the family behind him know he was ready to move on.

Noah passed his original camping spot. It had been a good one, but he worried it was too close to the highway. The road went at least another mile, branching in a few places before it petered out. However, there was a short distance between it and one that branched away just before the main one looped west. He'd noticed a well-used deer path that cut between the two roads and on to where the stream flowed into a lake. It was wide enough that, in a pinch, he could maneuver his vehicle to the other road as an escape route if needed. He turned. Tree branches brushed against the cab of his truck, getting thicker and closer as if reaching out to stop him.

This is crazy. He'd never contemplated an escape route before, except in the case of a forest fire, but if everything Dexter said was true, not everyone would have died. Dexter's family were proof of that. But if millions *had* died, as stated in the newspaper, then people would become—or had become—desperate. Maybe he had missed the panic. Not everyone could have died so quickly. *Could they?* His mouth dry, he took a swig from his water bottle, making a face at how warm the water had grown.

Whether they were still panicked or not, the last thing he wanted to do was to run into any of those people. No doubt some would bolt to the forest. It was his first instinct, and he couldn't be the only one feeling that way. Plenty of people were preppers now, and there might already be some in the forest. He wondered whether he should avoid them—and if they would avoid him. He hoped so. But if they didn't, he would have to protect himself. He had a few weapons on hand, but what he had was only meant to defend against an attack from a bear or a drug trafficker. Either would be a short-lived encounter. Noah had never planned to bring enough ammunition for long-term defense.

But he was getting ahead of himself. There was no reason to think that anyone was going to attack them. After all, other than Dexter, his family, and the crazy people in the vehicle that almost hit him, he hadn't seen a soul. And both of those encounters had been on the road. If they hunkered down in the woods, chances were good that they would never cross paths with anyone else. Noah pulled his truck as far into a copse of trees as he could, parked, and got out, waving the other car in beside him.

While he wanted to be away from any possible contact with others, they still needed to be near water, preferably running water. Although he had some purification tablets and a water bottle that had a UV light that killed almost every pathogen in the bottle, it could only purify about twenty ounces at a time, and he wasn't sure how long it would last. They would need to recharge it with the cars, and eventually, the cars would need more gas.

Overwhelmed as one problem seemed to lead to another, Noah

pushed the thoughts aside as he returned to the cab of his truck. *Get through right now. Find a camp, pitch tents, make dinner for tonight.*

Dexter pulled alongside and rolled down his window. "What's the plan?"

Noah pointed into the forest. "We can park just past those bushes. They should conceal the cars. Then we're hiking into the campsite. I want to go as deep as we can."

Dexter nodded. "Got it."

Sighing, Noah shifted into drive and cursed himself for appointing himself leader. The last thing he wanted was responsibility for other people's lives. He'd been there and done that in Afghanistan. He eased the truck forward, bouncing hard as the tire dipped into another depression. He went a little beyond the bushes then backed into a slot that concealed his truck from all but the front but left room to get his supplies from the back. It also allowed for a quick escape if needed.

He watched for a moment as the other car parked, copying his maneuver to back into the brush. It was a tight fit, but it would do.

Before exiting the cab, he gripped the gear shift. It was his chance. He could leave and be gone before they could find him. He knew that the road intersected the deer path again about a quarter mile ahead. Instinct screamed at him to flee. *What are they going to do, chase me like zombies in a B movie?* As he debated his next move, he watched as Dexter reached into the back seat of his minivan then pulled back, tenderly holding his daughter in his arms. The sleeping child's head lolled on his shoulder. Noah drew a deep breath and exited his truck even as his instinct still shouted, *What the hell are you doing?*

FIVE

Repeated knocks and pressing the doorbell produced no results. Alice and her husband were in their seventies but were extremely active. *Are they even home? When did I see them last?* Rewinding her recent interactions, she tried to place them on a timeline. It had to have been at least a week before. *Could they be out of town? They have a daughter and grandchildren down in Texas, near San Antonio. Had Alice mentioned going to visit them?*

Rubbing the heel of her hand against her forehead, she struggled to recall her last conversation with the older woman. The cute older couple usually spent a lot of time keeping their lawn immaculate. At times, it seemed as though they were out there catching the leaves as they fell from the trees before they even hit the ground.

In comparison, her lawn was a mess. It had needed to be mowed days before, but she hadn't gotten around to it. Cassie frowned at the scraggly mix of crabgrass, a smattering of bluegrass, and a scattering of dandelions. But there was nobody dead in the middle of it, which was something. Her lawn was the fucking jewel of the neighborhood.

A bubble of hysterical laughter slipped out as the random thought raced through her mind. Clamping a hand over her mouth, she stifled a sob. *What the hell is going on?*

She couldn't just leave Dave there. Authorities had to be notified. Dave's brother had to be notified. That's what she would do—she would call Noah. He was next of kin, not she.

Noah's number came up in her contacts. *Thank God!* The call wouldn't go through. Cassie opened the text box. Giving the news over the phone would have been hard enough. She couldn't send it in a text, but she could ask him to call right away. It was urgent. She composed the text, but it wouldn't send. Tears spilled down her cheeks, dripping onto the face of the phone. She wiped the screen on her jeans and tried again.

The sirens were farther away, or maybe there were fewer of them. Regardless, they weren't as pervasive as they had been, and that should have been a good sign, but instead, her stomach clenched. If she hadn't already been sick, she would have vomited again.

She scrubbed the tears from her eyes and drew in a deep breath, scanning the homes across the street. Just a few more houses, then she'd check on the kids. At least nobody was out walking around. Other than dogs barking and distant sirens wailing, it was eerily silent.

Cassie carefully skirted a dead mailman at one house. A dog barked, and at first, she ignored it, but then the animal must have stood on a sofa or chair, because its head popped up in the front picture window. She recognized a yellow lab she had seen being walked before. She'd even petted her a few times with the kids when they'd passed the owners walking her to or from the park. Feeling silly, she said, "Hey there, sweetie. Where are your owners?"

With the racket the dog made, it was clear the owners weren't home. Or—she glanced at the dead mailman—they were in the same shape. *What will happen to the dog if they're dead?* The scratch of toenails on the other side of the front door and the whining of the dog had her worried. She couldn't leave her in there alone. A line of ornamental stones created a border around a flower bed beneath the picture window. She thought about breaking the small pane of glass on the front door but didn't think she could reach the doorknob to unlock it.

Hesitating, she tried the doorbell a few times, standing up on tiptoe to peer into the small window in the door. Cassie heard the sound of toenails scrabbling across a wooden floor. The whining and barking escalated. Drawing a deep breath and vowing to pay for the damages if the owners showed up, she cocked her arm and heaved the rock at the picture window. It went right through but didn't shatter the window like she'd expected. *Damn.* She pried up another rock and threw it more toward the center of the window. This time, it hit the sweet spot, and the glass cascaded down into the bushes.

Before she could caution the dog and not sure how she could have conveyed the danger to a canine, anyway, she took a few steps back as the yellow lab jumped through the jagged hole. She crept up to Cassie, half-crouching as though waiting to be scolded. The stench that followed the dog out of the window was a mixture of death, urine, and feces. Gagging, she retreated a few more steps. The stench and the dog's desperation told her all she needed to about the owners. She knew what she would find and didn't think she wanted to know if the dog had disturbed the remains. She didn't seem like a vicious animal—she wriggled her whole scrawny body when Cassie tentatively stroked her head.

"I'll bet you're hungry and scared. I'm scared too."

The dog sniffed the ground and peed.

"Well, that's good. At least you must have had access to water." She cast an eye at the neatly maintained brick home and sighed. She bent, inspecting the dog for any cuts. "Easy there, sweetie. It's okay." The dog appeared unharmed and seemed healthy except for the scrawniness. She reached for her collar, but before she could get ahold of it, the dog bolted down the street.

"Hey, wait!" Cassie took a few steps after the animal but then stopped. She had to get back to the kids. Even as a breeze swept the scent of death away, it brought the smell of smoke. Something was burning. Fear and uneasiness drove her to abandon her search for survivors. She'd already left the kids longer than she'd intended.

Jogging back to her house, she dodged a delivery woman who had apparently deposited a brown smiling box to a front porch then promptly keeled over beside it. Cassie glanced at the brown truck parked in front of that house and tried to remember how long it had been there. She had received a delivery three days before, and everything had been fine then. She hadn't seen who had delivered it, though, and couldn't determine if it was the same woman. Maybe there was a manifest in the truck. Cassie was tempted to check, but it wasn't the time.

Keeping her house in sight, she tried a few more homes as she worked her way back to hers. Nobody answered at any of them, and when she found one door ajar, she called out, "Hello?"

With no reply yet again, she bit her lip, darted a look at her own house, and not seeing any activity, decided to risk it. Five minutes, not a second more. She pushed the door open wider. Taking a tentative step in, she halted, a scream frozen in her throat. Two kids not much older than her own were sprawled on the floor, their faces contorted into macabre grins. Blood splattered the walls, floor, and sofa as if someone had recreated the prom scene from *Carrie*.

Cassie tore her gaze from the children only to lock onto the unseeing stare of a man—the father, presumably—seated in a recliner, a remote still clenched in one hand, an empty beer bottle tilted toward his lap. A thick coating of blood covered his chin and had formed a pool in his lap.

A glance toward the back of the house and into the kitchen revealed the feet of a woman. She wore dress pumps as if she'd been on her way to work. Cassie backpedaled, stumbling down the steps, then flew across the yard, the urge to reach her own children racing through her. Even though they had been fine just minutes before, she had to know they were still okay.

Tearing open the front door, she raced up to the second floor, jerking to a halt just before she reached Bella's room. She couldn't panic in front of the kids. She had to be calm. Even as her heart thumped against her ribs, she drew a few deep breaths then entered Bella's room.

Bella glanced up and grinned. "Hi, Mommy. I stayed in my room like you said, and when Milo woke up, he cried for you, but he's playing now."

Milo had one of Bella's Barbies, gripping it by the head and using the feet like a dagger. He jabbed the toes into the back of the miniature armchair as if he was a matador stabbing a bull. Relief made her sag against the doorframe, and her next instinct was to hug them to her, but she didn't. She felt dirty and contaminated.

"Good job, honey. I'll be right back. Don't go anywhere."

Bella gave her a quizzical look, as if asking where she would be going on her own. Cassie smiled at her as she turned into the hall, the smile dropping from her face as soon as the kids couldn't see her. Hands shaking, she scrubbed her hands and face until both were so red that she looked sunburned. She swiped a towel across her cheeks, hung it to dry, then changed her clothes, tempted to burn them.

Maybe I should burn them. As she contemplated how she would do that, she caught sight of herself in the mirror. She looked like a crazy woman. Her hair stuck up in wet spikes, a few locks stuck to her forehead. She pushed it back, staring at her reflection, unseeing. *What had happened in the world? And how had I not known?*

She had to know what was happening. She needed information.

Telling the kids to play quietly for a bit, she headed to her computer. Her laptop sat on her desk, her last session on the Internet still open. She clicked the tab she'd opened to read the news. *When was that? Yesterday? The day before?* News of the virus had been elevated to the top story. She was able to view cached articles, but when she clicked on newer stories, she received error messages. Devouring all the news, her heart felt like it was about to pound right through her chest. *How had I missed all of this?*

What should I do? What do I have on hand? Her first priority was securing the house.

She went to her children. "You guys, I know I keep saying this, but it's really important. You have to stay in your room for a bit longer. I need to make some… repairs on the house." The lie flew off her lips, and she ignored Bella's wide eyes. She must have sensed Cassie's panic, but there wasn't anything Cassie could do about it now. As if propelled by a giant slingshot, she dashed down the stairs and raced out to the garage.

She threw a hammer and a few other tools into a big blue Rubbermaid bin then grabbed the sheets of plywood that Dave had bought before he'd gone to prison. He was going to finish the basement and make it into a playroom and had purchased all the wood and Sheetrock, but that was as far as he'd gotten. It had sat in the back of the garage since then. Some of it was warped, but she didn't care. It would do.

It took her an hour to bring everything she thought she might need into the house, including the hose. She glanced into Alice's backyard. The woman had put in her garden already. Cassie noted it without really knowing why, but her mind was whirling. Snippets of news she'd heard in the background while she'd been baking over the last few days charged to the front of her mind. A virus had been the big story, but it had been far away, or so she had thought, confined to some island or something. She'd dismissed it as insignificant, and with the huge cake order looming, she'd paid it little mind.

Her kids had been home with a stomach bug all week, and while she knew influenza wasn't the same as a stomach virus, she'd bundled the viruses together in her mind, assuming that if a virus had hit, that her kids had probably already caught it. It was just a virus. Kids caught them all the time. As they recovered, she had kept them home because they were only in preschool and kindergarten. One more day before the weekend wouldn't make any difference. And if she was being honest, she had to admit that part of the reason she'd kept them home was so she wouldn't have to ferry them to and from school when she could have been finishing the cakes.

Cassie checked on the kids again. Bella was playing with her stuffed animals. Cassie told her she was going to run over to the neighbor's really quickly and just keep playing. Bella was deep into some imaginary play world and only nodded.

Milo followed Cassie down the stairs, running his Hot Wheels up and down the bannister and making car noises. He grinned at her when she stopped at the bottom of the steps and turned to face him.

"I wanna go to the park." He loved the park, and it was a beautiful day.

Tears sprang to Cassie's eyes. If only she could take them. Blinking furiously, she dropped a kiss on top of his head. "Maybe later, sweetie. Right now, I have to go next door to tell Ms. Alice something."

"Can I come?" He leaped down the last two steps, nearly landing on her feet.

She squatted, smoothing her hands down his shoulders. "Not today. We don't want to give her your stomach bug, do we?" She had explained how he had probably caught it from a classmate, so he had a concept about that.

He shook his head.

"That's a good boy. I'll only be gone a few minutes. I need you to stay here for me."

His face started to screw into a pout. He was normally a very even-tempered child, but several days of being ensconced in the house had left him antsy. She couldn't blame him, but he absolutely couldn't follow her next door. Glancing around to find something to distract him, she ran through their movies—but the kids had been watching movies for the last few days. She didn't think any would hold his interest for long, so did something she hated to do and bribed her son. "I've got an idea. Want to play a game on my tablet?" She rarely let him play on it.

His eyes lit up, and he nodded hard, his dark hair flopping into his eyes. He needed a haircut.

She smoothed it back. "Okay, sweetie."

She crossed to her desk and unplugged the tablet from its charger. "Here you go." She pulled it back as he tried to grab it. "Uh-uh. You know the rules." When he was allowed to use it, he had to sit on the sofa. He wasn't allowed to walk around with it.

He raced to the couch, hopping onto it, turning as he did so to face her.

Unable to suppress a smile, she handed it to him. Within seconds, she heard the sounds of his favorite game. He would be mesmerized for at least an hour if she let him use it that long. It gave her more than enough time for what she wanted to do.

She rummaged in her junk drawer for the spare key Alice had given her. She'd only used it to take in the mail and water the plants when the couple went out of town. She dug through random buttons, batteries, miniature flashlights, and loose change before finally finding the macramé key ring that held the spare key.

Cassie paused at her back door, gripping the rough, beaded ring, the key cold in her hand. Guilt chipped at her resolve. *Am I blowing this out of proportion? What if Alice returns and finds me in her house?* Biting her lip, she wished she could remember if the couple had mentioned anything about going somewhere. She couldn't recall the last time she had seen one of them. Surely, they had been out recently if the garden was planted. It had only been warm enough for a couple of weeks. And if they left for more than a few days, they always told her, because God forbid their ficus tree should die while they were visiting their grandchildren out of state. *What if they're sick with the virus? Maybe that's why they didn't answer their door. Will I catch it if I speak to them?*

At the last second, she grabbed her rubber gloves from beneath the sink and retrieved a mask from her pantry. She had an allergy to pecans, but as a baker, she sometimes had a request for them. Her doctor told her not to inhale any dust from them, so she kept a few boxes of masks for the times her baking called for the nuts.

Cassie felt silly with the mask on and bright-yellow gloves pulled up to her elbow. *What would Alice think if she was home and answered the door?* She could say she didn't want Alice or her husband to get the stomach bug. Yeah, that was it. Drawing a deep breath, she knocked on the back door of her neighbor's house.

She hadn't expected an answer, and she'd been right. Fumbling with the key, she finally managed to get in the lock and turned it. "Alice? Frank?"

Everything seemed to be in order. That was a relief. She glanced about the tidy kitchen and moved into the living room. It, too, was neat as a pin. Relaxing, Cassie started to pull off her gloves so she could more easily remove the tight mask when she glanced through the open bathroom door. A scream lodged in her throat when she spotted Alice lying in a full tub stained red with blood. She was clearly dead. Sobbing, Cassie backed away from the scene. *Where is Frank? Why didn't he come seeking help for his wife? Why hadn't he called 911?* Or maybe he had and nobody had responded, just like nobody had come when Cassie had called.

She didn't want to look, but she drew a deep breath and stepped forward to see if she could determine how Alice had died. There was enough blood for her falling and hitting her head to be a possibility, but that didn't explain where Frank was.

Upon closer examination, Cassie guessed that Alice had been dead for a while—not that she was an expert, but the body was bloated, facedown. A murder-mystery buff, she had read enough murders that she knew that a day or so after death, a body would float in water. Cassie looked away, tucking her face against her shoulder. Poor sweet Alice. She would never want to have been found naked, bloated, and floating in her bathtub. Impulsively, Cassie grabbed a fluffy bath towel hanging on a rack and draped it over Alice's exposed backside.

Heaviness filled her, and dread weighed her steps as she turned from the tub and went in search of Frank. If he was alive, he would have helped his wife.

"*Frank?*" Her breathing quickened, and her hands were sweaty inside the hot rubber gloves. It took everything she had to force herself not to flee back to her home. It made sense. Her house was safe and secure, or it would be. She would make sure it was. Whatever had killed everyone on her block wasn't going to get her or her children. Panic began to bubble inside of her as she thought about this happening to Milo and Bella—whatever "this" was.

"Frank!" Cassie wanted to fling off her mask, fearing her muffled voice wasn't carrying, but some instinct refused to let her do it. She raced up the stairs to the master bedroom. "Frank?" Maybe he was inside and needed help. But the room was clean, the bed made. Alice liked to take long baths in the evening after gardening. She even confessed to Cassie that sometimes she read racy romance novels and had a glass of wine while relaxing in the tub.

That cemented her belief that Alice had probably died the night before at the latest. Her neighbor didn't take baths in the morning. She struggled to remember what Alice had told her about what Frank did in the evenings, sure she'd been told. Alice was a talker when she brought over baskets of her garden bounty. One basket jumped out in Cassie's mind. It was more of a bowl, a solid wooden bowl. Frank had made it, she recalled Alice telling her. He liked to work with wood and had a little shop in his basement. Alice had called it his "man cave" and giggled about it, as if she had coined the term.

Cassie had never been in their basement, as Frank didn't keep plants down there. She knew where the door was, though, because the house was a mirror image of her own. "Frank?" At least she was prepared, sort of, when she spotted his body lying beside his workbench. A piece of sandpaper lay beside his hand. A quick glance around showed he had spewed blood into a large trash can, as if caught by surprise, and had fallen, spilling the can in the process. A few empty beer cans had rolled up against Frank's body. Another can of the same brand sat on the workbench.

Closing her eyes and saying a silent prayer, she asked forgiveness for what she was about to do next. She didn't dare touch the bodies and didn't think anyone would come if she tried to call. Nobody had come to take away any of the bodies out in the neighborhood, and those were in plain sight.

Thinking of her kids and in a hurry to get back to them, Cassie grabbed Frank's toolbox, dumped all the nails she could find into it, then added his nail gun, staple gun, and drill. She found the chargers for the tools and hesitated. *What if the power goes out? How long will it stay on if everyone else dies?* She tried to push the fear aside, overwhelmed by the possibility that so many people might die that the power could go out. It wouldn't happen. It couldn't happen. *Could it?* When she saw a battery charger that could be used by plugging it into a car's cigarette lighter, she took that too. There were cars all up and down the street. She could recharge some things for a while, anyway.

SIX

Ethan awoke to a buzzing noise nearby and a tickling sensation on his nose. He bolted upright, swatting at the flies that swirled around him. His movement caused the flies on the blanket-covered bodies to lift in a cloud of black. Disoriented and confused, he scrambled back on his butt before he leapt to his feet. *What am I doing outside?*

But then the stench caused him to gag, and it all came back to him. His family was dead, and soon, he would be too. Retching, he took another few steps back, averting his eyes from the blanket. He wasn't going to be able to stop nature from taking its course, but he could bury them and not leave them to the scavengers. That much, he could do.

He turned, ran to the garage, and pulled out the garden shovel and a bright-blue tarp Dad had used to use to cover their snowmobile before they sold it. Ethan scanned the front yard, wondering where to dig the grave and whether he should worry about hitting buried cables, the sewer pipe, or the gas line. Then he shrugged. There was no power, so the worry about hitting buried power lines was gone, and if he hit a sewer, it wouldn't make much difference. If he hit the gas line, maybe it would spark and take him out. But the gas to the stove had quit the day before, so he didn't think it would make any difference if he hit it or not. It wasn't as if anyone would come and arrest him or anything. He wasn't sure what the punishment would have been before, but whatever it was, nobody was around to enforce it anymore.

It took him two hours to dig a hole long and wide enough for his family. It wasn't as deep as he would have liked, but a sewer pipe stopped his efforts. Frowning, he stared into the hole, which was about eighteen inches deep, and hoped it wasn't too shallow. He looked at the pile of dirt he'd tossed to the side and realized that he could always get more dirt from another yard and make a mound, of sorts, over the grave.

Sweating, thirsty, and hungry, Ethan moved to the front stoop and sat, panting as he waited for the light-headedness of hunger to pass. He couldn't remember the last meal he'd eaten—maybe it was it that peanut-butter-and-jelly sandwich the day before. His parents had a warehouse club membership and bought in bulk. They'd never been able to pass up a deal, so food, or lack of it, wasn't an immediate concern. Even water was okay, for the time being, and he had plenty of soda, coffee—which he didn't like—and even beer, although his dad had put a dent in that just before he died. It wasn't a lack of food or water that was an issue, but guilt for even feeling hunger and thirst and guilt for wanting to do something about it. If he really wanted to join his family, he would ignore his needs. Or better yet, he could use a rope and a chair and make it a short trip to meet Mom, Dad, and Amber in the hereafter, but Ethan couldn't picture ending his life—not intentionally, anyway. But if the virus wanted to take him, he was ready and willing to go.

An hour later, he used the back of the shovel to smooth the mound of dirt over his parents and sister. Then, with the wheelbarrow and shovel, he ransacked the neighbor's flower bed for large landscaping stones and mulch, using larger stones from the border of the bed to create a cross pattern among the smaller ones. Finished, he set the shovel aside and stood with his head down, willing some kind of prayer to surface from the depths of his brain. They had gone to church sporadically, and all he had were bits and pieces of prayers, so he abandoned that idea and just said his goodbyes, trying not to choke on the words.

Ethan plodded into the house, his energy spent as he stripped down to his boxer shorts as he went. His skin crawled from the memory of the bugs he'd seen while digging and the thought of what had been under the blanket. He reached to turn on the kitchen faucet out of habit but paused, wondering if there would be any water with the power out. Their well used a pump. That much he knew because his dad had to have the pump replaced a few years ago and had grumbled about it for weeks. Without electricity, the pump wouldn't work, but there was usually enough left in the hot water tank to get a little water pressure.

He knew that hot water was out of the question, though, despite coming from the hot water tank. Ethan grabbed a paper towel and kitchen cleaner to wipe out the kitchen sink and then plugged it so he could fill the sink while not letting any water go down the drain. When he turned the cold-water handle, water came out, but it didn't come out quickly. Glad he'd plugged the sink, he figured he could save what was accumulating for washing up again later.

His fingers slippery with dish soap, he scrubbed his scalp hard as if he could remove the stench of death over everything by simply washing it from his body. He rinsed into the stopped-up side, then plugged the other side of the sink and shifted the faucet, letting that side fill with clear water for whatever he'd need it for later. There was just enough water pressure to fill that side, too, before the water sputtered to a trickle then died. Ethan used his toe to open a bottom kitchen drawer, finding a neatly folded kitchen towel there, just as he'd expected. He dried his face and chest, sniffing deeply, drinking in the fresh clean scent of fabric softener. The smell immediately conjured up the image of his mom folding a basket of laundry while sitting beside him on the sofa as they watched television.

He tossed the towel onto the counter and pulled a bottle of water from the refrigerator, wrinkling his nose at the smell that wafted out. The lunch meat, milk, and eggs were bad, but he grabbed a jar of pickles along with the water, craving something salty.

Pickles don't go bad, do they? He opened the jar, sniffed the contents, and shrugged. They smelled like dill pickles. He fished one out and crunched it. Other than being warmer than he preferred, it tasted fine. Pickle in hand, he dug through the pantry and found a box of crackers with peanut butter. He used to eat them every day when he still took a lunch to school. Salivating, he tore into a package then shoved three into his mouth at once.

As if sparked by the food, his stomach growled, and suddenly ravenous, he opened a can of tuna and ate it right from the can. It clashed a bit with the crackers and dill pickle, but he didn't care.

When he finished eating, he sat at the kitchen table. *Now what?* Maybe it was the odd food choices, or maybe he was getting what everyone else had, but his throat tightened, and his stomach churned. Two days before, he'd had a family. Not anymore. He was an orphan in a dying world. *Is anyone left alive? This virus couldn't have killed everyone, could it?*

Ethan scraped at a drop of dried maple syrup on the kitchen table with the edge of his thumbnail. Two days before, his mom had made pancakes. The gas stove had still worked, and the box pancake mix had needed only water. That had been their last real meal together as a family. His parents had been worried, he could tell, but had tried to hide it. His dad had cracked a joke about something Ethan couldn't remember, but they had all laughed. Amber had gotten syrup all over her face, and her hair had stuck to it, creating a little mustache.

He drew a deep breath. He couldn't do it, couldn't replay the scene. It was too soon and his grief too raw to think of that simple meal a few days before and how they hadn't known it would be their last together.

Squaring his shoulders, he swept the dried syrup onto the floor. He needed to make some kind of survival plan—not that it would make much difference, since the virus would probably get him soon, but he couldn't just sit there, waiting to die.

Guilt that he didn't really want to die and join his family washed over him, but he thought of his mom and dad and knew they wouldn't want him to die, either. He closed his eyes, wishing he could ask them what to do. *Should I stay here and hope for help? Or go out and find it?*

As he opened his eyes and glanced around the kitchen, he realized that remaining there would be impossible. It would be torture. Every time he turned a corner or opened a door, he would expect to see his parents or hear his sister babbling in her silly baby talk. Squeezing his eyes shut, he pushed that memory into the same corner where he'd parked the pancake breakfast.

He had to find help. It had to be out there somewhere. *Help has to come, right?* The National Guard or someone would show up with water and supplies. They always did when there was an emergency, and what was happening definitely counted as one. A tornado had torn apart a nearby town two years before, and he remembered seeing FEMA trucks driving down the road. His mom had told them that they helped after emergencies, along with the Red Cross. He hadn't seen any FEMA trucks on their street, but maybe they were helping someone else. He bet the Red Cross were on their way. Somehow thinking of them close by, maybe a town over, made him feel less lonely. Soon, help would arrive.

His instinct was to turn on the TV and see what they were saying on the news, but he knew that there wasn't anybody left on television, and there was no power, anyway. He reached for his back pocket out of habit to check social media on his phone, but it wasn't there. The last time he saw it, it was charging in his room. The night before, he'd used his mom's phone to call 911, snatching it from her hands as she had stood there, apparently unconcerned about the deaths of her baby and husband.

That had been the scariest part. *Why hadn't she cared?* It had to have been the virus, because no way would his mom have acted like that. She had to have already been sick with it and he just hadn't known, what with dealing with Amber's death then his dad's.

He could see her standing there, furiously pressing on the screen. He'd thought she'd been trying to dial for an ambulance because even with no service, emergency calls should have gone through. At least, that's what he had always thought. But when he'd grabbed the phone, he remembered a game had been on the screen. *Could that have been what she'd been doing? Playing some silly game?* White, hot anger had pulsed through him. Little Amber had died only hours before, and his dad—her husband of eighteen years —had dropped dead with blood gushing from his mouth, but she thought that was a good time to play blackjack. She should have tried to help him. She was—had been a nurse. She should have known what to do or even how to stop them from getting sick in the first place. *Why did she let them die? Why did she let herself get sick?*

Even as the thought crossed his mind, he knew it wasn't fair, but he had to pin his grief on someone because a virus was too abstract. It had no soul. No body. It was invisible, and he couldn't even conjure up an image of Sympatico Syndrome. *What the hell kind of name is that, anyway?* Anguish loosened the tight knot of anger in his throat, and he couldn't contain it. He swept a bowl of plastic fruit off the table.

"Why did you leave me, Mom? Why did you all leave me?" Ethan stood as he shouted the questions, flipping the table as he did, not caring about the crash it made. Stepping back, his foot landed on something, and a plastic lemon squirted from beneath his heel. His ankle twisted just enough to cause a twinge of pain. The pain was nothing. He'd have shaken it off or hammed it up around his friends, but that was before. But fear and anger made him draw back his foot and vent on the lemon, sending it ricocheting across the kitchen. He watched as it bounced off the baseboard and spun like a top for a few seconds. *Who is going to yell at me about it? Nobody.*

His mom's phone lay on the counter where he'd dropped it the night before, and he narrowed his eyes on it. *Blackjack!* Jaw clenched, he grabbed the device and drew his arm back to fling it against the opposite wall. There was nobody to call. Nobody to text. Nobody anywhere. *Nobody.* His chest heaved, and he lowered his arm without throwing the phone. Instead, he cradled the glass-and-metal rectangle in his hands as though it was a fragile bird. Tears dropped onto the darkened face of the phone until he dragged it across his chest, smearing the screen. It was almost all he had left of his family. It contained hundreds of pictures and at least a dozen video clips.

His mom had constantly taken photos of him, Amber, and his dad, and she had even learned how to do a selfie. He laughed and sobbed at the same time as he remembered her attempts and how he'd tried to give her tips. They'd laughed over photos of her at weird angles, her focus on the wrong part of the phone, fake smiles, and how she swore that wasn't how she really looked. Only it had been how she really looked, and it had been his real mom, not that crazy woman who had died the day before, sometime between the tears she'd shed for Amber and the game of blackjack, only her body had still been upright.

Ethan tried to turn the phone on, but it was dead, just like everything else.

At least he could do something about it—he could resurrect the phone. Somewhere in his room, he had a solar charger he'd received as a gift last Christmas but had never needed to use. He hoped it worked as well as the ads had claimed. The box still sat on the floor of his closet, where he'd set it five months before. A bit of gift wrapping still clung to it via a piece of transparent tape. After skimming the instructions, he plugged in his mom's phone and set it on the windowsill to charge. *There.* It was a small accomplishment, but at least he could save the pictures.

Ethan found his own phone on his desk, where he'd put it on the charger a few days before. The power had been out for days, but since he hadn't used the phone at all, it still had a fifty-six percent charge but no bars. He walked around the house and out into the backyard, willing at least one bar to come in, but he had no service. He hadn't expected it to work but had to check. Still, he tried to text several friends. All of his messages failed to send.

The week before, everyone on social media had been freaking out, and he'd freaked with the rest of them. Then, within days, his friends had gone quiet on social media. He'd searched for information, wanting to present it to his parents as hope for a treatment or cure, wondering how long it would take to create a vaccine. But all he found were clips of death.

His mom had told him to quit looking at the clips, but the few he'd seen were seared into his mind. The worst had been posted by those dying who, in their crazy stage just before death, took morbid selfies with bodies in the background while grinning as though at a celebration. Even after he'd put away his phone, the last hours of the news on television had shown video clips of raucous groups rampaging through streets, breaking into stores, with some people dropping dead mid-clip and the rest of the group stepping over the bodies.

All of that had stopped, from what Ethan could tell. At least the sounds of music and nonstop blasting of car horns had ceased, but that could mean that everyone was dead. He decided he couldn't just sit in the house and wait around to die. He had to get out and see what was going on in the world. There had to be other survivors somewhere. *Will they welcome me?* Ethan bit his lip. He'd watched plenty of zombie movies, and everyone was always fighting everyone else. *Should I seek out others? What if that isn't a good idea?* But if he stayed put, eventually, he would starve, anyway.

If he found anyone, he would watch them for a while before he approached. It was the only solution he could think of. If there were other people still out there, at least some of them had to be friendly. The trouble would be to figure out who would be friend and who would be foe. He would just have to trust his gut. That was it. *Trust your gut.* Ethan drew a deep breath and noted the slant of the sun on his windowsill. It was too late to head out, but he would leave first thing in the morning.

SEVEN

Noah pounded the first stake and tested it. It would hold. The tent was a good, sturdy one. He had kept the little two-man tent for himself. When he was awake, he was usually outside, anyway, so it didn't make sense to cram them into the small tent, even though little Ava barely took up any room.

Good thing he'd decided to bring the small tent. He'd learned that lesson before, when a previous tent had been destroyed in a terrible storm. He'd had to cut his trip short that year. Since then, he always brought it, and he'd found it great for an overnight excursion from his campsite. It was easier to just bring the small tent rather than break down a whole campsite for one night. He was glad he had it.

His larger six-person cabin tent had been meant for him and Miguel with a divider to make it into a front room and a place for their sleeping bags. Other years, on colder evenings, they would sit at the folding table, play cards, and drink beer, a small heater making the tent comfortable. This year, he hadn't bothered with the table or the divider, but he'd used the heater one night. He still had plenty of propane. He moved around the tent, pounding in stakes with none of the usual satisfaction he normally felt as the tent became taut and sturdy. There was too much to think about. It threatened to overwhelm him.

Noah had barely had time to wrap his mind around the whole world dying, let alone dig down into the cause. He didn't know how the virus, Sympatico Syndrome, killed or why it would spread so quickly. He knew a bit about microbes, but only what he'd learned in culinary school after getting out of the service. That had been all about food safety, but there was nothing he'd learned of that spread so quickly or was so deadly. It didn't make sense that everyone could have been infected in just a couple of weeks.

Before he'd left for his fishing trip, it had been business as usual. There had been nothing on the news. Maybe the country was attacked with some biological agent. In the military, he'd trained to take precautions and had been ready, but that was when he'd been in a war zone. *Is this truly global, or was it some kind of attack to take over the country? How would anyone know? And even if someone knew, someone high up in the government, would they tell?* Everything was compartmentalized. He'd learned that much while in the service. Everything was on a need-to-know basis.

Noah had so many questions and no way to find answers. He worried that he had made a huge mistake when he'd stopped the family and that he would have been better off on his own. He swallowed hard—it was possible that he had signed his own death warrant. Noah thought of what he would have found in the nearest town. From the little he had been told and had read in the newspaper, it would have been horrible. He would have been contaminated. He'd have stumbled along, alone and clueless, become infected, and joined the dead.

What would I do if someone tried to join them now? Shoot them on sight? While he was no stranger to warfare, he hadn't ever imagined taking up arms against his own countrymen. He wasn't sure he could unless the person was an imminent threat. But unlike in Afghanistan, he had more to fear than bullets and bombs.

What little he'd learned from Dexter was that those infected became extremely social near the end. If that was true, and a group of friendly folks appeared at the end of the deer trail, he didn't know how he would react. *Even worse, what if Dexter or someone in his family became cheerful and sociable?* For all he knew, that's how they normally were before the virus hit, and feeling safe might bring out their natural personalities, but he could mistake that for infection—and they could do the same with him. While he loved the solitude of the forest, he liked being around people too. Not for long periods of time, but give him a tall beer and an audience, and he could spin a good story. He only prayed his friendly nature wouldn't be the death of him. Noah already cursed that he hadn't kept strict quarantine. He could only blame his shock at learning the news. He hadn't been thinking clearly, but as his mind sorted everything out, he knew one thing for certain.

He glanced at Dexter as the man crossed behind him, carrying the portable generator. So far, he liked the guy and his family. The little girl was cute and well-behaved, especially considering the circumstances, and the son was, well, he was a young teen, and Noah supposed he was behaving as normally as possible, not that he knew what normal even looked like in such a situation. He would give the kid the benefit of the doubt—there wasn't much of an alternative. They had no tent, and he doubted they had much experience camping, let alone foraging in the woods for food. If they survived the disease, they would need his help to survive in their new environment. He would hate for them to show signs of the disease.

"Why are we trusting that man?"

Noah paused before rounding the corner of the tent, stiffening as he heard the fear in the Vivian's voice. The couple was in front of the tent and obviously didn't know he was just around the corner. He squared his shoulders and continued rounding the side of the tent.

"I get it. You don't trust me." His jaw clenched, and it took conscious effort to relax it. "But the way I see it, I'm the one who is taking the bigger risk. I'm sharing my supplies"—he waved a hand towards the tent and cookware set up near where the fire would be —"and even setting up camp for you. For all I know, you could be planning on—" He broke off when their daughter passed them. He'd been about to accuse the couple of planning on killing him, but at the last second, he realized how terrible that would sound. He didn't want the little girl to feel like he thought her parents were murderers. He drew a deep breath. "Listen, I have nothing against you folks. You may have saved my life by warning me, so I'm willing to share and help. Just... just give me the benefit of the doubt, please."

Dexter nodded. "And you do the same for us."

Vivian's eyes narrowed as she listened to Noah, but her regard seemed more speculative than hostile. "I'll give you the benefit of the doubt... for now." She nodded at him. "So, if you don't mind, I'm going to get things set up."

Noah motioned toward the door in the tent. "Have at it." It came out sounding more flippant than he'd intended, but he only shrugged when Dexter followed his wife into the tent, wearing a look that Noah could only describe as sheepish.

Arms crossed, Noah studied the flimsy door as it bounced against the door frame. *Where does she come off, treating me like I owe her something?* He debated leaving the family to their own devices. They weren't his concern. He would have better odds of surviving on his own, and he could see about Dave and his little family. His breath caught. He should go immediately, take his little tent, leave them the big one, and just head to Dave's house.

Still fuming, he saw Ava struggling to carry a box from the car to the tent. The box was nearly as big as she was, and despite his anger at Vivian, he couldn't hold on to the feeling. The little girl's determination, her tongue poking out of the corner of her mouth, elicited his admiration.

The cardboard box almost slipped from Ava's grip as she approached the door, and Noah instinctively jumped forward. "Whoa! Let me help you." Steadying the box, he peered at the contents, biting back a comment as he counted about a dozen boxes of mac and cheese. Those would last a few days at most. He wondered what else they had in the way of food.

He glanced at Ava, who returned the look with wide eyes as she tried to wrest the box away from him. "It's okay. I just thought you were going to drop it." Noah smiled, trying to seem unthreatening, but the girl must have picked up on her mother's fear and shied away. A second later, she darted back to the car.

She was scared, and he couldn't blame her. He was a stranger, and even if she hadn't heard the angry exchange he'd had with her mother, she probably sensed the tension in the air. She looked only a little older than his niece, Bella, had appeared in her latest school photo.

If he left, there was no telling what would happen to Ava. She was here and alive. If he left, there was no guarantee her parents would be able to keep her safe. Dexter, whose last name Noah had learned was Jackson, worked as a supervisor in a warehouse. He wasn't sure what

Vivian's job skills were, but it sounded like she worked in an office, from what he'd overheard. If he left, he could be sentencing the kids to death. He could stay and help the kids he knew were alive or leave to find out for certain if Bella and Milo were still alive, even though the odds weren't in their favor.

Noah sighed and took another look inside the box. In addition to the mac and cheese, there was powdered milk, oil, shortening, and envelopes of rice with veggies as side dishes. Altogether, it wasn't more than a few days of supplies, and it would be only if they used fresh ingredients to stretch it. He shook his head and hoped the fishing remained good. The woods had plenty to offer for those who knew where to look, but something told him the family weren't regular campers, let alone survivalists. Not that he considered himself a survivalist, either, but between his military training, his years of hunting and fishing experience, and his knowledge of food as a chef, he didn't think he'd have much trouble securing enough to eat for himself. Only it seemed he would have to show them how to acquire food too.

That settled it. His couldn't leave them just yet. No matter his feelings for the mother, there was no way could he leave a couple of kids to starve to death.

The oil was what had unbalanced the box, and he reached in, shifting it to another spot before turning to the tent. He stood awkwardly outside, questioning whether he should just go in. He'd told Dexter it was for his family's use, but it was still Noah's tent.

After hesitating for a moment, he decided it was probably better to just assume the family wouldn't feel comfortable with him barging in any time he wanted, so Noah cleared his throat right outside the entrance, trying to ignore the low-pitched but heated conversation near the back of the tent. As he adjusted his grip on the box, he realized he should probably be glad he couldn't make out what they were saying. "Uh, hello?"

The hushed conversation ceased as if Noah had thrown a switch. He squinted through the mesh, making out a shadow nearing the door. Vivian stood on the other side, her eyes shifting from Noah's eyes to the box as if trying to decide if he was helping or whether she should snatch it from him trying to steal it. Noah lifted the box slightly. "Your daughter was having trouble with it, so I helped her out. Here you go." He thrust it forward.

The door opened, and Vivian took a step out, taking the box with a mumbled "thank you." Then she scanned the area. "Where'd Ava go?"

Noah stepped back and turned towards their car. "I'm not sure. She was just here a second ago."

Shooting Noah an accusing look, Vivian dropped the box just inside the tent and rushed out. "Ava! *Ava!*"

"Right here, Mama!" Ava emerged from behind a bush, tugging at the waistband of her leggings. "I had to go to the bathroom, and Jalen said I had to go in the bushes."

Vivian sighed and shot a look around. "Where is your brother?"

Ava pointed beyond the bush. "He's down by the stream, trying to catch a frog."

Noah hid a smile. "Can I help you folks get anything else set up? If not, I'm going to get my own tent up then build a fire."

Vivian nodded, seeming to dismiss him, then focused on Ava. "You run down there and tell him to get back here this instant. There's a lot of work to be done."

As Ava headed toward her brother, Noah winced at the close proximity to where she had relieved herself and the stream. What they needed to do was get some kind of latrine set up. As the saying went, "don't shit where you eat." Although he was pretty sure it had another meaning, they needed to take it literally. He'd bring that up after dinner.

Vivian called to Ava's retreating back as the girl paused to pick up a stick, "And don't you be taking your good old time, neither! We have a lot to do!"

Noah skedaddled—her tone, while not directed at him, still dredged up memories of his own mother scolding him for goofing off. *Poor Ava*. Noah smiled.

EIGHT

"Hey, guys! I'm back!" Cassie kicked off her shoes, leaving them outside, then entered, dumping her load of tools by the basement door.

The sound of music from a favorite movie drifted out to her, and she peeked around the door from the kitchen. The kids were engrossed in a movie, not even noticing her. *Good.* The last thing she wanted was for them to run to her just then. Her skin crawled at the thought of them touching her. She was contaminated. Shuddering, she dashed to the sink and scrubbed her hands until they were raw. She found the kitchen disinfectant she normally used on the counters and sprayed it on the doorknobs she'd touched then doused the tools too.

It wasn't enough. She could almost feel the germs darting over her skin. Turning on the water full blast, she squirted dish soap on her hand and lathered her face. Through stinging eyes, she read the label of the yellow liquid: *anti-bacterial. Perfect. It should kill whatever was out there killing everyone.* She dunked her whole head under the stream of water, getting her hair wet and using the dish soap on it too. She'd have showered if she didn't have to go past the kids to get upstairs, but she didn't want to take a chance of tracking germs through the house. There was only a lone dish towel to dry off with, but she dried as best she could, wringing her hair over the sink.

Her shirt was soaked, and it could have had germs on it too. She ran downstairs and pulled clean clothes from a basket of laundry sitting on the counter beside the dryer. She tossed the clothes she'd been wearing in the washer. An overflowing basket beneath the laundry chute made her start a load, washing everything in hot water. She didn't care if anything shrunk. All the germs had to be killed.

Finally feeling clean enough, she climbed the stairs and found the children watching a movie she had downloaded on her tablet. They were supposed to ask, but, for once, Cassie was glad Bella had gone ahead and used the tablet. That little girl was too smart. Reading was her passion, and she knew exactly how to find the movies she wanted.

When Bella looked up in wide-eyed guilt at being caught, Cassie forced a smile and shook her head. "It's okay, hon." To think, the day before, she would have scolded her daughter for not asking, but yesterday might as well have been an alternate universe.

Tucking a wet lock of hair behind her ear, she sat on the sofa beside the children. "Listen, kiddos, Mommy has a lot to do tonight, so how about pizza for dinner, and you can have cupcakes for dessert?"

Frozen pizza was the quickest dinner she could think of, and she was in no state of mind to prepare a normal meal. Her thoughts zoomed chaotically through her mind like a million pinballs bouncing around in her skull. *What has happened? How did it happen? And what should I do? Most importantly, what should I do first?*

Bella looked at Cassie. "The cupcakes you made for your job?"

"Yes. The job... well, it got canceled, but hey, that's good news for us! We get to eat them all!" Cassie clapped her hands as if in excitement. Milo whooped with glee, and while Bella smiled, she looked at Cassie with suspicion.

"You'll let us eat them?" One tiny blonde eyebrow quirked.

"Yep. We can't let them go to waste. Remember that other time a job got canceled?"

Bella's eyes widened. "Is this like when that lady didn't want to get married anymore?"

Cassie managed a chuckle to keep up the charade. "Yep. Sort of."

She'd taught them to always ask before helping themselves to any desserts in the house, not just to keep them from eating too many sweets, but because most of the time, the baked goods were for catering jobs.

"While you're watching your movie and eating pizza, I have a lot of other baking to do, so I would love it if you guys watched another movie."

That time, Bella grinned, too, her earlier suspicion gone. If only they could keep their innocence a little longer. Cassie reached out, stroking Bella's hair then rubbing Milo's neck, doing her best to blink back tears. The little boy's dark hair curled around Cassie's fingers.

When the pizza was done, she took a few slices for herself, made plates for the kids, and then started a triple batch of cinnamon-raisin bread. It tended to last longer than regular white bread, and the kids loved it. She made it so often, she could practically do it in her sleep, and she needed to do something mindless so she could process what had happened.

While it was rising, she scoured the Internet for recipes, worried when it seemed to take forever for pages to load. She'd told herself not to look at social media, that it would only freak her out, but she couldn't help herself. The sidebar showing which friends were online was short, and when she tried to message the few showing as online, there was no response. The messages were never seen.

Images depicted on the timelines of friends, some dated only days before, showed how the country had collapsed. It had happened so fast, but still, she wondered how she had missed it. But maybe that was what had saved her and the kids. Whatever the reason, they were still alive, and as far as she could glean from news articles, they showed no signs of having contracted the disease.

There was speculation about losing electricity when too many died to run the power companies. She glanced up at the clock on her stove. While the stove was gas, it needed electricity to set the time, alarms, and temperature, and she doubted the oven would even work without a way to get the electronic ignition to work. Time was of the essence. She needed to cook as much as she could, but maybe it wouldn't get to that.

Cassie scrolled more, her non-scrolling hand balled in front of her mouth, stifling sobs so the kids wouldn't hear her. The feed was filled with images and videos of looting, riots, and crazy parties, all while she had been making cupcakes. In a million years, she never would have guessed that the world would end while she was pouring vanilla into a bowl and mixing it into batter or piping Swiss meringue into delicate, pretty swirls.

Her nose ran, and tears spilled down her face as she saw post after horrible post from friends whose loved ones had died and then posts from the friends who had gone off the rails as they became wild and almost jovial. Then nothing. No more updates.

Snatching a paper towel that had only a little flour on it, she wiped her eyes and blew her nose. *How am I going to tell the kids what happened?* She crossed her arms on the kitchen table and rested her head against them. *How am I going to survive this alone? How can I keep my children safe and alive?*

Overwhelmed, she sobbed until she was exhausted, used the paper towel again, then closed social media. From the signs on there, it was a miracle that the power was still on. She immediately had to prepare as much as she could.

She had bread going, but that would last only a few days. Her pantry wasn't well stocked with regular food—it mostly contained baking supplies. Food coloring, candy melts, a dozen different flavorings, even gold leaf, she had aplenty, but non-perishables, not so much. With the kids sick, she hadn't gotten around to doing her regular shopping that week.

Pushing away from the breakfast bar, she moved to the refrigerator. There were several cheeses. They would eat the soft ones, the mozzarella and American and the Brie, first. The hard cheeses would last longer at room temperature if the power shut off. With all the baking she'd been doing, she'd stocked up on eggs, and she was grateful. But they wouldn't keep for long once the power shut off. Sure, she could scramble or boil some, and she would, but there had to be a way to stretch them.

The back of her pantry contained shelves with the staples. She noted what she had. While she kept inventory, seeing everything she had on hand gave her a little comfort. She tallied a mental list of the flours, sugars, leaveners, oils, and shortening. At least she had plenty of those. In addition, she had powdered egg whites, powdered milk, powdered buttermilk, and cornmeal. She examined the flours. While much of it was cake flour or all-purpose, she had bread flour, almond flour, and even chickpea flour she used once for a gluten-free cake.

She pushed aside the almond flour, searching for the semolina she knew was there. She loved making pasta and had planned to make some a month or so before but had never gotten around to it. *There.* She found the bags, a total of three, which would make a decent amount of pasta with the eggs she had.

While the bread baked, she made the dough for the pasta, secured her pasta roller to the countertop, and rolled sheet after sheet. She turned it all into fettucine for simplicity then got all of the coat hangers she could find, washed them, and then hung the pasta to dry. Every curtain rod, every doorknob, and every towel rack got a hanger or two. Dried, it would keep for a long time.

Exhausted, she cut slices of the cooled cinnamon-raisin bread and took some out to the kids. They were sound asleep on the sofa, the darkened iPad lying between them. Sighing, she gave each a kiss before she sat beside them, eating her bread, too tired to make more plans but knowing there was no time to sleep.

CASSIE PREPARED AS WELL as possible in so short a time frame. All night, she scoured the Internet, looking for information, downloading and printing as much about survival as she could gather. She had a stack of how-to sheets on purifying water, finding food in the forests, building shelters, although she hoped she would never need that, making a compost toilet—something she found really enlightening and not too difficult—and first aid. Her biggest concern was fresh water. While she had found several cases and jugs of water in homes, it wouldn't last forever. She had to find a source for fresh water at some point and was at a loss.

She hadn't slept all night as she filled every pot, pan, jug, both bathtubs, and the washtubs in the basement with water. She knew it wouldn't last long.

She baked four loaves of bread and mixed up a sourdough starter batch in case she ran out of yeast.

When the kids became hungry, she gave them cupcakes and cooked all of the meat in the fridge, wishing she had a food dehydrator to make jerky. She'd made a few batches in the past, using the oven on low to dry it, but with bread baking every minute, she couldn't use it for that. With a little thought, she rigged up a makeshift dehydrator with foil funneling the oven vent into a foil-covered cookie sheet. She managed to dry a three-pound roast that she'd cut into thin strips and seasoned with salt, garlic, pepper, and paprika. It had looked like a lot of meat before she'd dried it, but it barely filled a one-quart bag. If only she'd gone shopping and stocked up.

Over the next few days, she was forced to lock the kids in the house for short periods of time while she went door-to-door, breaking and entering into as many homes as she could, raiding freezers of all the meat that wasn't spoiled. It wasn't until she had explored most of the homes on her side of the block that she realized there really wasn't much threat because everyone was dead, but the stench in the whole neighborhood nearly overpowered her. She smelled it in her home, too, but with all the baking she was doing, she was able to mask a lot of it in the house.

The deep freezers in people's basements yielded chicken, turkey, pork, and beef, as well as bags of vegetables. In one, she even found venison.

Then she grabbed her neighbor's propane grill and whooped with excitement when she found a good-sized smoker in one backyard. With it, the meat would last longer.

With the stock from the freezers and dozens of cans of tuna, salmon, and even pickled herring, she felt a little better about the situation. They had enough food for the three of them for months. It might not be their favorite foods, but it would sustain them.

"Mommy! *Mommy!*"

Cassie started awake to find Bella shaking her shoulder. "Huh? What?" She blinked in the dim light of what must have been early morning. She'd fallen into bed after two in the morning, completely exhausted from going almost two days straight with no sleep. Her eyes burned as she rubbed them as she sat up. "What's wrong, honey?"

"I'm scared. It's really dark out."

"It's night. Of course, it's dark out, silly bug." Cassie smiled and lifted her covers. She didn't need to offer an invitation as Bella dove in beside her and snuggled close. Cassie dropped a kiss on Bella's sleep-warmed cheek. "Go back to sleep. It'll be light soon."

"I'm glad, Mommy, because the lights in the bathroom are all broken, and I kind of need to go."

Cassie stilled, her lips pressed against the back of Bella's head. She lifted her face. "What do you mean, the lights are broken?" They had a night-light plugged in as well as the actual lights around the mirror. They couldn't have all burned out at the same time.

"The light switch isn't working."

"And the night-light isn't on, either?"

"Uh-uh."

Bella's drowsy response was almost lost in the turmoil inside Cassie's head. She rolled over to check her alarm clock. When she and Dave had been married, he'd had this side of the bed and she'd had the one with the alarm clock. She'd kept the clock on the far side so she couldn't just reach over and hit snooze. She had to actually get up to turn it off.

Immediately, she noticed the darkness and lack of the greenish hue from the clock. Even though she'd expected the power to go out, the fact that it actually had happened set her heart tripping in her chest.

Easing out of the bed on the far side so as not to disturb Bella, she checked the other rooms, hoping against hope that it was just a fluke. Maybe she'd tripped a circuit breaker with all of her cooking. She'd had the microwave, blender, mixers, and two crockpots going. Plus, she'd filled pans she wasn't cooking in and had frozen blocks of water to keep some of her cooked food good for a few more days.

Everything was off. She stood in the middle of the kitchen, glad she'd filled both sides of the sink before going to bed. She cocked her head. *Is water still running?* She tried the tap, and it came out, although it would all be cold except for what was left warm in the water heater. She tried the gas stove. The electric starter didn't click like normal, but she grabbed a match and was able to light a burner that way. She turned it off, not sure if she was using up what little reserve was left in the lines or if it would continue for a few days.

While every instinct prodded her to *do* something, there was nothing she *could* do. She turned and plodded back to bed.

NINE

ETHAN AWOKE TO THE SOUNDS OF DOGS SNARLING. HE BOLTED UPRIGHT in bed and found his room dimly lit with the pale light of early morning. He peered out of his bedroom window. Movement caught his eye, and he made out the dark silhouettes of dogs dragging something large down the street. He pressed his face to the glass, panic gripping him. It wasn't until he was sure his family's grave mound was untouched that he breathed a sigh of relief. He hoped it wasn't anyone else he knew, but there wasn't much he could do if it was. The threat of packs of dogs was something he hadn't considered. He had his own hunting rifle and his dad's, but they wouldn't be much help if dogs attacked him at close range. He needed to find a handgun somewhere.

For the next hour, he gathered anything he thought he could use. Food was his first requirement, and he tried to figure how much he would need. If the virus hit, probably not more than a few days' worth. But if it didn't, he would need more. He decided to bring enough for at least a week. After that, he would figure something out.

The pantry wasn't as empty as his mother had made it sound, but he guessed it might have been hard to cook once the gas on the stove went out along with the power. They had talked about heating a pan of soup on the propane grill, but that was just before Amber died. After that, there had been no more talk of meals.

A box of zipper-sealing bags sat on a shelf in the pantry, and he unzipped one and dumped almost three-quarters of a box of instant potatoes into it. He did the same with what was left of the flour, sugar, both white and brown, and several boxes of cereal. All but the cereal got their own bags, but he opted to mix the breakfast cereals. He sometimes created combinations, anyway, and now he had one big mash-up of the healthy stuff his parents had eaten and the sugary stuff he preferred. A bag of rice didn't require a bag as it was unopened, but he put it in one anyway because once it was opened, he could store it better that way.

Ethan found a few dusty boxes of macaroni and cheese, a box of dried chicken-soup mix, and a partial package of egg noodles. It was all light and portable. Water might become an issue, but he would look in stores and see if he could find bottles of it. He wasn't sure about drinking out of streams or rivers—he knew that water had to be purified, somehow.

Ethan found a flattened box from a delivery next to the recycle bin, taped it back into a serviceable box, then filled it with cans of peas, carrots, and baked beans. He grinned at that find. He could eat them right out of the can, and they would be pretty good. There were several cans of condensed soup, two pouches of tuna, and four old jars of baby food that Amber had never eaten before she moved on to real people food, as Ethan had once joked to his mom. The jars were hardly more than a mouthful for him, but he took them anyway.

He brightened at finding an unopened container of oatmeal shoved into a far corner. It wasn't something they ate a lot of, but occasionally his mom had made oatmeal cookies. Maybe that had been her intention when buying it. Even though he wasn't a fan of the stuff, if he was hungry, he would eat it. A half bottle of pancake syrup sat on the shelf, and he dropped it into the box. It would help him get the oatmeal down.

As he stepped backwards, he scanned the shelves. There was a box of baking soda and a small container of baking powder. He contemplated the difference—he had no idea. Then he spotted an old cookbook wedged against the wall and added that to the box along with the baking powder and soda. He guessed the answer would be in the cookbook. Rummaging past a can of brussels sprouts and another of spinach, he made a face. No matter how hungry he got, he couldn't imagine eating either of those.

Lastly, he added a plastic bottle of canola oil. His mom cooked with it a lot, so he knew how to use it. Almost everything tasted better when it was fried.

When there was no more room in the box and the shelves were almost bare, he used his foot to push the box into the kitchen. He faced his next obstacle, carrying the box while riding a bicycle. Even if he ditched the box and used his backpack, there wouldn't be room for a quarter of it even if he left his clothes behind. As he considered his options, he thought of the diaper bag his mom had used. It had a bunch of pockets, so it might work better than his backpack, but he still needed clothes. Maybe he could figure out a way to strap one bag to his bike and carry the other.

He considered taking his dad's car. It wasn't as if anyone was going to stop him for driving without a license, but just a glance down his street told him the situation on the roads. Cars were stopped or crashed everywhere. Even if he went around them on the sidewalks, he might not get through. Maybe once he got closer to the edge of town, he could find a car and drive it somewhere if the highways looked better. It didn't really matter where he went, although he hoped he would find some place that hadn't been touched by the virus, some place with living people, some place safe.

Ethan opened the door off the kitchen into the garage. His bicycle leaned against the opposite wall instead of where it was supposed to go, in front of the cars and out of the way. His dad had yelled at him for that at least a million times. Sighing, Ethan crossed to the bike, glad that only one of their cars was still in the garage. The other was on the driveway. It left more room for him to try to rig up some way to carry his supplies.

A short examination of his bicycle confirmed that there was nowhere he could strap anything except for on the handlebars, and even there, only a small pouch would fit. He glanced at his dad's bike, which had a flat cargo rack above the back tire. His dad usually put a red bag that was like a soft cooler but with extra pockets there. He thought he might be able to strap the bag on there instead, but the cooler would be a good thing to have too. Still, the rack wasn't large enough for the box.

Then his gaze landed on the baby trailer. *Perfect.* It could easily hold the box plus a lot more. Ethan grabbed the bungee straps from a hook on the wall and rigged them to hold his rifles, the tent, and a rolled-up tarp. Inside, he loaded the box of supplies, a couple of cast-iron skillets, and a pot. The diaper bag became the holder of utensils, pot holders, dish towels, and a few empty storage containers with lids that he decided would double as eating dishes. That reminded him that he needed bath towels too.

Sighing, he zipped the carrier closed. There was so much he probably needed that he hadn't even thought of. As he passed the charcoal grill, he added matches and a lighter to his list. He lifted the lid of the round grill and took the grates from it. Set on top of stones, he could cook with those anywhere. The metal left his hands greasy and smudged with soot. He tossed the grates onto the floor of the garage near the bike. If he stuck them in a trash bag, he could add them to the gear he'd strapped to the top.

Hot and sweating from the closed confines of the garage, he headed into the house and popped the top of a can of soda. He might as well drink it because taking it along would be wasting space. After grabbing a trash bag, he found a package of peanut butter crackers in a drawer—probably stashed there by his mom. She'd always kept a few in her purse for the baby and had probably put a package in the drawer after cleaning out her purse one day. He tore open the cellophane with his teeth as he returned to the garage, crammed crackers in his mouth, put the metal grill into a trash bag, and tied it securely onto the top of the baby trailer. He was mostly done. It couldn't be much past eight a.m., but the garage was already getting hotter. Glancing at the closed door, he realized he would have to pull the manual release to raise the door. Good thing he'd helped Dad with it once during a power outage last year.

He used a plastic pitcher to fill every water bottle he found in the kitchen from his sink of clean water. The water bottles, some insulated, some not, had various logos on the side, and he remembered winning one as a prize at a community track meet. Another was given to every kid at summer camp a few years before. One had his dad's work's logo on it, and another had the logo from the hospital his mom had worked at. He traced the logo with one finger before shaking his head, turning to what was left of the water in the sink, and washing his hands. He splashed his face, rubbing some soap into his hands, up and down his arms, and around to the back of his neck. He scooped up handfuls of water to rinse with, ignoring the mess he made on the floor. It didn't matter anymore.

TEN

"So, we'll have men going to the left and ladies to the right of the curtain." Noah had rigged up a tarp between two trees, with a third tarp strung perpendicular between two other trees, dividing the latrine into two sections. Bushes on either end made the site somewhat private. After several days of just going into the woods, Noah realized they couldn't continue doing that. He should have thought of it right from the start, but he felt as if he was operating with only half of his brain functioning, and judging from the lack of conversation he'd had with the other two adults, they were probably feeling something similar.

Noah waved toward the tarps. "We've dug a pretty deep hole for each side and have buckets of dead leaves from the stream on each side. After doing your business, grab a handful of the dead leaves and dirt and toss it over your... your waste." Noah felt his face heating as he glanced at Vivian.

Ava piped up, "Like a kitty does?"

Noah laughed. "That's it exactly." He paused, focusing on Dexter and Jalen. "It would probably be best if we do our standing business against a tree to keep the latrine fresher a little longer."

Dexter nodded, and Jalen shrugged. "Yeah, whatever."

Vivian elbowed her son. "That is not how I taught you to respond to adults. Now, say it properly."

Jalen ducked his head and muttered, "Yes, sir."

Noah didn't miss the subtle sarcasm in the reply, but let it roll off his back. The kid wasn't his, and it wasn't his job to instill manners. He wasn't a drill sergeant, after all.

Ava eyed the curtain, her expression unsure, even skeptical. "What about toilet paper?"

Noah grinned. He liked her straightforward approach. And when she gave him a tentative smile, he hoped she was starting to warm to him. Earlier, she'd helped him add some of his fish to their rice dish and had been amazed at the fiddlehead ferns and leeks he'd found to round out their meal. Too bad neither would be in season much longer.

"You can use some of that newspaper you have for now or regular toilet paper, if you have it. I have a few rolls, but that won't last long. When that runs out, we can use moss or leaves. I'll show you what kind, and collecting it will be a job that needs to be done every few days."

Jalen pursed his lips. "How long do we gotta use a hole in the ground?"

Noah raised his eyebrows and looked to Dexter then to Vivian. "Look, I'm not in charge here. That's a question for your parents, not me." Noah crossed his arms and took a step back. Getting between a teenage son and his parents had never been an item on his bucket list.

"When are we going back home, Dad?" Jalen shot his father a dark look.

Dexter stepped forward, jutting his chin as he leaned toward the kid. His pointed finger stopped just short of prodding the teen's chest. "We're going to be here as long as necessary, son. Now, listen to Noah. He knows a lot about this stuff."

Noah shrugged. "I know some, but I'm not a survivalist. But even if it's only a few weeks, we need a designated place to relieve ourselves. It's as simple as that."

Dexter stepped up next to Noah. "That's right. We have to cross one bridge at a time."

Jalen crossed his arms, his stance wide even as he didn't meet his dad's gaze. He lifted a shoulder. "I don't like the woods. There's nothing to do."

Dexter sighed. "You know what it was like in the city. We can't go back to that. We didn't have any water, and the toilets were backed up and spilling. It smelled like shit and worse. And the buzzing... you hated the buzzing of all the flies, Jalen."

The boy's arms dropped as he shoved his hands into the front pocket of his black hoodie, dragging it down and highlighting his painfully thin shoulders. His throat worked as he slowly nodded. "Okay, yeah, the flies were nasty."

Dexter spread his arms and nodded toward the woods. "Look around you, Jalen. Here, there's food, as Noah has kindly shown and shared with us, and the water is fresh, the air clean."

Noah smiled. "I can't promise there will be no bugs here, as I'm sure in a week or so, the mosquitoes will be bad—big enough to carry off a boy of your size." Noah's attempt at a joke fell flat when Jalen glared at him. "To get back to the subject, if we intend to stay here for more than a month or so, we'll see about building something a little nicer than this."

"A month!" Ava's eyes grew big. "We're going to have to live here a month?"

Noah looked helplessly at her parents, and Vivian took his cue. "Baby, it'll be fun. It'll be an adventure!"

She cast Noah a look that was part exasperation, part apology, but for what, Noah wasn't sure. He rubbed his hands together then clapped them. "Okay, then. I'm going to finish airing out my bedroll then heat a little water for washing. If anyone else wants to use some, let me know, and I can get an extra pot of it." He started to head back to his tent, set across the campfire from the family's, when Vivian caught his upper arm.

"Thank you for all you've done." She pulled Ava against her side, stroking the little girl's cheek. "She hasn't quite grasped what's going on yet."

Noah sighed. "I think I know what she's feeling. I haven't grasped it myself."

SEVERAL DAYS LATER, Noah awoke to what had become the familiar sound of the kids talking quietly as they headed to the latrine. They always went as a pair, and Noah was impressed that Jalen never complained about having to accompany his little sister if their mom or dad was busy. He still hadn't warmed up to Noah, but as Noah sat on the side of his cot, he wondered what it was about him that Jalen resented. Noah had caught the young man glaring at him for no reason that he could figure out. Sure, he gave them tasks, but only because Jalen's parents insisted that the children help. The tasks weren't difficult. They were simple things like gathering firewood in the form of fallen branches. Ava treated it like a treasure hunt and squealed with joy whenever she found a big tree limb, while Jalen sulked around, reluctantly dragging back the larger limbs for his sister.

Shrugging, Noah pulled on his jeans and T-shirt. The days were getting warmer, and with all of the physical work he'd been doing, he hadn't needed his jacket. He wished he had more clothes with him, but he couldn't have known that he was going to be living in the woods indefinitely. He tried not to think about winter. It was still months away, but they had to start planning. That was on the day's agenda. Jalen's question a few days before had Noah worried they would be unprepared.

Maybe they should find a way to head south and gather supplies as they went, he thought. In just the week or so they had been at camp, supplies had gotten tight. He'd had to save his propane, initially thinking they would need it when it was cold, but the meager supply he had wouldn't last them more than two days in the winter if they needed it to heat the larger tent. His dried fish was gone. He knew he had to fish that day, and protein was another worry. He would have to hunt a deer soon, but at that time of year, the animals kept to the cover of the forest.

Breakfast was oatmeal with a drizzle of honey. It was the last of the sweetener, and Noah wracked his mind for what they could use instead. There were tree saps, but it was the wrong time of the year. Maybe they would find a beehive, but even if they did, Noah had only the vaguest notion of how to safely get the honey from within one. He knew smoke was involved, but that was about it.

He took a bite of oatmeal. Even with the honey, it had little flavor, but it filled his stomach even as the chef in him resented the lack of taste.

Dexter was still in the family tent as the kids wandered up from the stream. They said their mom had gone to the bathroom. Noah hid a chuckle with a bite of oatmeal. *Bathroom.* He glanced across at the latrine. *Sure. It's practically a spa.*

The kids made a face at the bland oatmeal but ate it without any other complaint.

"Hey, what do you say we ask your parents if we could all go fishing today?" Noah sloshed his bowl in the bucket of water, removing all traces of the gummy oatmeal before setting it on the camp table to dry.

The kids took their turns cleaning their bowls, and predictably, Ava enthusiastically agreed while Jalen gave a sullen shrug. Noah hid a sigh. "We can follow the stream and see where it heads. There might be a bigger stream with more fish not too far away."

Dexter grunted as he exited the tent and grabbed one of the drying bowls. He cast Noah a wry look. "By now, you must realize that I'm a terrible fisherman." He sloshed oatmeal into the bowl and grabbed a spoon from a box beside the table.

"Anyone can have a bad day or two." Noah tried to be encouraging, but he had observed Dexter's fishing and the man was right. He was terrible. His casts tended to slap the water, half the time losing the bait. And if he managed to get a bite, he couldn't set the hook, and the fish escaped. "It just takes practice. Pretty soon, you'll be a master fisherman."

Vivian snorted as she returned with the water but patted her husband's back as she passed him. "Give him a fish, and he can tell you how many he would need to feed five hundred people down to the ounce, but teach him to fish, and you'll have nothing for him to work with."

Dexter scowled but nodded with a wry grin. "She's right."

Noah laughed. "Well, you would make a great restaurant manager."

After scraping the last of the oatmeal from the pot, Vivian took her bowl and sat on a camp chair to eat it. She spoke around a mouthful. "I'm not so sure I want to fish, but I'll try. And we can bring a few of the baskets. Maybe we'll find some of those ferns."

"Sounds like a plan." Noah went into his tent and dug five ready-to-eat meals from his stash. The MREs would have to be lunch on the go if they didn't catch anything. After that, he only had a few more left. He hadn't wanted to hunt because they all agreed that the sound of gunfire could bring unwanted company, but soon, they would have to take a chance. Not that they had seen anyone, but Noah thought he'd heard gunfire one night. It had been brief, and he thought he must have imagined it. Still, he grabbed his sidearm and the special vest he used to carry it. They hadn't explored beyond a hundred yards in any direction, and who knew what lay upstream. The kids had asked about his gun the first time he'd worn it, and Vivian had looked alarmed until he'd explained.

He looked around for a way to carry the MREs and grabbed his jacket. Even if it wasn't cold enough for one, with the mosquitoes starting to hatch, it would protect his arms. He shoved the meals into an inside pocket and returned to the fire. "Are you going with us, Dexter?"

The other man pushed up from his seat on the log beside his daughter. "I guess so. I'll try not to get in the way."

"Listen, I don't mind teaching you this stuff, but you might want to be a little more enthusiastic." Noah didn't intend to sound harsh, but damn it, Dexter had to learn some skills if he wanted his family to survive.

Dexter looked taken aback but then scowled. "I will never be enthusiastic, but I'll do what I have to do."

"Good. Because this is something you *have* to do. I can't be responsible for feeding all of you." The second the words were out of his mouth, Noah wished he could reel them back in. Not only did they sound insulting, but he should never have said them in front of the man's children.

"Nobody asked you to be responsible. We can pull our own weight."

Noah hid his doubt and simply nodded. "I'm sorry. I've seen you with your kids and know you'd do anything for them. I'm just... I'm not used to any of this."

He meant being in the middle of a family, but Vivian scrubbed her bowl then dropped it on the table with a plop. "You think any of us were ready for the apocalypse?" She rounded the small camp table and stopped in front of him, feet planted, hands fisted on her hips. "I'll tell you something, straight up. We'd have been just fine without you, *Noah*." She spat his name as though it tasted bitter in her mouth.

She stepped closer until she looked straight up into his face, her eyes narrowed.

Noah retreated a step. "I didn't mean—"

"While you were here, fishing and whistling 'Dixie' in the forest"—she flung a hand toward the surrounding trees—"we were surviving things you can't even imagine! People pounding on our doors, dying in our front lawn, shooting our dog!" Her voice broke on the last word, but she regained her focus. "So don't you even act like we're just some city slickers who don't know jack shit. We survived because we were smart. *Smart!*" She tapped her temple. "We hid. And when everybody around us was dead, we took everything we could and escaped. There was no time to gather supplies from anywhere but our home. You think we just fled to the woods without a plan at all?"

"Uh, no, ma'am."

"You're damn straight we didn't. Now, maybe we didn't take survival classes like you did, *Mister Army Vet*, and we don't hike, hunt, or fish, but you better believe that someday, people will gather together again and rebuild, and it's people like me and Dexter who will be important then. Who's going to teach the children? Me. That's who. And who's going to get things going again? Dexter. He knows how machines work. He might not be able to catch any stinkin' fish, but if you have a problem with how much he contributes, he can build you a damn bridge, so you can just get over it!"

"Yes, ma'am." Noah tried to explain what he'd meant. It wasn't doubt in them that had fueled his comments but doubt about himself and his ability to keep them alive. He'd already had men die under his command, and no way did he want them to be on his conscience too. "I'm sorry."

"Oh, you'd better be sorry, mister."

Noah glanced at Dexter, who seemed almost as stunned as Noah felt, and reached his hand out. "I'm so sorry, Dexter. I truly mean it."

Dexter stepped toward him and clasped his hand. "It's water under the bridge."

Vivian crossed her arms and stepped beside her husband. "That's right. The bridge that you built!"

Throwing his head back, Dexter laughed. "No worries, Noah." He clapped Noah on the shoulder. "Let's go drown some worms."

ELEVEN

The next week, Cassie did what she could to keep Alice's garden going. She weeded and hoped she'd pulled weeds and not actual vegetables. She found a bag of fertilizer in her neighbor's garage and spread it. Then she thought to check other neighbors' yards for gardens, and early in the mornings, before the kids awakened, she scouted the neighborhood, finding three more that looked to have been recently planted. She had no idea what they would yield but did her best to tend the rows.

"Is this a weed, Mommy?" Bella knelt beside something that Cassie thought might become a bean plant.

Not for the first time, Cassie wished that Alice had given an indication of what she'd planted. Even a seed envelope on a stick stuck in the ground would have helped to identify what was where. Alice had probably been planting the same vegetables in the same places for years. "I think those are green beans in that row. Let it grow until we know for sure, okay?"

Bella walked down the row, counting each sprout. "We'll have twenty beans!"

Cassie laughed. "I hope they grow more than one bean per plant."

In addition to the full-fledged gardens, she found several tomato plants, and herb planters abounded on Alice's deck.

Plucking a sprig of mint from one of the plants, she rubbed it then held it under Milo's nose. "What do you think of that?"

Milo grinned. "Is that gum?"

"No, sweetie. It's mint. It's what they use to flavor some kinds of gum." Her smile died as she realized she should have spoken in past tense. She doubted anyone was flavoring anything anymore.

She drew up a map of all the gardens and what she'd done for them so far. Alice's bookshelves had yielded a trove of gardening books, and when Cassie wasn't taking care of the kids, she read the books, learning what pests to watch for, what plants liked lots of water, which ones didn't, and a host of other tips. Maybe, if she was lucky, she would get a bunch of vegetables in the late summer. She glanced at her thumbs. *Damn.* Neither were green. She chuckled. If they were *really* lucky, maybe they'd get some strawberries before then. One yard had what she thought were strawberries in a plot behind the garage.

She'd lost track of the days until she thought to mark them off on a calendar. She thought she was pretty close to the actual date. After what she thought was ten days, she sorted the tools she'd taken from Alice's house. She'd heard gunfire in the distance the night before. After days of no sign of other human life, it had startled her, and she began to wonder who it was and what they were shooting at, worrying that someone might come and try to take their food. She decided to build a secret room in the basement. She'd helped her dad build before and had helped frame out the kids' bedrooms in what had been an unfinished attic upstairs. The basement room wouldn't even be that complicated. She just needed a long wall and a door, but she couldn't put a regular door there. The hard part would be disguising the door.

Cassie measured from one side of the room to the next and jotted down the numbers. In her backyard travels, she'd spotted a stack of two-by-fours in a pile beside a garage, where there had been several sheets of drywall. Getting the Sheetrock to her house would present a challenge. The building material was deceptively heavy, but she would figure something out.

After framing a wall three feet in front of the wall on the far end of the basement, away from the furnace and washer and dryer, she bolted it to the floor. She hoped if anyone came into the basement, they wouldn't notice that there were no windows on that wall when the outside of the house clearly showed windows, but she would make sure lots of weeds grew there. She just had to get the Sheetrock from the neighbor's house.

It took a lot of sweat and a bit of help from the kids, pushing, pulling, and tearing an old sheet to make a cross between a sling and a harness. It wasn't the weight of the Sheetrock so much as the unwieldiness of it. She balanced the front end of the Sheetrock on Bella's scooter and used the sling under the back corner attached to two ropes to keep it from dragging on the driveway. She wrapped the ropes around her hand and, with the kids, rolled the drywall to the basement entrance.

Cassie brushed dry, chalky dust from her hands after she'd propped the last sheet against the basement wall. She glanced around the basement. The black-and-white checkered tiles on the floor and pine paneling were dated, and she'd always hated it, but it was cooler than the rest of the house, and she contemplated bringing their things down here to sleep once she had the wall up.

"Mommy? Are we ever going back to school?"

Bella's question came out of the blue like a sucker punch. Cassie gasped. She'd been avoiding telling the kids the reality of the situation. When they were babies, she'd read parenting manuals about colic, sibling rivalry, bullying, and every other childhood issue the experts could think up. But no matter how much she wracked her brain, she couldn't remember ever reading a guide for this. There simply were no parenting manuals on how to explain the apocalypse to young children.

"No, honey. I mean, no, you're not going back to school, at least probably not for a long time."

She couldn't figure out how to explain what had happened. So far, the kids had only been in the backyard and in the neighbor's yard to help with the garden. If they thought it was weird that nobody was around, they hadn't said anything. She motioned to the shabby sofa on the edge of an old carpet that formed a small play area she used to use when the kids were younger and she had laundry to do. It had always been a safe place for them to play, and she'd often read them books while waiting to switch a load from the washer to the dryer. "Let's sit down."

Milo climbed into her lap, and Bella slid under Cassie's arm. Both looked at her with big eyes, Bella's brown like her dad's and Milo's blue like hers. Both had their dad's thick, dark lashes. Before speaking, she pressed a kiss against Milo's forehead, breathing in his sweaty but innocent little-boy smell. She leaned down and dropped a kiss on Bella's hair.

"I don't know how much you've noticed, but a few weeks ago now, a terrible, terrible thing happened." She drew a deep breath before continuing. "People got sick. Very sick." She paused, trying to decide how much to tell them, but there was no other way to explain what had happened, so she continued. "They got so sick that they died. And the sickness spread quickly. Too fast."

"Did they have to go to the doctor?" Milo's expression showed his empathy. He hated going to the doctor.

"I'm sure many of them did, but you see, there wasn't anything anyone could do. They—most of the people—they died, I think."

Bella grasped the meaning first, her eyes widening. "Everyone *died*?"

Biting her lip and trying her best but failing to blink back tears, Cassie nodded. "Yes. Probably. I know everyone around here seems to have died. I checked the houses, and I couldn't find anyone."

"Where'd all the people go?" Milo had the teeniest crinkle between his eyes. Perhaps when he got older, it would become a worry furrow, but for the time being, it was just a tiny dent. She kissed it.

Bella grew still, staring at her hands in her lap before raising her gaze, her voice wavering as she asked, "Are we gonna die too?"

Cassie wanted nothing more than to assure her that they wouldn't die, but she couldn't. Instead, she did her best to soothe Bella's fears by telling her what she knew. "I don't know, but we haven't gotten sick yet, and there's nobody left around here to give it to us. We missed getting it probably because of that week when you and Milo were throwing up, remember?"

With a start, Bella stiffened. "Was that it? Are we going to die now?"

"No, hon." Cassie pulled her in for a sideways hug. "What I meant was, because you were both sick, we stayed home and didn't see anyone that whole week, remember? I was baking cupcakes and taking care of you two. I didn't even know what was going on, and I guess it's kind of a good thing, because nobody could pass the bad sickness on to us."

"I don't like being sick." Milo said it with such conviction that Cassie had to chuckle.

She wiped her cheeks. "Me neither, sweetie."

"What about Daddy?"

For the second time, Bella left Cassie speechless. Biting her lip, she turned her gaze on first Bella, then Milo, before turning back to Bella. "I'm sorry, sweetheart"—she closed her eyes briefly—"but your daddy... he died."

"How do you know? Did you call him? Maybe he couldn't answer because he was in jail again?"

"Oh, baby, I wish he was in prison instead. Even that would be better, but he died in front of the house. I saw him."

Bella stared at Cassie, her eyes filling. "*No! You're lying!*" She jumped off the sofa and ran to her bright-pink beanbag chair, diving into it, and curling into a ball.

Milo's eyes filled with tears, too, and he buried his head against Cassie, but she didn't know if he understood what had happened or just knew that his sister was upset. She pulled him close, rubbing his back. "It's okay, Milo. Shhhh…"

Standing with Milo in her arms, she crossed to the beanbag chair. She had to set Milo down because she couldn't drop onto the low chair while holding him without falling. He didn't seem to mind and crawled beside his sister. He patted her shoulder and said, "Shhh… it's okay, Bella."

Cassie drew Bella to her, relieved that Bella's initial stiffness eased and she melted into Cassie's arms. She let the little girl cry until she stopped on her own. "I'm so sorry, Bella. I wish he was here to help us, but it's not his fault. Nobody wanted to get sick."

"Can we have a ceremony for him like we did for Noodles?" The cat had died in the winter, and Cassie had taken her body to the vet to be cremated. The kids had drawn pictures and said a few words in memory, then buried the box in the backyard with ashes Cassie had taken from the grill when the kids weren't looking. They didn't need to know that the animal hospital had disposed of Noodles's ashes.

Cassie nodded. "Of course, sweetheart."

"Can I draw a picture?" Milo asked around the thumb firmly

planted in his mouth. He had stopped sucking his thumb over a year before. Cassie didn't say anything. She'd suck her own thumb if she thought it would comfort her.

She rose and sighed. "Is anyone hungry?"

Neither replied, but Cassie knew they'd be hungry soon, so she headed upstairs to see what she had to give them. Pickings were getting slim.

Drained, Cassie fixed each child a thick slice of bread spread with strawberry jam and a juice box. She'd found the juice packs in a neighbor's house, as she'd rarely bought them. With all of the baking she did, the last thing the kids needed was more sugar, but with water at a premium, she took advantage of the juice boxes.

Bella had carried a piece of broken Sheetrock back from Alice's house earlier and was using it like a piece of chalk on the chalkboard easel she'd put down there last year when she'd been painting Bella's bedroom. A stick figure with a large circle head and what looked like pigtails took shape on the board.

"I wanna try!" Milo tried to wrest the Sheetrock from Bella.

"No! It's mine! Mommy!"

Stepping in to break up the scuffle, Cassie gave the chalk substitute back to Bella. "Sorry, Milo, but you have to wait your turn. We can get more pieces in a little while."

The kids were already going stir crazy and seemed to be acting out. Normally, when the weather turned nice, Cassie would take them to one of the various parks almost every day. Some they walked to, others they drove to, and often, they took a picnic to one of the local lakes' beaches. Cassie enjoyed watching them play, and it got her out of the house.

Milo pouted but leaned against Cassie's leg, wrapping one arm around her thigh, popping his thumb in his mouth again. She ran her fingers through his sweat-dampened hair. He needed a bath. They all did, but she didn't want to use the water. Maybe it would rain, and she could take soap and shampoo outside and give them both a good scrubbing.

TWELVE

Ethan pedaled across town. It had taken him nearly two hours to go as far as he used to ride in an hour. Between the weight of the baby trailer and trying to maneuver it around so many stopped cars, he almost regretted using it. But finally, he turned down a stretch of road that had fewer cars blocking his way.

The stench of death permeated his nostrils, and the sound of buzzing flies, squawking birds, and snarling dogs seemed embedded in his head. He had to get away from it all. It couldn't be so bad away from town. He paused and took a swallow of water. There had been numerous stores, mini-marts, and restaurants he could have stopped at to get more supplies, but he didn't have room for more. Besides, one look at the parking lots of all of them had made his stomach lurch. As bad as it was on the road, the parking lots were worse. The pavement steamed from decomposing bodies and crawled with vermin feeding on the decay. He wasn't that desperate yet.

As he pedaled, he caught the smell of smoke, and as he crested a hill, what he'd thought was a low hanging storm cloud turned out to be a thick cloud of billowing black smoke. A whole neighborhood looked to be on fire. Shocked, he stared, wondering how long the fire would burn and whether the whole town would go up in smoke. The highway seemed to be a divider of sorts, as most of the fire was north of it, although a few smaller fires were visible on his left. He was heading west and decided there was enough distance between what appeared to be actively burning and the highway heading west.

He wished he could Google his location so he had a map to go by. It was as far as he'd ever ridden his bike in town, and not being a driver, he wasn't sure where the road went, but he knew that farms dotted the rolling hills beyond the town. If he was lucky, he might find some people who hadn't been affected by the virus. After all, they were away from town. He remembered being taught in history class that people often fled the cities in the summer to escape heat and diseases. Although he couldn't recall what diseases they fled, he figured if the strategy worked a hundred years ago, maybe it still would.

By late afternoon, he was exhausted and starving. The town had to be at least fifteen miles behind him, but he still hadn't seen anyone alive. He pedaled slowly, looking for a good place to stop, which would have been easier if he knew what a good place looked like. He supposed water would be necessary and knew of several small lakes out that way. If nothing else, he could go for a swim.

He passed a sign saying that a small town his parents had gone to for an apple festival every year was eight miles away, but he didn't know how long it would take him to pedal the distance. In a car, it would have been less than ten minutes. He sighed and looked for somewhere to stop, rest, and possibly spend the night. There was a gas station and a fast-food place a mile up the road, where a state highway intersected the road he was on. Neither appealed to him. Every gas station he'd passed so far had been jammed with cars and bodies, and while he'd kill for a hamburger, he doubted anything would be edible at the burger place.

Just before he reached the intersection, he came upon an animal hospital. As he neared it, his mind returned to a few years before when they'd had to put their beagle, Ace, down due to cancer. Before the virus, it had been the worst time in Ethan's life. He scanned the building, wondering about the pets who had been euthanized inside. Just thinking about stepping inside made his stomach churn as he remembered the smell of disinfectant, urine, wet dog, and a strong citrus-scented air freshener on the receptionist's desk.

After Ace had been put to sleep, Ethan had stumbled out, his dad's arm around his shoulders as they passed cages of dogs and cats who were being treated, probably wondering what went on in the room at the end of the hall and if they were next.

Ethan slammed on the brakes. *What if there are animals still in cages in there?* He couldn't leave them trapped if they were still alive. He circled the bike around to enter the parking lot. The lot only held one car, but Ethan didn't know if that was good or bad. He parked the bike and tried the front door. It was locked. The interior was dark, but light from the doors and windows high on the wall of the reception area showed that the interior was undisturbed. That set the place apart from other businesses Ethan had come across. A lot of waiting rooms he'd been in had watercoolers with little paper cups. It could be worth it to check out the inside for one of them. He'd rather not use up his store of water if he didn't have to. Plus, he could sleep on a couch in the waiting room if the smell wasn't too bad. After seeing the animals that came out at night to eat the dead, he wasn't eager to sleep outside if he didn't have to, not even with the tent.

Before breaking the window, he circled to the back of the building, testing a couple of side doors, both of which were locked, but at the very back, he found an open door and wondered whether someone had forgotten it or if they were in there. Ethan opened the door a few inches, peering inside. The stench assaulted his nose, but it was mostly urine and poop. Dog poop, probably. He didn't smell the rot of death.

"Hello?" He wasn't sure what he'd do if someone replied. He held his breath as he strained to hear a reply. Finally, he did, but it was a whimper. He pushed the door wider. "Hey, anybody here?"

The hallway was darker than the lobby had appeared, and he unclipped his small flashlight from his backpack. The room on his right had an exam table. A few drawers were opened, and an empty box of gloves lay on the floor, but nobody was there. The next room was almost the same, only it had a cabinet door ajar. A canister of dog treats sat undisturbed on the counter beside a roll of paper towels. He tried a door on his left and found it locked. A plastic holder attached to the wall held a manila folder. He took it out and opened it. Some kind of paperwork. It looked like test results of some sort. Ethan returned the folder to the holder and moved to the next door.

As soon as he turned the knob, the faint whimper he'd heard before returned, louder than it had been. A dog! Ethan tugged the door open, finding it was a split door, so he had to reach inside to open the bottom half too. Along each side of the room were cages. Most were empty. A calico cat lay in one, but a glance at the stiff body told him he was too late to help it. Poor thing.

The whimper came again, and Ethan bent, shining his light along the bottom row of cages. A large black-and-tan dog thumped its tail once as though in greeting. He looked like a mix between a German shepherd and Labrador retriever, with the shepherd's longer fur and markings, but a lab's floppy ears and head shape. He was basically the perfect dog in Ethan's estimation. The animal lay stretched out in the cage, the hollows between his ribs dark in the shadows. "Aw, you poor puppy."

Ethan unlatched the gate and reached in, gently stroking the dog's head, drawing a silky black ear between his fingers before attempting anything else. "I'm gonna help you, okay, pup?" The dog tried to lick his hand, but the effort seemed too much, and his head flopped back to the floor of the cage. A clip with a clear plastic name holder read "Dino."

"Is that your name? Are you Dino?"

His tail flicked once more.

Before moving the dog, Ethan looked for something to wrap him in. The dog's plaintive whimper as he moved to a counter at the far end of the room pierced Ethan's heart. "Aw, I'm coming right back, Dino. I have to find something to wrap you with."

Dino looked so frail that Ethan was afraid of hurting him. He found a cabinet with towels on one shelf and folded blankets on another. He unfolded one of the blankets and returned to the dog.

"I'll bet you're thirsty and hungry, aren't you?" An overturned metal bowl rested against the back wall. A metal tube connected to a large plastic bottle poked between the bars, but the bottle was empty. "How long since you had a drink?"

Ethan took one of his water bottles from his supplies and emptied it into the empty plastic one. It seemed the easiest way to control how much water the dog had. He knew Dino needed water but wasn't sure how fast he could have it. Giving it too fast could hurt him, and gulping it could cause the dog to puke.

Dino couldn't quite reach the tube from his position even if he'd been trying, but he seemed too exhausted to make the effort.

"Whoops. I'll hold it for you." Ethan removed it from between the bars and held the bottle in the cage closer to Dino's head. The dog's dry tongue came out, half-heartedly sweeping over the end of the tube as if to say, "I've done this before and nothing comes out, but I'll humor you."

When water hit his tongue, Dino's eyes widened, and his tongue returned for a second pass. He found the energy to lift his head, seeking the tube. Ethan smiled and stroked Dino's side, his hand skimming over the skeletal rib cage. "That's it. Not too fast, though." But he didn't pull the bottle away until Dino seemed to sigh and let his head drop back, exhausted from the effort.

Ethan set the bottle aside as he wrapped the dog in the blanket and carried him to the front of the building. Early-evening sunlight streamed in through the windows, bathing the waiting room in a golden glow. Ethan bent, grabbing a cushion from one of the chairs as he carried Dino past it, letting the cushion drop in the corner of the room. Then he gently laid the dog on the cushion. "I'll be right back, boy. Stay!" Ethan backed from the room, making sure the dog wouldn't follow him. He didn't want him to expend any more energy than he had to.

He rummaged through the building and, finding a large plastic bin full of dog food, scooped some into the bowl he'd taken from Dino's cage. Ethan carried it and retrieved the water bottle, bringing both back to the dog.

"I wonder why you were here? Were you sick or hurt?" Ethan sat with his back against the wall, his legs outstretched and the dog's head on one thigh. He didn't see any injuries, but maybe Dino had been there long enough for one to heal. What the poor animal needed was food and water. That he knew for sure. "I suppose your family died." He drew his fingers through the dense, matted black fur like a comb then scratched behind Dino's ear. "Mine did too."

THIRTEEN

Noah sighed. None of them caught anything at the first few spots they tried to fish.

"I'm hungry, Mama." Ava leaned against her mother, her head pressed into the curve of Vivian's waist.

Jalen swatted a mosquito. "This sucks."

Noah caught the dirty look Dexter sent his son but pretended not to notice as he emptied his water from his purifying water bottle into Jalen's. It was the surest way of making certain the water was good to drink, but it was a slow process for a group. At the camp, they had boiled the water and added a few drops of bleach. Vivian had been horrified at that, but Noah convinced her it was safe. It was safer than drinking untreated water, anyway.

After scooping more water for his bottle from a spot where the water moved the fastest, Noah straightened. "Come on, guys. We'll just go a little farther, and if we don't find a good spot, we'll head back and see what we can do with that rice packet."

He didn't know how he'd stretch it for the five of them. He still had the MREs and decided he'd bring them out at the next fishing hole, but by evening, they'd all be hungry again.

Already, he'd noticed Dexter and Vivian claiming to be full so their children could eat more. He admired their strength to do that but wondered if it was the best in the long run. If they grew too weak to find food, that would leave the kids alone.

It wasn't his business, though, so Noah kept quiet and reduced his own portion in hopes the other two adults would increase theirs.

They hiked for another twenty minutes, following the stream. Close to the camp, the stream had been narrow enough to jump, but now it was close to eight feet wide with steep banks. Noah was about to call a halt in a promising spot when he heard a loon call. It echoed nearby, and he paused. It sounded like it was on water. "Let's follow this just a bit longer."

Jalen spotted it first as he rounded a bend in the stream. "Whoa! Look! It's a lake!"

Noah jogged up beside the boy and rested a hand on his shoulder. "It sure is. Nice job!"

Jalen shrugged off the hand. "I didn't do anything."

"You found the lake." Noah was trying to elicit a smile or something, but Jalen turned to his dad.

"Can I go swimming?"

Dexter bit his lip. "Let's see if we can find a spot."

Noah pointed to a bank overhanging a portion of the lake. "It'll have to be away from the fishing area." He swept his hand to the right. "It looks shallower over there, but it'll probably be pretty cold at this time of year."

Noah's comments didn't win him any favor with the preteen, but Noah had one more thing to offer. "MRE, anyone?"

Jalen and Dexter knew what they were and grinned. "What kind?"

"Spaghetti or beef stew. You know what these are?" Noah was surprised. Not about Dexter knowing, but about Jalen's knowledge of the meals.

"Yeah, my friend's brother was in the army and sent him some. Were you in the army?"

Noah nodded.

Jalen took a spaghetti meal and plopped onto the ground, all thoughts of swimming apparently forgotten. He looked as if he'd made an MRE once or twice, but Noah stopped him from using the purified water in the heater. "Get some from the lake. It doesn't need to be drinking water."

Jalen didn't even give Noah a hard time as he jumped up and raced to the lake's edge. Noah gave Ava the other spaghetti meal, and the three adults had the beef stew.

For the next several minutes, everyone ate with hardly a word. The hike and little bit of oatmeal had them all hungry. Even little Ava ate every bit of her meal. Vivian pulled a blanket from the basket she'd carried and spread it on the ground. "Why don't you take a nap, Baby?" She patted the spot beside her.

Ava smiled and curled on her side, her head pillowed on Vivian's thigh. In seconds, it seemed, she was sleeping. Dexter curled around her, one arm thrown over his daughter. Jalen sprawled beside them.

Noah felt like an outsider as he took in the domestic scene. He should have brought his own blanket. In normal times, a nap on the banks of a peaceful lake after lunch would have been the perfect way to cap off a hike, but he was restless. Food supplies were dwindling. The lake looked promising, and he grabbed the fishing gear he'd dropped on the bank. Before he did any fishing, though, he scouted the lake shore. Trees came up to two of the edges without a real beach except for the small sandy spit they had eaten their lunch on.

The opposite side of the lake had a marshy area with cattails. He started walking toward it, fishing pole on one shoulder and net dangling from his other hand. At the last second, he grabbed his jacket, which he'd discarded on the grassy bank. He could use it as a makeshift bag.

"Noah, where are you going?"

He stopped in his tracks and turned back. Vivian rarely addressed him first and had never questioned his coming and going. "I'm going to see about digging out some of those cattails over there. The shoots and stalks are good this time of year."

Vivian eased Ava's head from her lap and stood, brushing off her jeans as she passed her husband and kids napping on the blanket.

"I thought I'd give fishing a try." So far, she hadn't tried to catch anything but had learned how to gut and clean a fish along with Jalen. Ava was even learning a little bit.

Noah nodded. "Well, you're welcome to come along. I can get you started while I dig up the shoots."

Vivian fell into step beside him. They walked in silence for about a minute before she said, "I'm usually a good judge of character."

Noah glanced at her but remained silent, wondering what she was getting at. Wary of another tongue lashing, he didn't dare speak.

"I was terrified at the thought of setting up camp with you. I mean, I was sure you had the virus and would infect us all, and if that didn't happen, then you'd murder us in our sleep."

"How do you know I still won't?" Of course, he was kidding, but he slanted a grin at her just to make sure she understood.

She chuckled. "I don't know, for sure, but you've had plenty of opportunities. Instead, you've shared everything with us. I was pretty harsh with you earlier. I won't say I'm sorry because I meant every word of it, but I guess I could have expressed it differently."

"No, ma'am. I deserved it. And don't worry—I've heard worse from drill sergeants. Not that you're a drill sergeant." Damn, he was totally screwing up.

Vivian shook her head with a laugh. "Dexter and I, we're both city folks. I grew up in Chicago, and he in Milwaukee. We wanted fresh air for the kids, but for us, that meant suburbs, not country. We don't know anything about camping, hunting, or even fishing. So, I have a question that's been burning inside of me for days. Why? Why share with us? I guess that's why I'm so distrustful. I think you'd be just fine on your own. We've been nothing but a hindrance, my earlier tirade notwithstanding."

"That's your burning question?"

She shrugged and stopped when he did. They were just a short walk from the cattails, and he was hopeful the fishing would be good there. He dropped the net and set the handle of the pole against the ground, inspecting the hook where he'd attached it to an eyelet on the pole. "I guess in the beginning, I didn't have time to think. I was numb and…" He trailed off, thinking of his brother and his family.

"I just was on autopilot, I guess. But now, well, I suppose I would be okay alone, but I was already fishing for two weeks on my own, and it was getting a bit lonely. I didn't relish living out the rest of my days completely by myself. I didn't have time to think that all through on the first day, but now I'm glad we met. You guys help a lot more than you know."

He had pushed his grief about his brother, niece, nephew, friends from work, Miguel, and whatever had happened to him and his family, so deeply into a corner of his mind that he had trouble dragging it out into the light to examine it. A lump formed in his throat, and his vocal cords tightened. He scuffed a toe against a clump of mud, sending the clump rolling down the bank to rest beside the waterline. He darted a look at her to find her regarding him with what appeared to be concern.

"I'm not so sure about that, but I think I misjudged you. I was right that we don't know you, but I'm willing to hear you out before making any more judgements. I think you need our help too."

A warm feeling washed over Noah, starting at the back of his neck and moving to his face. He ducked his head to concentrate on the hook, baiting it with a bit of dried meat—the offal they didn't eat. When he felt the blush fading, he handed her the pole. "Here you go. Do you know how to cast?"

"Sort of?" Then she let out an uncharacteristic giggle when her first attempt slammed the tip of the pole into the edge of the water. "I guess not."

Noah laughed and gave her instruction. When she had made a couple of successful casts, he set the net beside her. "I'm just going over there. Call me if you catch something and need help. Remember, set the hook and reel it in."

He kicked off his shoes and peeled off his socks before wading a few feet into the cattails. Using his hunting knife to both dig and cut, he gathered dozens of the tender shoots and stalks, setting them on the bank that sloped down to the beach. When he felt he had enough, he removed his jacket and drew the drawstring tightly around the bottom of the jacket, forming a bag. He loaded it with the tubers.

After about thirty minutes, Vivian squealed and started reeling in the line. "I think I got one!"

Noah wiped mud from his hands and rushed to her side. "Steady." The water churned where the fish fought just beneath the surface. "There you go. Nice and easy. I'm going to get the net." Vivian had migrated several yards away from it as she'd fished.

When he returned, he followed the line to the edge of the lake, spying the fish twisting and flopping on the end of the line. "Wow! It's a big one! Looks like a large-mouth bass!"

"As long as they're good eatin', I don't care how big of a mouth they got nor how noisy they are!" Vivian grinned as she lifted the tip of the pole, bringing the fish above the waterline.

Noah slid the net beneath the squirming bass, scooping it safely to the bank. "I got it!"

Vivian whooped and did a little dance. "I am bringing home the bacon again!"

Grinning, Noah pulled a stringer from his back pocket and put it through the gills before lifting the fish. "You sure did. This fella has to be at least seven pounds. We'll eat well for a few days."

FOURTEEN

"Bella! Stay back!" Cassie pulled on Milo's hand, urging him to walk faster. She breathed a sigh of relief when Bella listened and waited until she and Milo had caught up. The door to the restaurant supply store was half torn from its hinges, but compared to other stores and restaurants, it was largely untouched. Tucked away in an industrial park, she'd hoped nobody had thought of it when looking for supplies. She'd run out of some of her baking supplies and hadn't found what she needed in neighbors' houses.

"Mommy, there's another one."

Cassie glanced to where Milo was pointing, grimacing when a bundle of clothes that had once been a person fluttered in the breeze. Thankfully, the breeze blew away from them, so they weren't treated to the stench. "Yes, hon. Don't look."

"Are there going to be more inside?" Bella held her hands in front of her mouth, her thumbs resting against her lips as she took a step back.

"I don't know. I hope not, but we'll just have to go around them and not look, okay? Promise me you'll try not to look, you guys."

Milo's eyes were still locked on the bundle between the parked car and the building. Cassie gently turned his face away. "Let's go."

It was the first time she had ventured away from the house, and it had taken three times as long to get to the supply store as it used to take. She'd had to detour four times when accidents blocked her way, and once where a fire must have burned through a building and toppled bricks and other debris onto the road.

Her old SUV had managed, but she worried about gas. "Stay close, you guys. I just want to get in and then get right out." She hated having to bring them with her, and even as she said the familiar phrase, she winced. It sounded as if they were on their weekly trip to the grocery store. She had said the exact same thing as they crossed the parking lot too many times to count.

As she entered the store, she paused, letting her eyes adjust to the dim interior. As she'd hoped, while it was evident from torn bags of flour on the floor, there still seemed to be quite a few bags remaining on the shelves. She grabbed a flatbed cart, rolled it down the aisles, and loaded four sacks of all-purpose flour, two of whole wheat, and one of barley. It looked like so much, but she wasn't even sure how she'd bake with it. Cassie grunted as she picked up a bag of rye flour. It had a small hole, but she tried to keep the hole on top so it wouldn't spill. As she turned to set it on the cart, a hiss made her drop it and back away, pushing the kids behind her.

The biggest rat Cassie ever saw gave another hiss before fleeing to find a new meal. Apparently, it had been working on the hole in the rye and had come back for more.

"Bella, Milo, get on top of the sacks of flour." The kids scampered up, needing no encouragement as Cassie grabbed the handle and headed for the door. Out of the corner of her eye, she saw two more rats scurry beneath shelving units.

Just before she fled the store, she slammed to a halt. They needed food. She couldn't let some stupid rat, no matter how big, scare her away. Not when her kids' lives might depend on it.

"Hold on, guys!" Tugging on the handle, she pulled a quick U-turn and marched back into the store. She found cans of shortening, jars of coconut oil, jugs of canola oil, and even one of peanut oil.

While she passed over any opened products, she grabbed everything she thought she might need, including more pots, pans, and utensils. It wasn't as if she'd be able to order more on Amazon when they wore out or became battered.

Sweating, she made three trips until her car wouldn't hold anymore. Then she had the kids get in their seats and rounded the car to the driver's side.

As she reached for the door handle, a shot rang out, and something ricocheted off the ground and skimmed her leg. Cassie screamed and flung open the door. Ignoring the burning pain along her calf, she turned the ignition and floored the accelerator. As she pulled away, she saw someone in the liquor warehouse across the street raise his arm and take aim as he screamed something unintelligible at her.

Who the hell was that, and why had he shot at us? Cassie glanced in the rearview mirror, meeting Bella's frightened gaze. "You guys all right?"

Bella nodded.

"What about you, Milo?"

"I'm okay, Mommy."

She took a second to look over her shoulder, seeing him crouched on the floor of the car, his hands clasped around his head. "Good thinking, Milo."

"Who was that, Mommy?" Bella asked.

"I don't know, hon, and I don't think I want to go back and ask him his name." She tried to chuckle at her weak joke, but it fell flat.

"I thought everyone was dead."

"I thought so too, Bella, but I guess some others survived, just like us." She wasn't sure if the person had the virus, though. What little she knew made her wonder. He hadn't said anything and had just shot without asking any questions. She hadn't taken the time to get a good look at him.

What if the bullet had ricocheted off something in the car and hit us? Hands shaking, she white-knuckled the wheel as she wheeled around crashes and debris in the road. "At least we got a lot of food, so we won't have to leave the house for a while."

Cassie sighed. She'd hoped to scout some other stores and see if there was more around, but she couldn't do that with the kids. It was too dangerous.

While she didn't see any other cars on the road, she took a roundabout way back to her neighborhood, just in case the guy had somehow managed to follow her. It wouldn't be difficult, since she was in the only moving vehicle that she could see.

When they got home, she sent the kids in the house and told them to get in the basement. She didn't want them around any windows for the time being.

It took her nearly an hour to unload the food and get it all into the basement and behind her false wall. It had taken her days to complete it, and she, with the kids' help, had lugged a tall bookshelf from the living room downstairs, where she'd turned it into a sliding door. When it was rolled over the entryway, it was impossible to tell that there was anything behind the door. She'd even rigged up fake cobwebs near the top of it to the rafters out of dirty cotton fibers glued to rubber bands and tied together. When she rolled the door out of the way, the bands stretched, and when the door was put back in place, it looked like the cobwebs had been there forever.

She used a bit of precious water to splash her face and unscrewed the top of a bottle of soda. After taking a sip, she passed it to the kids. "Drink up, you two. It's going to take me a bit to fix something for dinner."

Once she'd fed the kids and gotten them to sleep, she collapsed on the sofa in the living room, the gun beneath the sofa pillow. She'd had the gun with her earlier while getting supplies, but it hadn't helped because she hadn't even noticed the man across the street. She kicked herself for being so careless.

Tears welled in her eyes as she gave in to the emotion she'd tamped back since the incident. *How am I going to survive, and more importantly, how will I keep my children alive all by myself? And what's the point if all that's left are a few crazy people who are trying to kill us?*

FOR THE NEXT FEW DAYS, Cassie stayed close to home, gathering a few more cans of food, spices, and a few sealed boxes of cereal from neighbors. She thought one of the boxes of cereal was some kind of commemorative box, because when they opened it, the wheat flakes were stale. Some athlete graced the box, so she supposed someone had intended it as a collector's item. Oh well, it was edible, even stale and with powdered milk.

There were a few homes across the street and down the block that she hadn't yet checked, so she got the kids and all the empty jugs she had then pulled the wagon from the garage. It would be easier than trying to carry the heavy water back if they were lucky enough to find some.

Before crossing the street, she scanned it, her shoulders tense as she looked for signs of the shooter, as she'd come to think of him. The liquor warehouse was at least a mile away, but she still didn't want to run into him again. In a neighbor's house, she'd found another handgun, ammunition, and best of all, a holster. She hadn't had one before, and the holster held the gun within reach, just under her left arm. She'd worn a light shirt over her tank top to try to conceal the weapon from the kids, but Bella had still spotted it. She'd looked up at Cassie and said, "Is it loaded?"

When Cassie said it was, Bella had just nodded and said, "Good."

Her solemn answer had sucked the wind from Cassie. *Where has my happy, cheerful little girl gone?* Instead of skipping down the driveway as she might have a few months ago when going for a walk, she dragged her feet as if she was heading to her execution. Cassie tried to tune out Bella's whining about wanting to go to the pool. She was too busy watching the street. There was something different. She couldn't put her finger on it, but it made her uneasy.

Milo circled in front of Cassie, walking backwards, his face eager. "Can I go in this time?"

"No, sweetie. Remember? I need you and Bella to keep an eye out in case anyone comes around. We don't want to catch that nasty bug."

Bella grumbled about the nasty bug, and Cassie agreed with her and sighed. *What is the point of trying to survive? When our food runs out, then what? Eventually, all of the flour will run out or become spoiled. Rodents will get to supplies in stores and homes, and what do I know about survival?*

Maybe it would have been better if they had all died with most of the others. For a moment, she envied the billions who were gone. They were the lucky ones who didn't have to stay alive in this horrifying apocalypse. *What kind of life will my kids have, growing up alone at the end of the world?*

She drew a deep breath and did her best to shake off the morbid thoughts. She had to focus on surviving, on getting through the day, and the next, then the one after that. Water and food were the priorities. At least she didn't have to worry about shelter. Hell, she could probably take her pick of mansions if she wanted.

The pickings were slim, but they found enough water in the two toilet tanks and left in the water heater to last them for a few more days. As a bonus, she was thrilled to score a few cans of vegetables, a bag of rice, and one of egg noodles. Bella found a box of yellow sponge cakes tucked in drawer between a tablecloth and dish towels, and Cassie bet that the woman who lived there kept them as her own stash from her husband. It amused her to imagine the woman she'd seen in a photo on a bookcase, sneaking off to have her sugar fix.

Cassie had managed to convey to Bella that they could make it a surprise for Milo's birthday. Bella's face had lit up and she'd eagerly nodded. Cassie wasn't certain what day they were on, but if she calculated right, it was in three days. She'd considered baking a cake, but the kids were tired of her baked goods, and without a proper oven, she wasn't sure she could bake anything better than the cellophane-wrapped tubes of sponge and cream-filled goodness.

She paused at the top of the driveway to look around before entering the house, unable to shake the feeling that they were being watched.

There's no way that man could have found them. *Could he? What are the chances?* No, it was just her nerves. The guy had probably already died from the virus. It was the only way she could explain him firing his gun at her. She'd posed no threat, and there were plenty of places he could find supplies. Granted, maybe he had kids hidden away somewhere and wanted to claim everything to feed them, but she had children, too, and hers had been right there. Certainly, he'd had to have seen them. *What kind of person shoots a mom with children with her?* Giving one last, hard look around, her hand hovering over the handle of her gun, she almost wished he was there, right in her sights. She would give him a lesson he wouldn't soon forget. With a shake of her head, she turned back to the house.

Cassie almost tripped over the gallons of water the kids had dropped right inside the door, nudged the jugs out of the way, and locked the door. Just because she wanted to face the guy again didn't mean she wanted him to have easy access.

"Are you guys hungry?" Cassie ran through her meal options. While she had plenty of actual food, very little of it consisted of regular meal-type items. The great food pyramid was more like the Space Needle, with its wide base of carbohydrates, very skinny middle of fresh fruits and veggies, and a wide tip made of desserts and sugar. As a baker, she'd done her best to limit sweets for her kids. They got occasional treats, but she made sure her children ate their fruits and vegetables. She hoped the neighbors' gardens had a bountiful harvest. Then she'd have to figure out how to can what she could to last them into the winter.

The thought of winter made her shiver, and it wasn't from the idea of being cold. She didn't know how she was going to manage on her own then, even with canned produce. Cassie pushed the thought away. She had all she could manage to worry about piled high on her plate already.

The kids trooped down to the basement without her even telling them. At night, they slept behind the false wall, but Cassie knew if anyone was really looking, they'd see that the house had living occupants. The two fresh loaves of bread sitting on the counter were probably the first clue. She grabbed one loaf, a knife, and a jar of strawberry jam pilfered from a neighbor's house and took it down to the basement.

FIFTEEN

Noah stabbed the last bite of his cattail root then eyed the pan to see if there were any left—only a few. He left them for the others. They had been even tastier than he recalled. Maybe hunger was the best seasoning after all. He certainly found that food tasted better now, even though he was cooking over a campfire using the oddest and most basic ingredients.

"These were really good, Noah." Jalen moved the pan then took two more and offered his sister the last two.

"Thanks. I'm glad you liked them." For kids who had never foraged for food before, they were surprisingly open to trying whatever Noah cooked. It had to be the seasoning.

"Can we get more tomorrow?" Ava piped up as she bit into hers.

Noah set his plate beside his chair. "I don't know. It's quite a hike." He had planned to scout for deer.

"I wish we lived by the lake. We could have these every day. And go swimming!"

Noah looked at Dexter and found both him and Vivian looking at him. "Are you both thinking what I'm thinking?"

Dexter nodded, flashing a look at his wife.

"Moving the camp?" Vivian answered for both of them.

Noah nodded. "It's a great idea, actually. We'd be deeper in the forest, for one." The gunshot they'd heard had come from the west, which meant the lake was farther from it. Every mile they could put between themselves and someone else was a good thing. The lake was buried deep in the forest. He wasn't even sure how close they could drive the vehicles.

"We'd have fresh running water from the stream that feeds into the lake, plus the lake itself for fishing, cattails, frogs, ducks, and other animals who come to drink from it."

"Frogs?" Ava made a face.

Noah grinned at her. "The French consider them a delicacy, *cuisses de grenouille*. You'll like them. They taste like chicken."

THE NEXT DAY, they moved the camp. It hadn't taken as long as Noah had expected.

Fighting to find a path through the woods to the lake had been the hardest part, but they had found an old logging road that ran only a hundred yards or so away from the lake. They were able to wind a path around trees to get to within fifty yards of the lake.

While it was still far from perfect, over the next few weeks, the cattails added starch to their diet, and the stream and lake provided a steady diet of fish.

Noah hiked deeper into the woods one day, his hunting rifle loose in his arms. He'd hoped to find signs of deer, but it was as if they had all found somewhere else to live. He saw occasional tracks in the mud near the lake but hadn't been able to find any. He'd had a few sightings, but only after they had spotted him and bounded away. Clearly, he wasn't a very good hunter. Maybe it was holding the rifle that triggered the memories, but too often, his mind drifted to walking patrol in Afghanistan, his rifle at the ready. Instead of searching for deer, his brain automatically searched for the enemy.

When he was able to push those thoughts aside, it was usually because he focused on the plants nearby. He'd make mental notes of something they could come back later to harvest or stopped to gather whatever it was he knew was edible.

The cattails had rounded out many of their meals, but they needed more. Every day, the kids looked skinnier, and even his own pants had loosened considerably. Dexter and Vivian hadn't fared any better.

He took a different, parallel route back to the camp then ducked behind a tree when he heard men talking. Holding his breath, he strained to hear what they said and pinpoint their location, but their voices were low and muffled. He peeked from behind the tree and saw them not more than fifty paces away. They wore an arsenal of weapons. Each carried a semi-automatic rifle and wore holsters around their waists. Hunting knives were sheathed on their thighs.

He glanced down. Okay, he was dressed and armed similarly, but there was something about their stance and the way they darted looks around them. Noah had to pull back when one of the men suddenly turned in his direction. He'd barely drawn a breath. When the men started talking again, he caught a few words, something about a woman. Then his heart almost stopped when he heard one say something vulgar about a little girl, laughing and using a racial slur. *Are they talking about little Ava? And Vivian?* He had to know.

He dropped to a crouch then onto his belly, timing the sound of his movements to when they walked and when the wind rustled the trees above. They weren't going anywhere but seemed to have set up a small camp. A tent lay flat against the ground, but he didn't know if they had just arrived or were preparing to leave.

"You gonna get that girl, Don?"

"Dunno. Maybe. It's been weeks." Don hawked up phlegm and spat. The wet sound of it hitting the ground made Noah gag. It had sounded close. Too close.

"Ain't she kinda young even for you?"

Don laughed. "What do you care, Junior? You got your eye on the momma!"

A red haze clouded Noah's vision. His muscles coiled.

Junior's voice came closer, sounding only feet away. "Someone's gotta keep her occupied while you're having your fun!"

Noah's finger twitched on his trigger. He'd never wanted to kill anyone before. He had killed in uniform, but only because he'd had to, to protect his squad. Anger had never been involved.

Maybe he should give them the chance to explain themselves, he thought. Maybe he'd misunderstood, but he didn't think there was any way he could have misunderstood that conversation—there weren't that many mothers and daughters around, and even if it wasn't Vivian and Ava, that simply meant it was some other mother and daughter.

The sudden gush of liquid mere feet away and the smell of urine made Noah recoil.

The stream stopped. "Who's there?"

Noah's options were over. He leaped to his feet.

Junior dropped his jeans as he struggled to reach his weapon, tripping over his pants and face-planting in the undergrowth. Noah took that extra second and switched his aim, pulling the trigger. Don dropped.

Noah pivoted to aim at Junior, who was on his knees, his pants still around his ankles.

"Don't shoot!"

Adrenaline coursed through Noah, and it took every bit of willpower to keep his trigger finger still. "You, get your shit and get the hell out of my woods."

"Why'd you kill my buddy?" Junior stood slowly then bent and fumbled for his jeans. "You didn't hafta shoot 'em."

"You call that piece of filth your buddy?" Noah sneered.

"He wasn't so bad."

"It sounded to me like he was going to rape a little girl."

"Oh. That." Junior had the grace to duck his head. "Well, he did like 'em young, but I never did." He pulled his belt tight and reached for the rifle he'd left propped against a nearby tree.

"*Don't!* And leave your weapons here. All of them." He motioned to the gun belt, and Junior sighed, letting it fall from his hips. "And the knife."

"What am I supposed to use to defend myself?"

"Seems you didn't care about a woman and child and how they could defend themselves."

Junior's shoulders sagged. "Fine. But I wasn't gonna hurt anybody. I just wanted to have a little fun. Don, now, he was sick. I admit it, okay, but I'm not like that."

Noah shook his head. "You think you're innocent? I *heard* you. You were just going to 'keep the momma occupied.'"

Having the grace to duck his head, Junior whined, "I said I wasn't gonna hurt her. It's just there ain't many women, and what's a man supposed to do?"

"You're no man. Now, I'm not going to say it again. Get the hell outta my woods before you join your friend."

"Can I take my tent?"

"No. Get in your truck and drive away. If I see you again, I'll shoot you on sight. You have thirty seconds." Noah began counting.

"I'm going." He stopped beside Don's body, bending to reach before stopping. "I... he had the keys."

Noah moved closer. "Use one hand and keep it where I can see it... eight... nine... ten..."

Junior cringed has he reached into Don's bloody front pocket and pulled out a set of keys, dangling them for Noah to see. Then he turned and ran to the truck. Noah had nearly missed seeing the vehicle—it was so dirty and covered in mud and leaves that it was almost perfectly camouflaged.

As he peeled out, Noah sagged against a tree. They could have had the virus. He'd never seen anyone with it and had only descriptions from Dexter and Vivian to go by. He might have gotten close enough to get it. He wanted to take the weapons, for their own use and to keep Junior from getting them if he came back, but they could have been contaminated. Noah pulled a plastic bag from his pocket. He'd taken to always having one to gather any edibles he found while roaming the woods. He slipped it over his hand like a makeshift glove and gathered all the guns along with any ammunition he could find, dropping the weapons onto the deflated tent. Noah carefully rolled it all into a bundle then tossed away the bag. He didn't like littering, but it had to be done to decrease his own risk.

He trudged through the woods, his mind still whirling. He'd killed a man. His stomach churned, but there was no regret.

"NOAH?" Dexter spotted him as he entered the camp and buried the ax he'd been using to chop wood in a large branch. His eyes went right to the rolled bundle over Noah's shoulder. "What's that? Did you get something? A deer? We heard a gunshot."

Glancing around the camp, he spotted Ava and Jalen on the shores of the lake. Jalen had the fishing pole, and Ava had the net—sort of. She looked to be spending more time making a rock tower than paying attention to Jalen's fishing. Noah sagged in relief. She was okay. He darted a look around. "Where's Vivian?" The urgency in his voice must have alarmed Dexter because he spun around.

"Last I saw her, she was trying to wash clothes in the stream." He walked a few paces and bracketed his mouth. "*Vivian!*"

The stream was down a steep embankment, almost a ravine. Dexter jogged in the direction, shouting one more time.

"I'm right here. Is something wrong?" Vivian rushed into sight, wiping her hands on a towel as she zeroed in on her children. Then she slowed, and a look of annoyance crossed her features. "This better be important."

Dexter turned to Noah, eyebrows raised. "Uh, I think it is."

Noah nodded. "We need to talk."

"Jalen! Ava!" Dexter waved when they looked.

"Without the kids. But keep them close."

"You guys catch anything?" Vivian covered when the kids responded to being called. "You guys just keep on fishing. Gotta earn your keep." She smiled at the children, but it dropped from her face when she turned back to Noah. He lowered his bundle to the ground and rolled his shoulders. "Let's go in the screen room." When they'd set the tent up, they had used the partitions to have a bright, bug-free work area in the day. Dexter had found a shack that looked so old it might have been from the 1800s. He'd taken planks from it and built a table and five chairs. The table wobbled a little, and the chairs were rough, but it gave the small room a homey feel. Noah motioned. "Have a seat. I'm going to get a drink of water first."

He moved to the bucket of water they kept in the shade with a piece of screen over it. He dipped the mug on a string they kept attached to the handle and took a long drink. Then he poured a little bit over his head, still feeling contaminated from the scene at the other men's camp.

"Did you get a deer?"

Dexter motioned towards the bundle outside of the tent.

Vivian turned to look at it. "Looks kind of scrawny."

Noah gave her a wan smile. "It would be if it was a deer, but no, I didn't get one. I don't know how else to explain this, and you may want me to leave after I do. I'd totally understand." He had been judge, jury, and executioner, and the man hadn't even committed the crime yet. *Does that make me a cold-blooded killer?* He swallowed hard, his mouth dry despite the long drink he'd just had.

Vivian shot Dexter a worried look then focused on Noah. "What happened?"

"That bundle is a tent, and rolled up inside of it are weapons I took from two men. I killed one of them." He didn't even try to sugarcoat it—he couldn't. He tried to smooth down a loose sliver of wood but then decided someone might get it stuck in their hand and plucked it off instead, flicking it away. The weathered wood had been lightly sanded, but there were still a few splinters.

"You killed a man?" Dexter sounded shocked, but Noah couldn't lift his gaze to see for sure. In the weeks they had spent together, they had become his family, and the thought of losing them twisted his gut.

"Why?"

Noah glanced at Vivian when he sensed her lean back as she'd asked her question. *Was that revulsion in her voice?* He spread his hands, palms up on the table. "I heard them talking. They were making... *plans*."

Dexter's voice was low and intense. "Noah... what kind of plans were they making?"

Noah swallowed. "They were talking about a little girl and her mother and what they were going to do with them. I-I just lost it. I went off and didn't even give them a chance to explain. The one guy"—Noah paused, the words Don had spoken too filthy for him to repeat—"he preferred young girls. The other was going to keep the mother from interfering."

"*What* mother? *What* girl?" Dexter straightened, his expression dark. Noah tried not to take comfort from that. The other man looked how Noah had felt.

Noah shrugged. "I haven't seen any other mothers or young girls around, have you? And even if there was... I couldn't just let them go and do those things." He turned pleading eyes on Vivian. She'd turned to look out at Ava, who had completely abandoned any semblance of helping her brother and was busy making a sandcastle.

Vivian turned to him, her eyes hard. "Did he die quick?"

Noah nodded. "He did. He didn't suffer." Noah didn't know what he'd have done if Don had survived. He wasn't sure if he could have shot him again. His throat squeezed tightly as he thought of what he'd done—as he acknowledged his lack of remorse. *What is wrong with me?*

"Damn." Vivian clasped her hands in front of her. "Lord have mercy. I am so sorry. I will probably go to hell for saying this, but I wish he would have suffered."

Startled, Noah stared at her.

She shrugged off his gaze, her eyes hard. "That's my baby he was going to harm. Nobody does that and gets away with it. He's lucky you shot him before he did anything, because he'd have suffered long and pitifully if he'd touched a single hair on her head."

Dexter reached for his wife's hands, clasping them in one of his own. "You'd have to get in line behind me." His tone brooked no disagreement. He looked at Noah. "What about the other one?"

"I let him go." He dipped his head, running his fingers though his damp hair. "Told him I'd shoot him on sight if I saw him again."

"What if he comes back? Damn, Noah." Dexter stood and paced to the wall of the tent, peering through the screen as if expecting Junior to enter their camp at any second.

"What was I supposed to do? Kill him too?" He sat back against the rough wood of the chair back. "He was scared out of his mind and left. I don't think he'll be back."

"What if he has friends?" Vivian's eyes narrowed. "What if he and his nasty buddies come back here looking for us?"

"I thought you guys said everyone died? I was shocked just to see other people, but now you're saying there could be more survivors?" Noah stood, clutching the back of the chair at the idea.

Dexter paced back to the table. "We didn't take a damn census. It looked like everybody died. All the power was gone, and we didn't see many people moving around who weren't just about to die, but we survived. You survived. There are probably a few out there. Maybe these men were out in the woods like you were and missed the whole thing?"

Noah nodded but reviewed their campsite in his mind. It didn't look like one set up by regular campers. He'd seen no signs of fishing gear, for one. It was too warm for snowmobiling, and hunting season was months away.

"I guess he could have friends, but I didn't see signs of other people. Just one truck, which Junior drove away."

"Junior? You stopped to get their names? Did you shoot the breeze with them too?" Vivian sounded incredulous.

"No. I heard them call each other by their names." He didn't like the insinuation that he might have socialized with the men. He shook his head. The conversation was getting off track. "Listen, I killed one and let the other go. Now, maybe I shouldn't have let him go, but it's not easy to shoot a man point blank. I'm sorry, but it's not." He stalked to the screen, crossed his arms, and watched as Jalen pulled in what looked like a little bluegill. He looked disgusted, but Ava pranced around, clapping her hands.

"I'd do anything for that little girl out there. I would never, ever put her in harm's way. But I'd already killed one man." He pulled a hand down his face and sighed. "I just couldn't do it again. This guy, Junior, he practically shit himself. He was pathetic, had his pants around his ankles. Probably fell into his own piss. I don't know. I felt like the other guy was the leader." He turned and faced Vivian. "I didn't know what to do with him. It's not like I could call the police, and so it was either kill him or let him go."

Dexter blew out a breath. "Okay, so, the threat is gone. For now, anyway. What did you do with the body?"

"What did I do with it? I left it there."

"You didn't bury him?" Dexter plopped back onto a chair.

Noah joined him, resuming his seat at the table. "No, I didn't bury him. I didn't have a shovel, and I sure as hell wasn't going to give him a proper burial. Nobody buried the billions of dead people out there. One more body isn't going to make a difference."

Vivian tipped her head, nodding. "True. Just let us know where it is so we don't stumble upon it, picking berries or something."

Noah nodded. "Fair enough."

"So, what do we do now? Are we safe here?" Vivian looked at her husband then Noah.

"I don't know. I think we should plan on leaving, and sooner rather than later. I don't think that guy will be back in the next few days. He was too scared, but in a few days or a week, after stewing on it for a while, he might get up enough courage to show up, and he'll be sneaky about it."

"When do we leave?" Dexter sat forward, his gaze intense.

Noah calculated. "Any time, honestly. Where do you want to go?"

"We can't go back to a city, that's for sure. Too many bodies." Vivian shuddered.

"I'll take your word for it, but the forest probably has more like Don and Junior. Plus, it's going to be hard to store enough food for the winter. We already cleaned out the closest town. There hadn't been as much as we expected."

"Okay. It's late today. How about we pack tomorrow and leave the next day?" Vivian offered.

Noah nodded. "Sounds like a plan."

SIXTEEN

Noah rolled over on his cot, kicking off his lone blanket, sweltering in the heavy oppressive heat. The dank, humid air combined with the constant loop of the encounter with Junior and Don playing in his mind made sleep impossible. A mosquito whined past his ear and he slapped it. Another bit him on his shoulder. As much as he'd tried to keep the entrance secured, the damn pests managed to find their way in. His repellent had run out the week before. He sighed and reached for his water bottle, taking a long swig before pouring some on a cupped hand and splashing his face and chest with it. What he wouldn't give for air conditioning. Just twenty minutes was all he needed, enough to fall asleep. A whine at his other ear had him growling and beating the side of his head. Why did they always pick the ears? He sat up, bracing his elbows on his thighs and rubbing the back of his neck. The truck had AC in it.

He stood, grabbing his pillow, but after two steps, he returned to the cot and plopped back down. Running his engine just to cool down would be a complete waste of gasoline. With them leaving the day after tomorrow, he couldn't waste gas. Only a half tank remained, and he didn't know how far they'd have to go to get more. He had driven it only a bit since meeting Dexter on the road, but he hadn't arrived at his original campsite with a full tank. It had been about three-quarters full since he had filled it in a town about seventy miles from here. If he'd have known at the time that getting more gas would involve trying to siphon it from other vehicles, he definitely would have made a trip into the nearest town to top off his gasoline, and his propane for that matter.

Noah shuddered at the memory of his first trip to a closer town west of their campsite. They'd wanted to find supplies. *Wanted.* He gave a sharp snort. Needed was more like it. Dexter had run out within the first week. It wasn't his fault. Nobody knew an apocalypse was just around the corner. If anything, Dexter and his family had been better prepared than most with jars of peanut butter and jelly, crackers, tuna, and such. Dexter credited his wife with being a coupon freak who couldn't pass up a bargain. What had seemed like a lot had disappeared quickly with two kids. But what they had found at the town had been beyond anything Noah had seen, even in the worst of the war. At least then, there had been survivors walking around amid the rubble. Now, there was no rubble, but no survivors either. None that they had seen, anyway. Most of the bodies had been in advanced stages of decomposition and clearly animals had been at many of them. He rubbed his eyes as if he could rub away the vision of skulls with bits of hair and flesh remaining in clumps. He picked up his bottle again and drained it. He might as well take a splash in the lake and cool off. The moon was nearly full and once out of the shelter of the trees, he shouldn't have much trouble finding his way to the shore.

He shoved his feet into his sneakers and grabbed his towel from the line outside of his tent. Noah paused outside of the tent and glanced at the fire. They'd learned to bank it at night to save on matches, but he sniffed, certain that he smelled smoke. A few glowing coals peeked out from beneath a layer of ashes, but other than that, all looked well. A small tendril of smoke curled up to disappear into the darkness above. Satisfied, Noah headed to the beach a few dozen feet away. The moon reflected on the surface of the still water, and he paused a moment to admire the beauty. The Milky Way arched overhead, the absence of light pollution making the night sky brighter than Noah had ever remembered seeing it. The first month, it hadn't been. Every night, the stars appeared dim, as if obscured by high clouds, and during the day, the sky was hazy. It reminded him of when he'd been in Los Angeles during a smog alert day. But the last month, it had all cleared. He and Dexter had speculated what had caused the haze. He said it came from the cities burning. Noah had no other explanation.

Slipping out of his shoes, he waded in the water. As tempting as it was to dive in, he didn't relish going under in the dark. Maybe it was some kind of phobia created from watching too many monster movies as a kid, but he couldn't shake the thought of some creature rising from the depths and grabbing him. Chuckling, he settled for sitting waist-deep and lying backward so his head rested out of the water while the rest of him was mostly submerged. It felt heavenly and he closed his eyes.

He didn't know how long he'd been lying on the beach, but a bite from what must have been a mosquito the size of a small airliner woke him. He slapped his neck, sitting bolt upright, then jumped to his feet swiping his back clean of sand the best that he could. He shivered as water sluiced down his chest from where the ends of his hair had soaked it. How long had he been sleeping? He glanced at the moon to find it farther down in the sky than he'd remembered.

Refreshed, he retrieved his shoes and headed back to his tent, pausing when he caught another whiff of smoke, stronger than before. This time, there wasn't even the glow of coals in the fire pit. Whatever he was smelling it wasn't coming from their fire. Could it be Junior was nearby still? But if he was smelling a single campfire, that meant Junior was close and the guy hadn't looked that bold. Not this soon, anyway.

Could there be a forest fire somewhere? Straightening, he scouted the sky, looking for a glow, but saw nothing but hazy stars.

He froze. The stars had been crystal clear when he'd fallen asleep. Either a weather front was moving in with high clouds, or something else was obscuring the constellations. He wished there was a nearby hill or something. He wasn't much of a tree climber, especially in the dark. The forest had ranger towers to spot fires, but he had no idea where the nearest one was. Why hadn't he thought of that? They should have explored and tried to find one before now.

Ducking into his tent, he used his lantern to gather all of his clothing and personal items, shoving them into his duffel bag. He had rarely used the lantern, not wanting to waste the battery, but he couldn't shake the anxiety that had suddenly taken over his senses.

He rolled his sleeping bag into a tight bedroll and set it all outside of the tent.

When he scouted the area again, he still didn't see anything. The smell of smoke blew on a hot breeze, searing his nose.

He jogged to the Jacksons' tent. There was no way to really knock, but he slapped the flat of his hand against the door. *"Dexter! Vivian! Wake up!"*

Noah didn't want to shout *"Fire!"* because panic wouldn't help anything right now, and he could be wrong. For all he knew, other survivors were camped out due west, and it was their smoke he was smelling. He didn't know if that would be a good or bad thing, but he didn't have time to ponder it before Dexter opened the door and stepped out, tugging a T-shirt over his head.

"What's wrong *now*?" He sounded annoyed.

"Don't you smell it?" Noah ignored the emphasis and looked west. The sky was pitch-black in that direction, but when Noah looked east, it was several shades lighter. Dawn was nearing.

Dexter sniffed, his brow furrowing. "Did you stir up the fire?"

Noah shook his head. "I couldn't sleep, so I took a little dip in the lake. I fell asleep on the beach and woke up just a few minutes ago and smelled the smoke."

Eyes wide, Dexter searched the sky, no doubt also looking for a source of the smoke. "Where's it coming from?"

Noah pointed east. "The wind coming from the west, so I'd say there's a fire out in that direction somewhere."

"How far away?"

Noah knew that sometimes smoke from fires traveled hundreds of miles and maybe what they were smelling was from a fire in Minnesota. It had happened one year during a fishing trip, but then they had been able to tune into the news on the radio and learn that they were safe where they were and had continued to enjoy their fishing trip. This time, they were on their own.

The trees protected them from sun and being seen by others, but they also hindered and kept them from seeing anything going on around them. "I wish I could tell you, but I haven't a clue. I think we should pack up everything though, in case we have to get away quickly."

Dexter glanced around. "Everything?" His shoulders rose in a heavy sigh. "I thought we were going to pack tomorrow anyway. Do you really think the fire is very close?"

Noah followed his gaze. When had their camp turned into something so permanent? They had a good-sized woodpile, and while it wasn't much, they had saved a bit from two months' worth of foraging. Noah had intended to take it and head to a cabin by the time October rolled around. "There's no way to really know for sure. Not from here, but if we wait until we know for certain, we may well be trapped. *Dammit*. This sucks." He ran a hand through his still damp hair. Tomorrow, they'd have had plenty of time to pack, but now they'd have to rush. "I don't think we can risk it. We'll have to hurry and pack as much as we can in the next fifteen minutes or so."

Dexter nodded. "I'll get the kids up and let Vivian know what's going on."

"I'll start packing my truck. When Jalen is up, send him out to help me get the stuff from the trees." The scant supplies they had were all lifted up out of reach of hungry bears. Mostly, he just needed someone to guide the rope so the tubs didn't crash onto the ground when he loosened the knot from where they were tied off.

Noah had his tent stakes up, and his tent folded, ready to roll, but he hated rolling it with dew still damp in the folds. There was nothing he could do about it now though, and he quickly had it tied tight and stored in the back of his truck. He lugged a box of tools to the truck, leaned the camp chairs against the side, to go in later, when more important things were packed, and paused to wipe the sweat from his face. He glanced at the deep red sunrise, too worried what the fiery color meant to admire its beauty. Smoke in the atmosphere was causing the bright color. It just confirmed what he already knew, but it spurred him to go faster.

Jalen headed towards him, his eyes wide, but his mouth set in a firm line. "What do you need me to do, Noah?"

"Just the man I'm looking for. I need your help getting the provisions down. When they get low enough for you to reach them, ease them to the ground so they don't crash and spill everything. Then we'll load some in my truck and some in your vehicle."

Jalen nodded. Noah wished he had time to praise the kid's bravery. He'd come a long way from the sullen kid he'd been just weeks ago.

Ava ran from the tent just as they had finished stowing the bins in the vehicles. She must not have been told too much because she broke into a grin when she saw Noah. "Are we going swimming today?" He forgot he'd promised Ava he'd take a break from fishing and hunting for a half a day or so and relax and teach her how to swim. Neither of the kids knew how.

Vivian trailed after Ava, carrying a small backpack. "Baby, Noah can't teach you to swim today. We're going to take a little trip today."

Ava's eyes grew wide. "In the car?" She sounded shocked. Of all of them, Ava had adapted to their new lifestyle the most easily. Noah credited her age and her inherent good nature.

"Yes, Baby, in the car. Here, take your backpack and hop in the car. I don't want to be looking for you when it's time to go."

Noah nodded. "Good thinking, Vivian."

She flashed him a tight smile. "Thanks. There's enough to do here without worrying. Where's Jalen?"

"I think your husband called him to help with your tent."

Vivian turned to look. Right at that moment, half the tent sagged. Dexter and Jalen must have pulled the stakes on the far side. "Shoot. I was hoping we could leave it up and just come back to it if there was no real fire."

Noah bit his lip, then said, "I can't say for sure the fire is heading this way, but there is a fire, and the smoke is getting thicker." The sun was a red ball low in the eastern sky. No traces of blue showed through the trees. The sky was gray and hazy, and even as he studied it, he noticed something falling. He caught a bit of it. Ash. He rubbed his thumb against it to make sure, frowning at the streak of soot staining his skin. He looked up to meet Vivian's eyes. Gone were any traces of doubt, replaced by stark fear. "We have to hurry.

"I'm going to head back to the main highway. If we somehow get separated, I'll wait for you in town." They had looked on the map and chosen a town about twenty miles south and east of where they were now, deciding to meet at the first gas station they came to. Every small town had a gas station, and the road cut through the middle of town. It was sure to have one. If they were in luck, they might even be able to get gas from the tanks, but he wasn't going to get that far ahead. It would be enough to get away safely. He hoped it was far enough away to be safe from the fire, but that it was also safe from the virus.

Once everything was packed, Noah stood on the driver's side of Dexter's car, his hands on the window ledge. "You sure you have enough gas to get there?"

Dexter glanced at his gauge and nodded. "We have just under a half tank. And I know how to get more from cars along the road. I do have a few skills." He smiled as he said it, but Noah heard a tint of defensiveness. It was true that in the woods, Noah took the lead, but Dexter was right, he had plenty of other skills. He knew more about machines and cars.

"Good, because I have never done it before." Thank god he'd filled up at the last big town on his way into the woods. What if he'd have let it get down and planned on filling up on his way home after his fishing trip? "And you have your safety precautions within reach?" He didn't want to say "gun" because of the kids, but Jalen answered before his parents could.

"Sure do. I'm locked and loaded!"

Dexter half turned in his seat. "I knew you were playing too many video games. Locked and loaded," he mocked, shaking his head before pointing an index finger at his son. "And you better have the safety on!"

Noah bit back a chuckle. "Awesome." A sharp wind hit his face, and he sobered as he glanced at the tree line. The ash fell thicker, and now he could see smoke roiling just beyond the trees on the far side of the pond. If only the pond was bigger, it might have offered safety, but Noah didn't trust that the heat wouldn't cook them even if they were in the middle of the water. Smoke would probably get them before that happened. Shaking off the morbid thought, he tapped a hand a couple of times on the roof of Dexter's car. "Safe trip."

"You too."

Noah ran to his truck and hopped in, starting it, sighing with relief when it started right up. Dexter had reminded him to start his engine about once a week so the battery wouldn't die, and he was glad now for the advice. He shifted into drive and took off as fast as the bumpy, rutted path would allow.

The deer path twisted and turned so much, Noah lost track of his direction more than a few times, but then spied the red sun like an angry eye and did his best to steer towards it. His teeth cracked against each other when he went over an especially hard bump, and he looked in his side mirror to see Dexter's car bounce over the bump. At least it hadn't gotten stuck. There had been very little rain, so the ground was hard. That was a good thing for driving off-road, but probably a factor in why they were trying to escape a forest fire, to begin with.

It seemed to take forever, but finally, they reached the logging road. It was marginally better than the deer path, but while Noah knew he'd turned the correct way when leaving the deer path, the road turned back on itself so many times, he wasn't certain it wasn't going to lead them back towards the fire. He glanced at the compass on his mirror. How could they now be going southwest? He rolled to a stop and waited until Dexter stopped behind him, then got out and trotted back to the other car.

"I think we need to turn around. Somehow, this road doubled back, and we're heading the wrong direction now."

"There's not much room to turn around." Dexter checked his side mirror. Trees bordered the dirt road.

"I'll go up a little way and try to do a three-point, then I'll wait for you to do the same."

"You want me to lead the way then?"

Noah shrugged. "Doesn't really matter."

"Yeah, I guess not."

Noah returned to the truck and drove a few hundred feet until he found a small gap in the trees along the road, did a three-point turn, then pulled along the side of the road as far as possible. He waved Dexter to pass him so the other man could get to the same wide spot.

In the time it took them to maneuver their vehicles, the air had darkened with smoke.

Noah glanced to his left and started when flames became visible not more than a hundred yards away. The wind picked up, blowing smoke and ashes into the road. Noah rolled down his window. Even from a hundred yards away, he could feel the heat from the flames. He rolled the window back up and floored the accelerator.

As he rounded a turn, three deer raced across the road. He slammed on the brakes, barely missing them, and when he checked his mirror, he saw Dexter's car had nearly hit the truck. Noah pressed the gas again, but this time, he didn't go quite so fast. Hitting an animal could do enough damage to disable his truck. If that happened, Dexter's car would be trapped behind his.

Noah forced himself to take a deep breath and steady his hands. It was just driving. If he didn't go crazy, they'd get out of here just fine.

Suddenly, a flaming branch dropped in the road ahead of him. Not stopping to think, he grabbed his leather gloves from the glove box and jumped from the truck. Grabbing the end that had fewer flames, he dragged it out of the way, swatting at his jeans when a branch brushed against his calf and his pants started smoking. Ignoring the pain in his leg, he hopped back in the truck and floored it, praying no more deer jumped in the way.

Dexter was right on his tail. Noah wished he'd back off a tiny bit in case there were any more surprises in the road, but he didn't blame the guy. His whole family was in the car while flames sped through the forest behind them and to their left.

Noah didn't even want to contemplate if the fire was south and east of them. That would almost completely cut them off. He wasn't sure how far north the highway went. He'd never taken it that far before.

The main highway had to be just ahead. It didn't seem like they had driven far when they had come through a few months ago. His headlights automatically came on when the smoke shut out most of the sunlight. It swirled in the lights like a living malevolent form. Leaning forward, he squinted as he tried to peer through the curtain of smoke, breaking into a harsh cough when smoke started coming through the vents. He closed the ones he could reach, straining to reach the far vent on the passenger side. His eyes streaming, he turned his head to wipe first one, then the other on his shoulders. Suddenly, the bouncing of the logging road gave way to the smooth feel of pavement. They had reached the highway.

The highway might have been smooth, but after a few months of no cars, already weeds encroached. In one place, a downed tree blocked both lanes, but Noah navigated around it and saw that Dexter had too. His plan of going south seemed to be working. The fire was behind them, going from west to east, and when he reached a rise, he looked in the rearview mirror and did a double take. Flames and smoke swirled over a hundred feet in the sky like some great fire breathing beast was consuming the forest. He shuddered to think what would have happened to them if they had slept just a little later.

NOAH YAWNED, swiping his hand down his face in an attempt to stay awake. It had been a long day already. They had driven for several hours, reaching rolling farmland. They'd stopped for a brief lunch and bathroom break, then had continued heading south. They had no real plan except to leave the forest fires far behind. None of them wanted to be anywhere near the woods. He hadn't seen any signs of human life. Cows, when he could identify them, lay dead, their bodies strangely flat after two months of decomposition.

His gas gauge was almost empty, and this particular stretch of road was devoid of vehicles of any kind. A tractor driven into a big oak tree in the middle of a field gave a hint as to why. The pandemic hit during planting season. Farmers were busy in the fields, and it looked like several of them had died in the middle of plowing. But this was dairy country too, so much of the land was pasture. From the lack of mud and the tall grass, it was clear it hadn't been used in weeks. In some places the grass was so thick and green, he knew that's where a cow had probably died.

After a few more minutes on the road, he hit the brakes when he spotted a black-and-white shape moving in the distance. Was that a cow? He squinted and shaded his eyes. Damned if it wasn't! He grinned. They should get it. It was the first farm animal he'd seen alive. He knew some of them had to have escaped. They couldn't all have died. He didn't know if he'd still get milk from one, but if not, they could use the meat.

He rolled his window down and pointed at it. Dexter flashed his lights in response, so Noah turned onto a gravel road that looked like it led to a farm a quarter of a mile off the highway. The cow was only a hundred yards or so away from the brightly painted red barn. Most of the barns were faded red, if a color could be made out at all, but this one looked to have been painted recently. A long white building looked more like a dairy than the barn did though, and Noah wondered if that was where the cow had come from.

He parked beside the barn. It smelled, but not any worse than other farms they had driven by. Dexter parked beside him and got out. "Do you know how to catch a cow?"

Noah laughed. "No. I was hoping you had experience here."

"Nope. I got my cows in the supermarket in the form of steak, hamburger, and milk. I simply dropped it in my cart."

"Same here, but how hard could it be?"

Jalen bounced out of the car. "I want to try! I can do it."

Noah shrugged. "You have a better chance than I do."

Vivian rolled her window down. "You better be careful, Jalen. Those cows aren't as gentle as they look."

Jalen laughed and waved his mom's advice away. "It's a cow, Mom. Not a bear."

It ended up taking Noah, Dexter, and Jalen an hour to get close enough to the skittish cow to catch her with a piece of rope and a leash Vivian had found under the front passenger seat. It had been their dog's, and Vivian eyes had teared up when she saw it. They fashioned a noose of sorts out of a piece of rope, making a small loop to hook the leash onto, then a wide loop with a slipknot to put over the cow's head. Noah tested it when it was ready. It seemed like it was strong, but was it strong enough to hold a half-wild cow? Noah had skidded in a pile of manure once and fell, luckily on a clean bit of grass, but that hadn't stopped the kids from busting a gut at Noah's expense. He sent them a dark look, then grinned, and he, Dexter, and Jalen formed a triangle with the cow in the center. Noah distracted her while Jalen, the quickest of them, dodged in and slid the loop over her neck before she knew he was there. She shook her head and pulled away, but Dexter approached, a bunch of dandelions in his hands.

"Here, Daisy. Taste this. So delicious!" Maybe it was his tone or maybe it was the greens, but the cow calmed and took a step towards him, literally eating out of his hand. Dexter shot Noah a triumphant grin. "I guess I have the magic touch."

"I guess you do." Noah dragged first one foot, then the other over an exposed boulder, cleaning the muck from his boots.

After the treat, the cow trailed after Dexter like he was the Pied Piper, and would have gone right into the white barn, but Vivian stopped him.

"I think we should make sure it's clean first." She slanted a glance at Ava, and Dexter stopped in his tracks.

"You're right. I bet the water trough is dirty too. Maybe we can put her in that pasture." He pointed to a fenced pasture on the far side of the white barn.

Once safely contained in the paddock, they looked into the barn and reeled when they opened the doors and hurriedly closed them again. Nope. It wasn't useable.

"Let's just leave her in the pasture for now and see if there's any corn stored in the silo." He pointed to the cylindrical metal building near the center of the farm.

SEVENTEEN

Ethan felt something warm and wet on his cheek and opened his eyes. "Dino!"

He laughed and swiped his hand across his face, removing most of the dog's slobber. Scooting up to sit, Ethan drew Dino into his lap, running his hands along the dog's head, down his neck, and along his sides. "I think you're getting a little fatter. You definitely feel heavier!" He grunted when one of Dino's paws came perilously close to a sensitive area.

Shifting, he eased the dog off his lap and stood. "I guess it's time for both of us to have breakfast. You have plenty of food, but I'm going to have to open a can of beans, I guess."

The second day he'd set up camp at the animal hospital, Ethan had used one of the dog runs that looked the cleanest as a place to build a cooking fire. He'd already burned several chairs and a lot of paper. One of the desks in the office area had contained a lighter and a pack of cigarettes. Ethan didn't smoke, but he took the cigarettes anyway. In an old war movie, he'd seen cigarettes used to trade for other items. He didn't know if there were any smokers left in the world, but just in case, he'd have something he could trade that he didn't need himself.

In addition to the cigarettes, he'd found several packs of ramen noodles, crackers, individual packs of peanut butter, jelly, and even one of a chocolate-hazelnut spread. He set that one aside for a treat later.

He'd eaten one pack of ramen but stuffed the others in his supplies. He rummaged until he found the beans. They were baked beans, normally his favorite, but his mom must have done something different to them because, while he still ate and liked them, they didn't taste the same.

After dumping the beans in one of his pans, he crouched over the fire and set the pan on a grill he'd rigged from a cage door. He had a grate packed away but decided not to unpack it when he had plenty of options right in the animal hospital. The beans soon bubbled, their scent making his mouth water. If he closed his eyes, he could imagine he was at a summer cookout with his mom's baked beans sitting on the long table of food contributed by everyone. His family had always helped organize the annual block-party cookout, and that's where he went in his mind. He smiled at the memory of the egg toss from last year's party. His dad had caught the egg, but he'd caught it too high, and it had broken in his hands right in front of his face. Yolk and slimy egg white had slid from his nose as everyone about died laughing. Ethan grinned at the memory.

A bean popped and hissed, and he opened his eyes, blinking at his surroundings. Nobody was laughing anymore. They were all just dead.

He took the beans off the grill and poured water into a coffee mug acquired from an office desk. The office also had a large jug of drinking water, and while it was no longer cool, it was clean, and he used it for drinking, cooking, and washing.

Ethan studied the beans on his spoon. They weren't as dark. He wished he could ask his mom her secret ingredient. He ate the spoonful, swallowing extra hard past the lump that had risen in his throat.

Finishing, he sighed and rinsed his spoon. The day loomed long and boring. He had already explored every inch of the animal hospital and had scrounged just about everything he thought he could use. There was only so much he could carry.

He'd been forced to stay at the animal hospital while Dino recovered, but the dog seemed okay. Still skinny as could be, but he trotted through the rooms, his nose to the ground, as though searching for answers to what had happened to him.

Giving a low whistle, Ethan snapped his fingers, and the dog immediately came to his side. "Good boy!" He gave Dino a piece of pork he'd fished from the can for him. Scratching behind Dino's ears, he said, "What do you say we get out of here today?" He didn't know where they would go but supposed he'd keep going until he found survivors he could join. He only hoped they actually existed.

It had only taken him a few minutes to finish packing his blankets and stowing his last-minute finds in his pack or bike trailer. He worried that Dino would run off, but he didn't want to put him on a leash because Ethan wasn't sure he could steer the bike and trailer and also keep the dog from becoming entangled with either of them. "You're just going to have to stick close, okay, pup?"

As if he understood, Dino trotted along as Ethan slowly pedaled, mindful of the dog's fragile health. He didn't want to overdo it on the first day. A few times, Dino approached stopped cars, but his tail would tuck down between his legs as he sniffed, his legs stiff. Ethan never bothered to check the cars afterward. He knew what he'd find.

After a long lunch and a short nap, they set out again. A small town was only five miles or so ahead of them, and Ethan hoped to reach it before they had to stop for the night. He reached the top of a hill and paused for a drink, squirting some water into Dino's mouth as well. After returning the bottle to its holder on the bike, Ethan looked around. From that vantage point, he could see that several miles stretched out to the horizon. Normally, the fields below would have been plowed, and corn would be starting to poke through. He hadn't known he knew that until he looked out and didn't see it. It looked wrong.

When he peered closer, he noted a few fields that were darker, as if the soil had been turned recently. *Could that mean people survived? Or had they just been in the midst of plowing season when the virus hit?*

Biting his lip, he tried to plot a way to get to the nearest cleared field, but he couldn't see a road to it. No doubt there was one, but from where he stood, it wasn't visible. He decided to try the town first. If he found someone alive, it would probably be there. Maybe it wasn't as hard hit as his own city.

By late afternoon, they rolled into one end of town. They'd already bypassed several warehouses and a factory. A river wound not far from the highway and seemed to lead parallel to the main street.

Ethan looked into the water, daydreaming about swimming in the river. A plunge into a refreshing pool of water was just what he needed to feel clean again. They crossed a bridge, and he paused to look down. Birds skimmed the surface, occasionally diving down to grab something. The water seemed to bubble, almost as if it was boiling, and he wondered if some breed of fish was spawning. *Did they do that here like in that documentary about salmon?*

Ethan whistled for Dino, who'd taken the break to plop down in a bit of shade created by a girder. The dog rose and trotted to Ethan, his tail wagging expectantly. Ethan patted his front pocket, where he kept a handful of treats he'd snagged from the animal hospital. The pocket felt flat and empty. "Sorry, pup. I'll get you a treat when we make camp. But you're a good boy, aren't you?" He scratched under Dino's chin, and the dog didn't seem too disappointed.

A few minutes later, they reached the end of the bridge, and Ethan parked the bike, curious about the river. If he could catch a few fish, that would be a welcome change from canned food and ramen noodles. Holding his arms out for balance, he descended the steep bank, grabbing a tree branch as he leaned over the water. It moved more quickly than it appeared from above. He doubted he could swim in it, at least not there.

As he studied the current, something white bobbed to the surface. Confused, he found a long stick and stretched to poke the thing. As the end hit it, the object rotated.

Ethan recoiled as the remains of a human hand seemed to reach for him. Falling back onto his butt, he dropped the stick as if it had caught fire and half scooted, half climbed up the embankment. Shuddering when he reached the top, he turned back, watching dead white blobs bob and spin in the current. What he'd thought had been fish spawning had been remains of countless people.

Ethan turned as his stomach heaved, spewing the bile and water. He spit a few times, gasping. "Okay. Get a grip, Ethan." Hearing his own name calmed him for some reason. It had been at least ten days since his family had died, he thought, but he wasn't certain. Closing his eyes, he clasped his hands on top of his head and let his head fall back as he drew deep breaths. It wasn't any worse than all the dead bodies he'd seen when he'd left his town, and it wasn't even half as bad as burying his own family. Thinking about his family pushed all the images of the bodies from his mind, but instead of seeing strangers, he saw his mom, dad, and sister. "Dammit!" He picked up a rock and flung it as hard as he could, but it barely made a splash as it plopped into the river.

Dino looked at Ethan then trotted down the bank and dipped his head to lap at the water.

Horrified, Ethan yelled, *"No, Dino! Get away!"*

The dog startled and darted a few steps away before scampering up the bank to Ethan.

Dropping to his knees, Ethan hugged the animal, burying his face in the dog's sun-warmed scruff. "They're dead, Dino. They're *all* dead."

ETHAN DIDN'T EXPLORE the town to see if anyone was around. He pedaled as fast as he could while still making sure Dino could keep up, weaving between stopped cars and crashes, around bodies, and up onto sidewalks, avoiding the same things there too. *How had all of those people ended up in the river? They couldn't have all fallen in.* He slowed as he approached a school. He read the sign in front: *Home of the Proud Riverton Eagles.*

The school in his town had closed a few days before the virus killed everyone. His mom had said it was for a few days, to keep the virus from spreading. She hadn't known—nobody had—that it had already been too late. He'd ridden by his school after he left home on the way to the highway, and the parking lot had been mostly empty. A few cars had crashed into the front of the building, and he'd seen remains of several bodies, but he was certain it would have been much worse if school had been open.

This school must have been in session, and Ethan felt sorry for the kids who hadn't been with their families at the end. The lot was full. Beer cans, bottles of whiskey and vodka, and even empty bags of weed littered the grounds. It looked as if a party to end all parties had taken place. Toilet paper clung to branches, fluttering in the breeze, some of it plastered to the trunk in a wrinkled white blob that reminded him of the bodies in the river. He turned away, glancing at a toppled eagle mascot near the front door. One wing had snapped off.

Ethan gazed around. He knew the virus made people act weirdly happy, and that had clearly happened here, too, but he couldn't figure out where everyone had gone. He'd seen remains outside bars and taverns and even outside of office buildings, although there wasn't usually weed at those sites. Mostly beer and cigarettes. While he hadn't gone too close because of the stench and the gruesomeness of it, he'd seen the same signs. There had been a big party, then people had died.

Here, there were just the signs of the party.

"Come on, Dino, let's look around back." He rode around to the back and found the football field and track. All the same signs were there, but again, no bodies. Or not many. He spotted a few, but not anything like he'd seen outside even a small bar. The liquor bottles and toilet paper formed a trail toward the back of the field, through a far gate. He followed it.

The gate led to a forested area, and he hesitated. Taking the bike and the trailer would be a hassle, but he felt like he had to figure out where they'd gone. Leaning the bike against a tree, he picked his way through the woods. He was no tracker, but even he could tell that the woods had been trampled not long before. Bushes were broken, branches were torn, and grass was beaten down to mud.

The forest sloped down, and he heard the sound of water—the river flowed right behind the high school. It must have curved around because he thought he'd left it behind at the bridge.

He stopped short between a bush and fallen tree. Before him, on the bank of the river, was a pile of shoes. Hundreds of them. Sneakers, boots, sandals, and even what looked like a pair of slippers were piled up as though everyone had decided to go wading at the same time.

Ethan closed his eyes as the hairs on his arm rose with a sudden realization. He knew how all the bodies had ended up in the river.

It took the better part of an hour for Ethan to leave the town and the river of death behind him. Even then, he still imagined he could smell the rot and stench. He knew the infected people would have died anyway, but knowing they had taken their own lives, even if maybe they hadn't realized what they were doing, sickened him.

What had they been thinking? Had they all been out of their minds? He hoped so, because then maybe they hadn't been afraid.

OVER THE NEXT FEW DAYS, Ethan skirted around most small towns, although he took a quick look from a hill if there was one nearby. He didn't want to chance coming upon another mass suicide. Then he reached a part of the state that was mostly rural, which was great for avoiding dead bodies but not so great for finding other survivors.

"What do you think, Dino? Should I head north? Madison is ahead of us if we keep going that way, and I don't think I can handle that many dead people."

The dog thumped his tail a few times then set his head on Ethan's knee. He'd found a park that looked like it hadn't been used in years. The road in was cracked with weeds growing through, and the asphalt had patches of loose gravel. The grills were rusty, but he scrubbed them with sand from an old playground. He heated up the last of his canned beans and opened a pouch of tuna to go with them. It was an odd combination, but he had gotten used to that.

Dino had plenty of food, but Ethan still gave him a few bites of tuna. "Yeah, I think we'll go north tomorrow. I bet all the survivors are up in the woods. That's where we should have gone instead of staying home."

"IT'S FLAT, DINO." Ethan sighed as he stared at the deflated bicycle tire. He was surprised it hadn't happened sooner. As far as he could tell, he'd gone around a hundred miles from his hometown. At least the flat had come in a small town. If it had happened out on a country road, he'd have been stuck unless he could have gotten a car to run.

He had plenty of food, but he wasn't much of a cook. While most of the stores were stripped, he found that if he popped the trunk on a stopped car, at least one in ten had a trunk full of food. Some of it was spoiled, but he found that a lot of people had been trying to stock up on things like rice, flour, and powdered milk, and he even found powdered eggs. There were also boxes of protein bars and cans of protein drinks, but his favorite was a box of cereal bars. The flavor instantly took him back to Saturday mornings, when he'd grab one and go to baseball practice. He wished there were more of them, since he liked the taste better than the protein bars, but he wasn't about to pass them up. A consequence of riding a bike all day left him ravenous, and he felt like he was constantly eating or wanting to eat.

He grabbed his water bottle and a chocolate-peanut-butter bar then shoved the bar in his back pocket. He rolled his bike out of the road, hiding it and the trailer in thick bushes near a sign that welcomed people to a town whose name he couldn't pronounce and had never heard of. The town was like all the others, with the only difference being the more advanced state of decomposition of the bodies that he saw. He wondered if there was something wrong with him that he barely noticed them anymore. When he saw one in his path, he walked or rode around it without a second thought. Even Dino ignored most of them and stuck close to Ethan—maybe he sensed that Ethan was the only human left alive. Ethan ripped open the bar and tossed a bite to the dog.

Making sure to note the names of the roads so he could find his things later, he moseyed into a neighborhood that reminded him of his own. The homes were small but mostly neat, or they had been. Weeds had sprouted in most of the lawns, although some had been so well cared for that their grass grew thick and green, even if it was probably longer than the owners would normally have kept it. He stopped in front of one such house and took a swig from his water bottle. The water was halfway down his throat when he heard a door slam.

EIGHTEEN

"When are you going?" Dexter set another log on the block and stepped back.

Noah took aim and cleaved it in two. Wiping his brow with the back of his arm, he waited for Dexter to set another log on the block. "Tomorrow, early. I figure you guys are set here, what with the cow and the garden coming in. Now that I know how to siphon gas"—he split the log then shot Dexter a grin—"thanks to you, it shouldn't take me more than a day to get there. I can go off road in the truck when I need to."

Noah bent to pick up one of the halves and handed it to Dexter to set on the pile. "I think that should do it."

The farm already had about a cord of firewood stacked behind a shed, but he and Dexter had added to the pile. They'd found a gasoline-powered chainsaw but wanted to save it for actually cutting trees down and trimming the branches. For splitting logs, they'd taken turns and had been teaching Jalen.

Dexter nodded. "Yeah. I think so." He brushed his hands together. "I won't lie. I'm going to be watching the road for your return. And I'm not sure how I'm gonna console Ava."

Noah smiled. "You tell her that if things go as I hope they will, I'll have another family with kids to bring back here." He looked around the farm. Not for the first time, he wished the owners had made it through the virus. Their bodies had been found outside, a few beer bottles scattered in the grass. It appeared as if they must have had a little party near a fire pit. He and Dexter built another fire pit on the other side of the house and covered the old one with dirt.

"What if you don't find them? Didn't you say your brother's wife divorced him while he was in prison? Do they still live in the same house?"

Noah looked at Dexter, touched at the concern in the other man's eyes. "I don't know. I guess maybe you shouldn't tell Ava about the kids after all. Chances are…" He couldn't finish the sentence.

Even if his brother and his family still lived in the same house and Noah remembered how to get there, the chances of them being alive were almost nil. He hadn't even spoken to his brother in a couple of years, and it had been through a plexiglass window at the prison. But Dave had gotten out. Noah knew that much from a text Cassie had sent him not long before the virus hit. It sounded as though his brother had made a nuisance of himself.

Noah hadn't seen the text until just before his trip and had sent a reply saying he would talk to his brother just as soon as he was back from his fishing trip. He hadn't received a reply, but he didn't know if it was because cell service went out before she could reply or if she had become a victim of the virus. He still didn't know how she had even gotten his phone number, although he supposed it probably showed up on some phone bill she must have looked through.

After dinner, they sat around the fire pit. It had become their routine in the last few weeks to escape the heat of the house. The fire was just to keep mosquitoes away, but it also gave them light to see each other as they told stories or took turns reading aloud. The farmer had several well-stocked bookcases, and surprisingly, the children were as caught up in the plight of Tom Joad and his family in the Steinbeck classic as Noah was. He'd always meant to read *The Grapes of Wrath* but had never gotten around to it. He couldn't help noticing how the Joads' exodus mirrored their own. With nothing left, they had to move on and learn to live by their wits.

"There ain't no sin, and there ain't no virtue. There's just stuff people do." Noah closed the book. The kids lay on a blanket, Jalen on his back, his hands behind his head. Ava curled on her side, her thumb planted in her mouth. Noah glanced at Vivian. Usually, she discouraged the habit, but she had her eyes closed, her hands clasped in her lap, and her legs stretched out, crossed at the ankles.

"I guess it's getting pretty late." He caught himself from speaking with an accent. Every time he read from the book, the twangy Oklahoma accent rubbed off on him. Jalen had mocked him just the other day, saying, "You got an 'idear'? Really, Noah? What's your great 'idear'?"

Noah had thrown a clump of dirt at him, saying, when the boy ducked, "I got plenty of idears, I'll have you know!"

"You really goin' tomorrow, Noah?" Jalen sat up. "Can I go with you?"

"Jalen!" Vivian shot forward. "You are *not* going. You're staying right here with us."

"Aw, man! There's nothing to do here!" Jalen draped his arms over his bent knees, shooting his mother a look of resentment. She cocked her head to the side, one brow raised in warning before looking at Dexter. Right at that moment, he let out a loud snore, dissolving the tension as everyone laughed.

Noah stood and set the book on the seat of his chair. "While I would love nothing more than to have your company, Jalen, I don't think I need to tell you that your mom is absolutely right. It's better for you to stay here with your family. They need you."

Early the next morning, Noah awoke before the sun and grabbed three gallons of water from their supply. He hoped he wouldn't have to use it but wanted to be prepared. He took only the minimum amount of food, in order to leave as much as possible with the others. With any luck, by the time he returned, his truck would be stuffed with more supplies.

The first rays of the sun broke over the horizon as he started the truck. He put it in gear and had started to pull away when, out of the corner of his eye, he saw Vivian approaching from the chicken coop.

He rolled his window down when she made a motion for him to lower it. "Yes?"

She held a basket of eggs out to him. "These will keep a few days."

The eggs would be a good source of a quick, protein-packed meal, but their flock still only laid about a dozen a day. He didn't want to take them. Every bit of food was valuable and might be needed in the winter. If he took the eggs they might have eaten for breakfast, they'd have to eat something else in their stores.

Noah held up a hand. "No, that's okay. Make the kids some scrambled eggs. I'll bet they'd really like that."

Her lips pursed to the side as her eyebrows rose. "Don't tell me what my kids will or won't like."

Damn it. He'd pissed her off again. After their talk at the fishing hole, they'd come to a truce of sorts, but they seldom spoke unless it had to with a specific task or instructions. "No, I mean, I just don't want to take anything—"

Her eyes softened with amusement. "I'm kidding, Noah." She paused and thought for a moment. "Mostly kidding, I suppose. They've never been too crazy about scrambled eggs, but even if it was their favorite food, I'd want you to take these. We'll have more tomorrow. I want to make sure you don't go hungry. Not after all you've done for us."

His mouth dropped open before he reached for the basket. "Thanks." He let the basket hang out of the window as he struggled to find something to add. "I'll bring the basket back."

She threw her head back and laughed. "Yes, I'm sure returning the basket will be your top priority." Her expression sobered. "Nobody is more surprised than me that I'm really hoping you will return here. And not just because you probably have a lot more to teach us about surviving, although I'm not gonna lie. We are still babes in the woods, literally. But I hope you return because Dexter would miss you if you didn't. And the kids... ugh. I don't even want to think of how much they're going to pester me about when you'll return. They're going to get on my very last nerve if you don't come back soon. Don't let that happen, Noah."

He wasn't sure if that was a threat or a plea. With her raised eyebrow and pursed lips, he took it as a threat, but he sensed that there was more to it that she didn't want to voice.

He raised his own eyebrow in question. "What about you?" He couldn't resist asking but hoped his grin let her know he was kidding. "Are you going to pine for me if I decide to find another family to hang out with instead of you all?"

"Pine? I do not *pine*, especially not for you, but I might give a thought to where you are. A *fleeting* thought, mind you."

Noah grinned. "I'll take it." He set the basket on the floor of the passenger side. "Tell the kids I'll see them soon, okay?"

"Sure thing. Take care, Noah."

Whistling, Noah took the road from the farm out to the main highway, noting how much clearer the road was since they had arrived. Several days a week, they'd worked on combing the wrecked vehicles for any supplies then pushed them out of the way. They'd managed to clear most of the wrecks close to the farm out of the way. *If only all of the roads were so clear and empty.* He glanced at the dashboard clock. With any luck, he could be to his brother's house in a few hours.

So much for lady luck, Noah thought as he nudged another wreck from blocking the road. He'd driven around a dozen wrecks and nudged three other small piles off the pavement. In an hour, he'd gone only ten miles. At this rate, he'd make one hundred miles, maybe, before it got dark. He glanced at his gas gauge and amended his timeline. He'd spent a good fifteen minutes siphoning gas from an older model car. Dexter had made a hand pump with a tube and something that resembled a small bellows, and he was thankful he hadn't had to risk swallowing fuel. Still, it had taken time for the can to fill. He'd made sure to look for older model cars, like Dexter had suggested.

As he drove, he noted fields of ragged corn and marked them on his map. So far north, only about a third of the fields had been planted. He had to breathe shallowly as he passed a dairy farm. The smell of rotten meat nearly overpowered him.

A curve in the road ahead drew his attention. The width of the road was completely blocked by a jackknifed semitruck. Out of habit, he glanced in the rearview mirror as he decided if he should go off-road. He shook his head and chuckled. *What am I looking for, a cop who'll give me a ticket?* If one showed up, he'd greet him with a hearty handshake and a thank you for the ticket.

A wire fence ran along the shoulder, but he thought there was enough room to squeeze by. If there was a wrecked car on the other side of the curve, though, it might get dicey getting out. But he couldn't backtrack. That would waste too much time and gasoline with no promise of finding a clear road.

Nothing ventured, nothing gained. He whipped around the wreck and whooped when the truck bounced into a trench hidden by grass and weeds. Despite the situation, a small part of him enjoyed the thrill of driving over terrain rougher than a smooth highway. Commercials always had shown rugged trucks climbing mountains and crossing streams, but he knew most people didn't dare treat their trucks that way. Repairs were too expensive. He laughed when the wheels gained traction and he sped through the weeds. The wreck had blocked traffic, so he remained on the shoulder for over a mile, weaving around a few vehicles that had crashed on the side of the road. One had knocked down a fence and ended up fifty feet into a pasture. He wondered if any cows had managed to escape. He hoped so.

About midmorning, he drove through a small town. A pack of dogs trotted down the middle of the road as if they owned it, and he guessed they did. He slowed, looking for signs of human life. It boggled his mind that so few people had managed to survive, and he wished he had more information about the virus. Vivian and Dexter had explained to him those two weeks while Noah had been blissfully fishing, and he'd seen evidence firsthand when they'd gone on their first supply hunt, but he had been with Dexter then, not alone. The knowledge that he could be the only one alive for miles and miles made him shiver.

He slowed as he approached an intersection with a hospital on one side, and a gas station and several fast-food restaurants on the other. Ambulances, at least a dozen, looked as though they had simply run out of gas as they'd tried to deliver their patients. They snaked into the drive marked "emergency" and disappeared behind the building. Noah looked for a way around them then changed his mind. They could always use medical supplies, and while a few of the ambulances sat open and had no doubt been ransacked, from where he was, it appeared that those in the middle of the drive were still intact. *Do we need supplies badly enough for me to deal with the stench and mess of decaying bodies?* He had a few masks and gloves. Sighing, he drove off the road parallel to the drive and stopped beside one of the ambulances. He grabbed the crowbar he'd brought with him but first tried the driver's side door. He stopped in shock when he found the cab empty. *Had the driver abandoned the vehicle?* He'd assumed the driver had died like everyone else in the cars he'd found, but for once, he was able to reach into a clean vehicle. He still wore the mask and gloves, though.

A quick survey of the cab revealed nothing worth taking, so with a sigh, he rounded to the back and pulled on the handles. A thick stench erupted from the squad like Mt. Vesuvius, swallowing him in a cloud of flies, moths, and steam just as lava had swallowed Pompeii. He gagged and reeled backwards. *Nope.* There was nothing they needed that badly. He stumbled away, his eyes watering, but he dared not rub them.

He carried soap and water in the cab of the truck. He opened the passenger side door and ripped off his gloves, tossing them away as he soaped and rinsed, splashing his face and eyes even though he was certain nothing had actually touched him.

Climbing back into the truck, he sat for a moment, looking around at the ghost town. Weeds already had sprouted around the tires of some of the stopped and wrecked cars. The whole town was dead. Everyone was gone, most without even burials. His eyes burned, and not just from the water.

A daycare center was tucked into a lot between the hospital and medical building. *If I went in there, what would I find?* For the first time, the true scope of the horror washed over him, and a lump rose in his throat, threatening to choke him.

His brother was dead. He had to be. Nobody else was alive. He rested his head on the steering wheel. Afghanistan had been bad—horrible, in fact. He'd seen bodies blown to bits, and some of them had been good buddies of his. But this was a hundred—no, a thousand times worse.

Noah didn't know how long he sat there, but eventually, he lifted his head and wiped his eyes. He had to keep going. He had to know for sure if Dave was dead.

NINETEEN

"Damn." Noah looked up from his gas gauge. He needed to find gasoline, and soon—he had an eighth of a tank. He should have found some in the last town, but his gut had forced him to flee. He should have ignored his nerves and just done what he needed to do. After nearly two months with the virus, he should have been used to it, but he had to admit that he'd lived a sheltered post-apocalyptic life, if that was possible—first, out in the forest and then, after the fire had driven them out, on the farm with Dexter, Vivian, and the kids. Sure, they'd had to find their own food, but he had a knack for it. They'd done okay.

He looked back at Dexter and Vivian's anxiety in the beginning and how he'd felt, deep down, that they had been exaggerating the reality. Noah dragged a hand down his face, grimacing at the stubble under his fingers. If anything, they had minimized what had happened—not intentionally, he was sure, but either because they hadn't seen much in their isolation or because they had then fled as fast as they could without stopping anywhere.

Seeing the utter devastation under bright, sunny skies hit home even harder than if he'd seen it in the gray, smoky landscape of post-apocalyptic movies. The bodies in advanced states of decomposition, sitting in late model cars or lying in front of expensive homes, still shocked him. Large, shaded homes still looked inviting, even with the lawns overgrown. They still sported fewer weeds than a regular field

—it was as if a gardener had merely taken an extended vacation and would be back any day to mow the grass.

Noah glanced at a sign announcing that he was entering a small town. He recognized the name of it as being the same as a famous Ivy League school. As he drove through it, if he ignored the death and destruction wrought from half of the town having succumbed to a fire and the other half dotted with the usual death and debris, he would have described it as a picture-perfect small town. When he turned down a side street in search of a parked car that wasn't wrecked or dripping with decomposing bodies, the homes looked so normal—modestly sized, mostly white, but with an occasional blue or yellow house to break up the block. Wide, neat roads, recently paved, would have given the town a fresh look if it hadn't been for the cars haphazardly stopped, crashed, or just abandoned, doors wide open.

The stopped cars had too often proven to have little gas in them. Maybe that was why they were abandoned to begin with, Noah thought, driving deeper into town. He came across a dead-end street that had no crashed vehicles. A few cars were parked along the curb but appeared to be normally parked. Only the grass brushing the passenger-side-door handles gave away that times had changed.

Noah pulled over beside the first car and took out his siphoning gear. Dexter had shown him how to use a second, shorter tube stuffed into the tank with a rag wrapped around both to form a seal of sorts. All he had to do was blow into the second tube to get gas flowing into his gas can.

The flow trickled to a stop, and he'd only recovered a few gallons. After he put it in his truck, he moved on to the second car, glad to find that its tank filled two five-gallon jugs. Twelve gallons should easily get him the rest of the way to his brother's town.

After filling his tank, he put the tanks in the back of his truck. The few supplies he had were in the cab of the truck, so for once, the covered bed was almost empty. He'd only thrown an air mattress back there to sleep on. He glanced at the homes. They looked well cared for, not trashed in the way some homes had become as victims of the virus had partied and destroyed property in the last throes of the disease. Noah looked at the house he'd parked in front of, which was dark blue on the top half and dark-red brick on the bottom half. It had a deep front porch covered by the roof. If the owners had wanted, they could have simply added windows to have a three-season room, but Noah liked the way it looked as it was. Two pots with wilted, dead flowers adorned the base of the wide stairs leading to the porch. No doubt, those planters had been filled with colorful petunias or poppies. He wasn't sure what the dried-up stems had been, but he would have bet that it had been colorful. If the same care went into the house, he guessed there were tools and canned goods to spare inside.

He wiped his hands on his jeans then reached behind his seat in the cab and took out a screwdriver and crowbar to get access to the house. Taking the broad steps two at a time, he bounded up the porch and tried the doorknob. At least half the time, he and Dexter had found homes unlocked, but to his dismay, it wasn't one of those times. Too bad. He hated having to damage a beautiful home like this one, even if nobody lived there anymore.

The dead bolt was solid, and jamming the screwdriver wasn't going to do the trick. He stepped back and surveyed the front of the house. It might have been easier just to break a window, but when he walked to the end of the porch and looked down the side of the house, he saw that all of the windows were right around six feet off the ground. He would have to get a stepladder to get inside or pull his truck alongside the house and use that as a platform to gain access. Shrugging, he wedged the crowbar between the frame and the door.

It took three hard pushes before the frame cracked and the door gave way. He stumbled into the house and heard a strangled scream before something slammed into his side, spinning him around. He heard only the echoes of a gunshot as his fell to the floor.

Noah gasped, stunned. *What just happened?* For a second, there was no pain, just the smell of cordite and the feel of hardwood beneath his back. He stared up at a stained-glass light fixture. He bet it had been beautiful when it was lit.

Then the pain hit. He turned on his side, clutching where it hurt, drawing his knees up and groaning.

"Get up!"

The sharp voice sounded so much like his sixth-grade teacher that Noah reflexively answered, "Ms. Audrey?"

"I said, *get up!* And then get out!" There came a strangled curse, and then, "Look what you did to my door!"

His legs scrambled on the hardwood floor like a newborn colt trying to get to its feet. Noah reached for the curving bannister of a stairway in the entry hall, cursing when his bloody hand slipped and he fell back onto his injured side. Biting his lip, eyes scrunched, he tried to wait out the worst of the pain, but it pounded over him in relentless waves.

"*Get up!*"

Something, probably a toe from the feel of it, bounced against his right hip.

"Jesus, lady! Can't you see I'm trying?" Noah rolled onto his back and glared at the woman. Her hair, mostly gray but shot with dark streaks, hung wild around her face. She wore a black T-shirt adorned with the name of a heavy metal band on the front, blue jeans, and black boots suited to riding a motorcycle, but what he noticed most was the scowl she wore—she looked as if she'd just squished a cockroach. She held a Glock but wasn't pointing it at him at the moment. Still, he scooted back against the stairway as if it offered some kind of protection.

He'd left his gun in the cab of the truck. *How could I have been so stupid?* The biggest threat he'd seen on his trip had been packs of wild dogs, and he hadn't heard any around there.

She gestured with the gun, and Noah tried not to flinch. "Why'd you break into my house?" She waved the gun as if indicating the whole area. "You could have gone into any house in the town, but you picked mine! Why?"

Grunting, Noah finally managed to stagger to his feet, hanging onto the bannister for dear life. "Shit. You think I *knew* someone was living here?"

"*Really?*" It sounded more like a sneer than a question, and her curled lip left no doubt.

With his head spinning and warm blood spilling over his fingers and dripping onto the floor, Noah shouldn't have sneered back, but he wasn't thinking clearly. "Why would I come in here when there's a whole world full of empty houses? I thought this was another one. That's all. Hell, I haven't seen a living person in over two hundred miles." He tipped his chin to the door. "Get outta my way, and I'll be gone."

The woman's sneer faded. "Two hundred miles?" Her gaze grew distant, and damned if tears didn't come to her eyes. "I guess they really are all dead." She set the gun on the hall table and wandered into what looked like a den or office, judging from the desk in front of the window and the bookcases on either side of the window.

Noah breathed a sigh of relief, wincing as he took a step forward. "I'll just see myself out." His attempt at sarcasm fell flat when the woman merely waved without even turning to look at him. The gun was within reach, and he thought about taking it for his own safety, if nothing else, but he would have had to veer to the left, and he wasn't certain he could make that change of direction.

The woman stood gazing out of the front-facing window as if she expected visitors any moment. Then her head bowed, and she sank to her knees. Bending forward, she covered her face, her shoulders heaving as a sob escaped her.

The action tugged at Noah's sympathy, but as he took another step and had to freeze as the pain flared, it retreated. Teeth clenched, he tried to breathe through the pain. He couldn't give in to it. He had to get back to the farm. Dexter had probably been right. His brother and his family were all dead. He should have listened to him all along. *Now, what will happen to them? They need my help.*

Little Ava's face popped into his mind. Her parents and brother joined her there, and he gasped as his knees buckled. *Breathe!*

Dexter and Vivian had learned a lot in the short time he'd known them, but they had two kids. They needed him. *Dammit!* He should have never left. Anger boiled inside of him, crowding out the pain. He put the foot on his uninjured side down flat and pushed up, looking for something to grasp, but there was only a short wall jutting out between the front door and the den. He reached out, bracing against it.

The woman came out of her stupor long enough to glance at him and at the bloody print he had smeared onto the paint.

"Gonna shoot me again for messing up your wall?"

Shaking her head, she looked like she was trying to smile, but he must've been hallucinating.

What can she possibly be smiling about?

"No, it's all right." She wiped her eyes with one hand and stood. "Are you okay?"

He was sure he was hallucinating. "Are you serious?" He looked down at his side. Blood saturated his shirt in a wide swath from just under his ribs to his belly button and down into his jeans. He couldn't tell how far around him the swath extended. "Do I look okay?"

"No. I guess that was a dumb question."

Then she approached him, and even though she'd set the gun down, he didn't know what else she had—a knife strapped to her calf, maybe, or a club on the other side of the jutting wall.

Noah inched away, wishing he could turn and run. "*Whoa*. I'm going! Or I will as soon as I can get my legs to work again." Truthfully, he was afraid to take one more step for fear of collapsing. He tried to use the open door to prop himself up, but it swung on its hinge, and he almost fell.

"Let me help you."

"No! Stay back!" Noah tried to turn to go out the door, but the room swirled around him and turned black.

TWENTY

"*Milo!* Come back here!"

Ethan choked on the water as he scanned the neighborhood. The slam sounded close. He darted behind a battered car and crouched down. Judging from the gray primer covering part of the vehicle, it had been battered even before the virus hit. He listened, not certain why he was even hiding. But he stayed hidden, his arm wrapped around Dino, hoping the dog wouldn't give him away. "Shhh… lay down."

Ethan hadn't been consciously training the dog, but he had either already known the command or had picked it up from Ethan using it casually over the last few weeks. He lay and put his head on his paws, his tail thumping against the blacktop.

Peeking over the trunk, Ethan watched as a woman and two little kids, a boy and a girl, walked down a driveway. The woman carried three empty gallon jugs in one hand, and each child held one too. They all wore backpacks, but the packs appeared flat and empty. The mom pulled a green-and-tan plastic wagon. Several more jugs were piled in the wagon.

"Why can't we just turn on the faucet and get water like we used to, Mom?" The little girl trudged, her toes scraping down the slight ramp down the drive.

"It still doesn't work, hon. You know that. We have to go see if we can find some in a neighbor's house. Come along. The sooner we get the water, the sooner we can get back home."

"I don't wanna go home. There's nothing to do there. It's hot. I wanna go to the pool."

"We can't go to the pool, sweetheart, but maybe we can bake cookies. How does that sound? I think our little oven will work in this sunshine."

The girl shrugged, her head down, and her mom swept her hand over her head, letting it rest on the girl's shoulder.

"Can I go in this time?" The little boy—Milo, Ethan guessed—raced ahead of his mother and turned around, his face eager.

"No, sweetie. Remember? I need you and Bella to keep an eye out in case anyone comes around. We don't want to catch that nasty bug."

"It's a nasty bug!" Bella's voice held more hate in it than Ethan would have thought possible for such a little girl.

"I agree, Bella. It is a very nasty bug. And that's why we can't go anywhere like the pool. We could get sick."

"But there's *nobody left*, Mommy. They're all gone." Bella sounded matter-of-fact, as if her mom was dense and unable to comprehend the situation. It would have been funny to hear that tone in any other situation, but there was nothing to laugh about anymore.

They walked past the car and out of Ethan's earshot, but the mother's words echoed in his head:*"We could get sick."*

Somehow, the family hadn't died. Like Ethan, they'd managed to survive. *How? Did they watch their family and neighbors die like I did?* At least they had each other. He watched, circling the car to stay hidden as the mother and children crossed the street. He reached into his pocket and pulled out a treat for Dino when the dog stood, his ears perked as he watched the little family head down the street.

Ethan stroked the dog's head and gave one more treat. He'd found several packs of them in a pet store. The pet food had been ransacked, but bags of treats had been knocked to the floor and ignored. They must have been deemed not worth taking by someone trying to keep their family alive.

They would be returning his way, and he didn't want to risk giving them the virus. Every day, he woke up surprised he was still alive and still not showing signs of the illness. Maybe he was a carrier, though, like Typhoid Mary. He'd watched a show on a streaming service about her. She never believed she was contagious and kept working and cooking for families even as the families sickened and some died.

Even though he didn't want to chance passing the virus to them, he wanted to watch them a little longer. He ran up to a set of thick hedges in front of the neighboring house. When he was younger, he and his friends would hide in bushes all the time and pretend they were in forts. When the shrubs were right up against a house, there were often gaps covered by the top of the bush as it spread out at the top. Checking to make sure they weren't on their way back yet, Ethan crept behind the bushes, the brick at his back cool and the ground covered in moist dirt. He patted the ground beside him, and Dino followed him in and promptly turned in a tight circle, lying down with his head on his paws.

Ethan scooted to where he could see, hoping the long grass and the weeds in the flower beds in front of the bushes would keep Dino and him hidden.

He didn't have long to wait, as the woman and kids made their return trip a few minutes later. Bella had half a jug full, and the little boy's appeared empty. The mom's water bottles looked full, though, and all of their backpacks bulged. Bella carried an armful of books, while the boy had a box of building blocks that snapped together. Bella must have forgotten her boredom because she smiled and skipped ahead of her mother. Milo walked slowly, but only because he held the bucket of blocks in front of his face, probably examining the different spaceships he could build with it.

The mom looked like Ethan's mom did when she was worried. Her brows came together and formed a little wrinkle between her eyes, while her lips formed a thin, tight smile when she looked at her daughter.

Bella stopped on the driveway that ran beside the bushes near Ethan. He checked to make sure Dino continued to sleep.

"Can I take a bath tonight, Mommy? I want to read one of my new books in the tub like you do."

"I wish you could. I really do, but there's not enough water for a bath."

"Oh."

"If it rains tonight, we might have enough tomorrow. Remember the barrels I put next to the house and garage? I hope they'll get filled with rainwater."

"Did those other houses all have rain barrels that emptied into their toilets?"

"No, they just had water leftover in there. When someone flushes a toilet, it fills the tank behind the seat with clean water."

"What are we going to do when there are no more toilets in the neighborhood to get water from?"

The mother's only answer was a sigh.

The mom's idea of making rain barrels gave Ethan an idea. He might not be able to go near them, but that didn't mean he couldn't help. He knew what a rain barrel was. They'd studied water-conservation methods in science. If he could find the supplies, he could set up more nearby so the mom wouldn't have to go so far for water. Filled with an energy he hadn't felt since before the virus hit, as soon as the mom and kids went into their house, he and Dino left their hiding spot. He tried to hurry the dog when Dino paused to stretch and yawn. "Come on! We have a lot of stuff to do!"

The first thing he had to do was find a new bike, but that proved a lot easier than he expected. He saw a car in a driveway less than a block from Bella and Milo's house that had a bicycle rack on the back. Ethan crept up the driveway and peeked in the windows. As expected, he saw the remains of someone inside. The garage door was locked, but he broke a window, looked inside, and saw a nice mountain bike hanging on hooks on the far wall. He located a garbage can, pulled it to the window, and climbed in.

Every time he did something like that, he felt guilty, as if his mom or dad would yell at him when he got home. Then he would remember that he had no mom or dad and no home.

The bike tires seemed fine, and he saw a hand pump on a hook near the bike and took that, too, along with a patch kit. These people must have been serious bicyclists. He opened the side garage door and wheeled the bike out. "Come on, Dino." He gave a low whistle.

That afternoon, he connected his trailer to the new bike and hauled his things six houses down from the mom and kids. He chose the house once he saw that the toilet lids were off and the tanks empty, concluding she must have already been there and wouldn't be back.

After parking his trailer in the backyard, he disconnected it and left Dino in the house after closing off the bedroom where the dead bodies were. The rest of the house was okay. He left the dog a bowl of water and another of food. "I'll be back. Don't worry, okay?"

The dog whined as Ethan closed the door.

He rode toward what he hoped was the business part of town, looking for a hardware store. He didn't find one, but he saw a garden center and stopped there instead. They had barrels for planting right outside. *Will those work?* He found plastic inserts, and when those fit inside, he decided they would work to make the barrels watertight. He tried to figure how he could he get them back to his new house.

A delivery truck sat near a loading dock, and Ethan tried the door, almost falling backward in surprise when it opened easily. He looked around, feeling as if someone should be stopping him, but of course, nobody was around. Climbing in, he frowned when he saw the empty ignition. *Shoot.* He checked under the seat and in the cup holder. *Nothing.* He flipped down the visor, letting out a shout of triumph when a key ring with three keys fell in his lap.

He didn't know why he felt like he was sneaking, but he glanced around again, as if waiting for someone in authority to run up and yell at him to get out of the truck. If only someone would. Sighing, he bit his lip. *Can I...? Do I dare?* He had to. If not yet, then at some point. Vehicles were everywhere. He could take his pick if he could get them started. At least he had the keys to that one.

Grinning, he loaded up barrels, several hoses, and tape. *How to get the water to run into the hoses and barrels?* Ethan picked up several items, discarding them when he didn't think they'd work, then spotted what looked like funnels. He wasn't sure if that's what they were, but they would serve the purpose of directing the water.

When he had everything he thought he might need, he tossed his bike in the back and got behind the wheel. Finding the right key by trial and error, he fit it into the lock, his left hand gripping the steering wheel as if it was a rope around a rodeo bull and the chute was about to open. He'd backed his parents' car out before and had backed up in the driveway a few times. It hadn't been hard, and it wasn't as if there was any other traffic. It started. He did a fist pump and put it in gear, swearing when the truck lurched and died. "What'd I do?"

After making sure he was in Park, he turned the key back and then forward again. The truck started again, and he remembered to put his foot on the brake before switching from Park to Drive.

Despite the grim situation and death all around, he laughed as the truck moved forward. It was his first time *really* driving. He imagined how proud his dad would have been to see him as he maneuvered around crashes and drove up on parkways and sidewalks whenever it was necessary. At one point, he nearly collided with a fire hydrant when the right front tire ran up the curb. With a sharp turn of the wheel, it bounced back down, and he laughed. His driving definitely wouldn't qualify him for a license, but it'd get him from one point to another. In just a few minutes, he was back in front of the house he'd chosen.

It took him several tries to get the truck up the driveway, but in spite of his best efforts, he couldn't get it all the way out of sight because of the homeowner's car still in the driveway. He could unload everything and park the truck around the corner. He doubted the mother had memorized every abandoned vehicle on her street, let alone around the corner.

After unloading everything, he rested in the fenced in yard, letting Dino do his thing while Ethan tore open a blue package of salted peanuts he'd picked up from the checkout counter of the garden store. Washing it down with a bottle of orange soda, he felt almost as if he was home. The yard wasn't very different from his own. A stockade-style fence enclosed the overgrown grass, but from the lack of weeds, he guessed the owners had applied weed killer and fertilizer before the virus hit. Flowers fought for dominance with weeds in a raised flower bed around the garage, and an empty bird feeder swung from a shepherd's hook jabbed into the bed.

His dad had also spread weed killer and fertilizer in early May. Ethan had been roped into digging up and turning over the soil in last year's garden. His mouth watered at the memory of the ripe tomatoes they'd harvested late last summer. He loved to sprinkle a little salt on them and eat them like an apple, with juice dripping down his arm. He hoped someone had planted tomatoes, that they survived the summer, and that he'd find them at some point, if he was still alive.

The pragmatic thought didn't seem odd anymore to Ethan. He'd lived his whole life with the assumption that he had decades and decades left to live. While the future had always seemed hazy and far off, there always *was* one. But now he lived moment-to-moment and day-to-day. He was surprised he'd made it so long without catching the virus and wondered if staying in a house with dead bodies, even behind closed doors, would infect him. He might die from the stench first, he mused as he threw a handful of peanuts into his mouth. He'd been in close proximity so much that the worry of catching the virus was on the back burner. In his mind, it was a given it was going to happen at some point. Today, tomorrow, a month from now… it was just a matter of when. Eventually, he would be caught. But in the meantime, at least he could help Dino survive. The dog kept him going. Every morning, his cold nose woke Ethan, prodding his cheek or hand, lapping his warm tongue along Ethan's cheek, bringing him awake with a start as he swiped the wetness away.

Ripping into a cheese-and-breadstick snack pack, Ethan called the dog over and tossed him a cheese-dipped breadstick. "Tomorrow, I'm going to go out and see if I can find more food. You could always use more, and I wonder if I can find some for that mom and her kids?"

Dino yipped, probably asking for another breadstick from the snack pack rather than answering, but Ethan laughed and said, "Yeah, I bet I can."

He'd leave whatever he managed to find on her driveway with a note or something so she wouldn't freak out. Excited to have something to do, he jumped up and began working out how to make a rain barrel. The sky was clear, so he didn't have to rush. If he was successful and the mom was okay with it, he could get some rigged up on her house soon.

TWENTY-ONE

Noah awoke to find himself on a wooden floor in a room that looked vaguely familiar in the dim light of either twilight or dawn—he wasn't sure which. He started to sit up, but the sharp pain in his side slammed him back to the floor. As he panted it into remission, he remembered being shot. *Where is the crazy old woman?* The witch had to be around somewhere. A glance around reassured him that he was alone for the moment.

How bad am I hurt? His next thought was that he had to leave while he could. He rose upon his right elbow, pushing aside a heavy comforter. It slid to his waist. His bloody shirt was gone. He felt his side, shocked to find a thick bandage over it. He bent forward, grimacing but noting the white-gauze bandage wrapped tightly around his torso. *How had that gotten there? For that matter, why is there a thick layer under me?* And a soft pillow had cushioned his head.

As his eyes adjusted to the light, he spotted a glass of water just a few feet to his right. Beside it were two white pills. A third pill, larger and more oval than round, lay beside them. Darting a glance at the doorway, he reached for the water, realizing how thirsty he was. He took a sip, wondering if it was poisoned, but it tasted fresh and clean. He tilted the glass, draining half of it in two gulps.

"Go slowly."

He nearly choked, managing to swallow the mouthful of water as the woman emerged from the shadows. She wore the same clothes, and back before the virus, that would have hinted that it was the same day, but he doubted if she followed convention anymore.

She squatted beside him in one fluid motion. He had to give her credit—she was in good shape for her age. "If you drink it too fast, you might bring it back up, and you need fluids right now."

"You're the one who shot me, so why do you care?" He knew it sounded harsh, and he was in no position to ask such a rude question, but he didn't understand what she was up to.

A soft laugh escaped her mouth. "I'm sorry. You look like you think I'm about to eat you for dinner. I'm not that hungry."

Noah relaxed slightly, and as his stomach gurgled, he conceded she was right. He knew better than to guzzle water when dehydrated, which he guessed he was, after losing a lot of blood. "Why are you doing this?" He gestured to the bandages and pills.

She dropped to sit cross-legged on the floor, her hands clasped in her lap. "I'm sorry I shot you. I was scared."

Noah studied her face. Dark eyes held his own, her eyes roving his face too. "I'm sorry I scared you. I wouldn't have busted in if I'd known you were here."

She blinked, dipping her head and nodding. "It's okay. I'm fine, as you can see. But, you... not so much."

Noah looked at the bandage. "Did you do this?" The bandages were neat, and when he looked closer, he saw something that looked like a surgical drain hanging out of it.

"Bandage you? Yes, I did."

"Are you a doctor?"

"I am, actually." She started to put her hand out but then pulled it back. With Noah leaning on his right arm, shaking would have knocked him flat. "I'm Leona Turner."

He nodded. "Noah Boyle. Well, I guess if I had to be shot, at least I got shot by someone who can fix me. What are you? A surgeon?"

"Well, I have done my share of surgeries, but probably not the kind you're thinking of. I'm an obstetrician and gynecologist."

Noah blinked as he processed that bit of information. "Um, I've never been to one before."

She tossed her head back and laughed. "No, I imagine you haven't." Then she leaned forward and put her hand against his forehead. "You're a little warm. I had some antibiotics I was able to scrounge up from my office before things got crazy. Samples, mostly, but I have enough for a full course. Are you allergic to any medications?"

Noah shook his head.

"Good. The big pill is the antibiotic, and the two little ones are acetaminophen with codeine. I wish I had something stronger for you. I have enough to get you through a few days, to take the edge off."

He managed to get the pills with his left hand, moving ever so carefully. He dropped them into his mouth and chased them with what was left of the water.

His arm started protesting his weight, shaking enough that he was forced to lie back, resting flat on the floor except for the pillow under his head. "Thanks. I'm not sure you should be doing this. I could be contagious."

Leona drew a deep breath and let it out slowly as she nodded. "I know. I thought of that. Believe me. When you busted in here, I was certain that you were infected. I saw plenty of infected people destroying things, drinking, shooting guns into the air and into random homes until they dropped dead, but you weren't acting like that. I mean, yeah, you broke my doorframe, and that sucks, but I believed you when you said you didn't know anybody lived here."

Noah's eyelids grew heavier, but he fought the urge to sleep. "What if you have the virus?"

"I don't."

She sounded so sure of her conclusion. Noah blinked slowly. "But how can you be certain?"

"I haven't seen anyone for two months. I secluded myself before things got bad."

Struggling to stay awake because he had so many questions, Noah gave up when his lids dropped shut. He would have needed the strength of Captain America to pry them open again.

TWENTY-TWO

Ethan put the final touches on the second barrel he'd set up on the front corner of the house. It was none too soon. Dark clouds roiled on the horizon. He grabbed the extension ladder he'd found in a garage three doors down and laid it beside the house. After a low whistle for Dino, Ethan raced into the house just as the first crack of lightning arced across the sky.

He stood in the kitchen, watching the dark, menacing clouds approach through the screen door. The air felt charged and energized, and he loved the feel of it. His dad had always loved to watch storms and had passed that love onto him. Ethan pulled a kitchen chair over to the door and watched in fascination as a low-hanging shelf cloud approached. Last summer, such a sight would probably have been followed by the sound of the tornado warning siren. As much as he loved storms, that siren had always freaked him out. He'd hated it.

Dino sat beside him, his body shaking as he leaned against Ethan's leg. "Aw, it's okay. I won't let anything happen to you." He scratched behind the dog's ears and ran his hand down in gentle stroking motions as thunder boomed and lightning snapped. The wind picked up as rain—first, a few big drops and then a torrent—poured from the sky. Ethan opened the back door, still in the protection of the eave, and grinned as rain started to trickle into the barrel at the back corner of the house. He wondered how much it would collect. As he thought of it, he slapped his forehead. "I should have set out pots and pans."

He shrugged and jumped up, opening what he'd learned was the pots-and-pans cabinet, and found a cake pan, a pot, and a long, flat pan that he thought was the kind his mom used to make lasagna in.

Laughing, he raced onto the driveway and set the pans down then scampered back into the back door. Even his quick dash had him soaking wet, but he didn't care. It felt good. He'd been working hard for two days, and his hair had felt matted. Getting another idea, he ran into the bathroom. *Yes!* There was a bottle of shampoo in a caddy in the corner of the tub. He grabbed it and hoped the downpour would last long enough for him to wash his hair. If he met that mom, he didn't want to look like a bum.

When the rain let up, he took the truck out and drove it around, looking for someplace that might have food. The parking lots of the stores he passed were a mass of crashed vehicles, some right into the stores, and dead bodies. He kept going, pausing when he came to a high school. The parking lot was mostly empty. The schools must have closed before the pandemic hit too hard. He thought of his school and the vending machines and the food in the kitchen. He drove around to the back, guessing which door might be closest to the kitchen. He parked and hopped out, Dino at his side. "We have to find a way in." The doors in the back were all locked with no windows even to break.

Ethan circled the school, standing back to take in the front windows. *There.* One was open. Not a lot, but it was an old school, and the windows tilted out. Only a bottom window was tilted, but it gave him access to the taller window above. He reached in and was able to unlatch the taller window. He gave it a little push with his hand inside the glass. When it was out far enough, he scrambled up to the slight ledge and climbed in. Dino sat outside, whining. "I'll go to the closest door and let you in. Hang on, Dino."

In his hurry to get to a door, he rushed through the classroom and out to the dim hallway. He turned left and found an exit. Grabbing a book lying on the floor, he used it to prop the door open then whistled for the dog. In moments, Ethan and Dino set out exploring the rooms. Classrooms didn't hold much that they could use, so he didn't take much time, but he did grab a few backpacks he found hanging on hooks in a couple of classrooms. He dumped the books but pocketed a candy bar he found in one pack.

ALONE AT THE END OF THE WORLD

The cafeteria's vending machine, after he tipped it over and broke into it, yielded toaster pastries, granola bars, chips, instant oatmeal, tortilla chips, and more candy. It fit into a couple of backpacks.

The kitchen held industrial-sized cans of vegetables, fruit, shortening, and cases of crackers, cookies, and small bottles of juice—apple, orange, and grape. Ethan grinned and unscrewed the cap on a grape juice, gulping it down. Even warm, it was delicious.

As the sugar rushed through him, he continued exploring, using a flashlight he'd taken from the garage at the house. Cans of tuna and sausages joined the other cans. Ethan stacked it all near one doorway, wondering if there was some kind of cart to help him get it all to whatever door was back there.

Although the school smelled dank and musty, there was no stench of death, which surprised him. He couldn't recall the last public building he'd been in that hadn't held the putrid smell of death everywhere. He thought about moving his living quarters there but decided against it. It was too big. He knew he would feel like someone was around every corner.

He found the back door, looked out, and was glad to see that the truck was only a little ways away. After he loaded up everything, he looked at the sky. There were still a few hours of light left. After the rain, everything felt cleaner than it had since before the virus hit. He wanted to explore the school some more and maybe even grab a few books from the library. He'd never been much of a reader before, but he'd found a few paperbacks on the shelves in the house, and out of boredom had begun reading one of them. It was a spy thriller, and he'd found that not only did the story intrigue him, but the simple act of reading about people interacting gave him a feeling of normality he hadn't known he'd been missing.

THE NEXT DAY, Ethan began collecting jugs to put his surplus rainwater in. It wasn't too difficult, surprisingly. Most houses had a recycling bin that hadn't been touched in weeks. He went from house to house, picking out the cleanest jugs. With an abundance of bins to pick from, he was able to select jugs that had only contained water to begin with and wash them with soap and water, figuring the little he used for washing was worth it if it kept them from getting sick.

A girl in his science class had asked the teacher if water in a rain barrel was safe to drink, and Ethan remembered the question because he'd had a crush on the girl. Everything she'd said had been burned into his mind. The teacher had said yes, as long as it was strained and boiled to remove impurities and kill any bacteria. So Ethan strained the water using a brand-new pair of pantyhose, still in a weird egg container when he found them in the dresser drawer of the house. After straining, he boiled the water, using every pot he could find. He wasn't sure how long it was supposed to boil, so to be safe, he boiled each batch for five minutes. Sweating from tending the pots and standing over the grill for so long, he sat and plucked a dandelion. He knew they were edible and thought about tasting the leaves, but then he noticed Dino lying in the shade and threw the leaves down. He didn't think the dog had peed on the leaf, but he wasn't about to take a chance.

When he had a half dozen jugs, he loaded up a wheelbarrow he'd found in the garage with the water, a can of sausages, and a dozen small bags of various flavors of chips. Then he waited impatiently for dark. He'd already prepared his note and taped it to one of the jugs.

He'd kept it short but tried to make it friendly:

Hi! My name is Ethan. I saw you and your kids the other day. I wasn't, like, stalking you or anything. I just saw you and didn't want to scare you or your kids. I heard you tell them you were looking for water. I'm alone and don't need a lot of water and don't mind sharing. I got the sausages and chips from the school cafeteria. If you need more or other stuff, just let me know. I'm pretty good at finding things. I even found a dog.

With the sickness around, I don't want to risk contaminating anyone— not that I'm sick. I'm not. At least not yet, but maybe I could become sick. I don't know. Anyway, I'm just leaving these here for you. I rigged up rain barrels around the house I'm in. They worked really good when it rained last night. If you want, I can get some set up for you. Oh, and I boiled and strained the water already. I hope it helps you out.

Ethan O'Connor

P.S. I guess that was stupid to not tell you how to let me know. It's not like you can text me. I guess if you'd like me to rig it up for you, just leave me a note in the mailbox. I can bring you some more water next time it rains. Maybe sooner if I find some.

He wondered if he should sign his name but decided to because it felt wrong not to, and he could almost hear his mom telling him it was the right thing to do. But as he looked at it, it struck him that putting his full name was silly. It wasn't as if there were a dozen Ethans out there, bringing water. The thought was both sobering and funny, at least kind of.

When it was dark, and he figured they were asleep, he wheeled the delivery around the corner to their house. The moon was almost full and the sky clear, but even so, the darkness pressed on him. He had always found shelter of some sort at night—not only because he needed sleep, but he didn't want to stumble over a corpse, nor did he want to see one under the eerie glow of a flashlight. It would have been like a real-life horror movie.

But that night, the sidewalk was nearly white under the moonlight, and he was able to stick to it for the most part, except when a blob of something blocked his way and he had to skirt around it. Maybe he should have brought Dino, after all. Worried he might bark, he'd left the dog at the house. It was far enough away that if he did make noise, it would blend in with the other dogs he'd heard barking in the distance.

After he delivered the water, he returned to the house he had started to call home, grimacing as the stench of the dead body in the back hit him solidly in the nose. After a while, he always got used to it, but every time he returned, the putrid scent turned his stomach.

When morning came, Ethan popped off the couch, his first thought whether she had found the water. He grinned, imagining her delight at finding it. She probably had already written him a note to thank him.

All day, he ran through different scenarios of her finding the water and food he'd left. Eagerness to find more for the mom and kids spurred him to explore a church. His goal there was mostly to find candles because churches always had candles, it seemed, but as soon as he opened the door, he reeled backward. Nope. No way he was going in there.

He returned to his bike and was about to wheel away when he saw a hall attached to the church, and it made him think of the times he'd gone to Sunday school at a hall similar to that one. There had been a kitchen in it. He rode the bike to the door. He expected it to be locked, but it opened easily. The kitchen looked clean, though, as if it hadn't been used in months. It wasn't until he checked the storeroom beside it that he found boxes of food stacked three boxes high. They were marked "Food Pantry."

When he pulled one down, he found it stocked with canned goods, rice, granola bars, jarred spaghetti sauces and noodles, and even a few bars of chocolate. He took one box with him. It would go to the mom. It was perfect. He could come back later and get one for himself. He had plenty of food.

TWENTY-THREE

When he next opened his eyes, it was due to the pressure of his bladder. The room was bright and sunny. Open windows provided cross-ventilation and he smelled something cooking. *Barbecue?* His stomach growled in response. His water glass had been refilled, and he fought with his desire to quench his thirst but held off. It would only contribute to his other problem. He squirmed. "Hello?"

When there was no answer, he rolled onto his right side and pushed until he was sitting straight up. He leaned back against the wall until the room stopped spinning. He looked for something to grab onto to lever to his feet, but the closest thing was the doorknob to the door into the den from some other room in the back of the house.

He leaned, getting his right knee beneath him and extending his reach to the side. His fingers hooked over the knob, and as he pulled, he straightened his knee at the same time. Upright but swaying, he rested his forehead against the door, only for the door to burst open, sending him flailing backwards, his forehead stinging where it had banged against the wood.

"Oh!" Leona stood with the other side of the doorknob in her hand, her mouth open in shock as she reached out to catch him, but he staggered back, coming up hard against the wall. He wasn't sure how he managed to stay on his feet, but in a second, Leona was at his side, draping his right arm over her shoulders as her arm went behind him, hooking his abdomen just above the bandages. "I've got you. Let's walk over to the sofa."

Noah would have nodded, but he was afraid the action would make him puke, so he simply moved in the direction of the piece of furniture, grabbing the armrest as he pivoted and carefully lowered himself with a grunt. When the darkness receded from his vision, he rubbed his forehead, feeling for a knot or blood.

"I am so sorry, Noah. I heard you get up and was coming in to help you. I had no idea you were standing on the other side of the door."

"Damn, you're doing your best to kill me, aren't you? Why not just shoot me again and get it over with?" Noah winced as he encountered a small lump above his left eyebrow.

Leona crossed her arms and stood back, eyeing him critically. "Maybe I should. It would save me a lot of trouble. And I could kill two birds with one stone."

Noah glanced up in irritation at her tone, doing a double take when she gave him a speculative grin. "What? Two birds?"

"You could probably feed someone my size for a good month or two." She waited a beat before she winked at him, her grin dissolving into laughter. "You should see your face!"

Maybe he had broken into the house of a madwoman, or maybe she was she infected. He tried to scoot away from her, shrinking back against the sofa cushions.

"Oh, relax. I'm not contemplating having you for dinner. I have plenty of food. I was just teasing you."

Noah gave her a weak chuckle. *Whatever*. She must have totally lost it.

Leona almost confirmed his thought. "I'm sorry. I've freaked you out, haven't I?"

"Sort of."

She examined her hands, clasped in front of her, for a few seconds. "It's just that I'm normally a people person. While I live alone, I had a large group of friends, and hardly a day went by that I didn't see one of them either for lunch or dinner, or even a movie or concert. And I miss it. I miss them…" Leona paused, her throat working. "Even more than I miss the conveniences of before and a steady supply of food, I miss talking to people. I miss joking, laughing, and even getting angry at them. How crazy is it that I feel like even though I shot you, you should be, like, my best friend or something?"

Noah wasn't an extrovert in any sense of the word. He had loved his weeks of seclusion in the woods before he learned of the virus. But he knew that his weeks of seclusion could easily turn into a lifetime of seclusion if anything happened to Dexter, Vivian, and the kids, and he found that he also craved human interaction. He was lucky he'd gotten that with the Jackson family and considered how well he would have coped without the Jackson family. Probably not well.

He started to answer, but sudden emotion locked his throat up. *What the hell is wrong with me?* He coughed to cover his embarrassment then gasped when the cough caused the pain from his wound to flare up. It was a few seconds before he could answer, but at least he no longer felt like his tongue was too thick. "I don't know about being best buds, but I don't *hate* you for what you did. I'd have done the same thing. Now, if you could show me where I can use the bathroom?"

The more he thought about the urge to empty his bladder, the harder it became to focus on anything else.

Leona straightened and dashed away so quickly that Noah thought he'd scared her away somehow, but she was back in an instant with a plastic urinal. "Here. I ran over to the hospital when you were sleeping and grabbed one. They still had plenty stocked in cabinets. I guess they weren't a hot item when people broke in to loot it for medications."

Noah took it gratefully then looked pointedly at the door that she'd smacked him in the head with earlier.

Leona nodded, taking the hint, but asked, "Do you need help? While I didn't usually deal with male patients, I did plenty of it when I was in medical school. Nothing embarrasses me."

"Yeah, well, I'm pretty sure I can manage."

"Good. While you're up, you can change out of those dirty jeans and clean up a little. I'll get you some water and a washcloth. I have clean sweatpants and a T-shirt ready for you."

"Great." He nodded and made a shooing motion with his hand.

A few minutes later, he sat on the edge of a recliner, catching his breath as Leona returned with water, towels, and clothes.

Noah glanced at the neat pile. "Hey! Those are my clothes!"

"Yes, they sure are."

"You went into my truck?"

"Of course. How else was I going to find something in your size? It's not like I have anything that would fit you." She set the stack and the water on the desk closest to the recliner and said, "The water is warm. Do you need any help? Once again, nothing—"

"No, I've got it." Somehow, he would clean up and get dressed. He managed pretty well then lay down on the sofa.

He didn't recall falling asleep, but he woke up with the most enticing aroma he'd smelled in a long time curling around his nose. He opened his eyes to find a plate of ribs and fresh green peas on a TV tray beside the couch. *Am I dreaming?*

Slowly, Noah sat up and swung his feet over the edge of the couch. He rested there, taking in the scent. It was what he'd smelled earlier. *Where had the meat come from?*

The door to the den opened slightly, and Leona peeked around the frame. "Just making sure you aren't on the other side of it this time." She opened the door and entered, carrying a plate filled with the same mouthwatering meal that was in front of him. "Do you mind if I join you?"

"No, be my guest. Or—I guess I'm your guest?"

Leona sat on the recliner, picked up a rib smothered in sauce, and took a bite.

Shaking from a combination of weakness and plain old hunger, Noah picked up a rib from his plate and sank his teeth into it. Succulent and juicy, the meat clung to the bone for a second, with just the right amount of resistance. "Wow. This is good."

He took a second bite then eyed the bones warily. He could have sworn they were baby back ribs, but he couldn't fathom where they had come from. Supermarkets were gone, and he didn't hear a generator running, so she couldn't have had a freezer to store the meat.

"What?" Leona licked her thumb, her eyebrow raised at him.

Noah lifted a rib. "What is this, and where did it come from?"

She took a dainty bite, chewing and swallowing before answering. "Well, you see, there was a kid down the street… such an annoying boy. He would ride his bike up and down for hours, yelling and almost knocking down the smaller children, and well, I figured he'd be pretty tasty. And guess what? The old rumors were true! Humans *do* taste like pork."

Noah gagged and grabbed for the glass of water sitting beside the plate.

Leona sent him a sideways glance before laughing. "Oh my God. Your face right now!" She bent forward until her head nearly hit her plate before she rocked backward, rubbing her eyes. "I am so sorry. That was such a bad joke." But her ear-to-ear grin belied her sorrow.

Noah narrowed his eyes. "So *not* funny. What is it? Really."

"It's pork. There are farms all around here. I went out one day a few weeks after everyone else had… well, you know."

Noah nodded and rolled his hand in a "continue" motion.

"I came to a farm where nobody was alive anymore. I couldn't help them, but they had several pigs and chickens that were still alive. They must have really topped up the feed troughs and water before they died, because the animals were still in good shape. The first thing I did was take one of the males and butcher him."

"You know how to butcher meat?"

"It's not so different from surgery, only there are no lawsuits." She took another bite.

"You… you have a sick sense of humor."

Leona nodded. "I do. It's a curse. But seriously, I grew up on a farm. I know how to butcher a pig, pluck a chicken, and shear a sheep. I hadn't done it in a long time, but it's kind of like riding a bicycle."

"What did you do with all of the meat? Surely, you couldn't have eaten it all by yourself." Noah eyed a rib, her earlier story about the bratty kid still causing his stomach to churn, but revulsion warred with his hunger. The hunger won, and he cleaned the bone and reached for another.

"I smoked most of it, salted some, dried a bit into a form of jerky, and even canned some for eating in the winter."

"Canned pork?" He scooped up a forkful of peas and ate them. They were fresh and sweet, the perfect balance to the heavy, rich pork. When his plate was cleaned, he sat back, stuffed. "You have skills. Everything was delicious."

Leona stood, her plate in hand. "Thank you. Let me get your plate soaking. If you'd like some cool tea, I have some I brewed and keep downstairs in the darkest corner of the basement. It's not quite iced tea, but it's refreshing."

"Cold tea? That sounds fantastic." Noah closed his eyes. An idea began to form in his mind. *Will she go for it?* She certainly didn't need their help to survive, but he had to try. They could use someone like her at the farm. *But will she want to leave what she has here and venture off into the unknown?*

"How about we take our drinks out to the porch? It's much cooler this time of evening than here in the house."

Noah conceded that the late-afternoon sun had warmed the room considerably. Setting his jaw, he stood, waited until he felt sure of his balance, and shuffled behind Leona, finally sitting in the rocker she indicated. He couldn't suppress the sigh as he leaned back. Leona handed him his tea and took the rocker on the other side of a small table that separated the rockers. Noah took a long drink. The cool liquid filled his mouth with a slightly sweet tea flavored with a hint of lemon. "Why am I not surprised that the tea is even better than I expected it to be?"

Leona smiled and sipped hers. "So tell me about yourself, Noah."

"There's not much to tell. I went on a fishing trip in mid-May, and when it was over and I came out of the woods, I found the world as I knew it was gone."

"I holed up here as soon as I realized what was happening. At first, I tried to get my closest friends to come and quarantine with me, but nobody believed it would be bad. In the beginning, the virus was on a small island in the Pacific, but once it hit the States and started showing up in countries across the world, I knew it wouldn't take long. It seemed to be spreading exponentially. One day, it was a single case, the next, a hundred, and within a week, the whole country was overwhelmed. It spread more easily than the measles but seems to have a nearly one-hundred-percent mortality rate. The only way to survive was to cut off complete contact with anyone."

"That's definitely how I survived." Noah sipped his tea and stared out toward the northwest, watching as the sun dropped in the sky. "I was supposed to be fishing with my best friend, Miguel. But at the last minute, he texted me that he couldn't make it due to a family emergency and to go alone. Maybe he'd meet me." He blinked and drew the glass close, rubbing his thumb over a drop of condensation. "Obviously, he never met me there."

"I'm sorry, Noah."

He shrugged. "I'm sure you lost friends too."

Her eyes grew misty, but she blinked a few times and didn't look at him. "Yes."

"I was lucky, in a way. I was still trying to piece together what was going on when a family in a minivan came along. Long story short, we teamed up and have moved into a farmhouse. The people who lived there had already started a garden and planted corn. We've been trying to keep it all going, but none of us are farmers. I'm not sure what we'll do with a hundred bushels of corn and soybeans, but I guess we won't starve."

Leona laughed. "That's a lot. Is it sweet corn?"

Noah shrugged. "We're still trying to figure that out. I think a field closest to the farm could be field corn."

"Somewhere, I have a cookbook that explains how to make masa from corn. I'll see if I can find it so you'll be able to put some of the field corn to good use. Do you have any animals?"

"Just a cow and some chickens. No pigs."

"Sounds like a good start, though, and the cow will like the corn."

Noah drained his glass. "For sure. I won't pretend that we know much about farming. There are some books in the house, but I think a lot of this is learned from growing up on a farm—like you did. Reading about it in a book is a lot different from the real thing. We just hope we have enough to keep us going. I was scavenging houses along the way."

Leona darted a look at him. "Along the way to where?"

Noah drew a deep breath. "It's a long shot, but I have a brother, Dave, who has a family living about fifty miles from here. I was on my way there when this happened." He gestured to his wound. "I don't know if they're alive, but I have to know for sure. They're the only family I have."

She nodded. "Of course. I'm sorry I've delayed your quest."

"Quest?" Noah smiled. She made it sound like something noble.

Shrugging, she returned the smile. "What else would you call it? You're searching for loved ones in the face of overwhelming obstacles. I'd call that a quest."

His throat constricted, and he wished he had more tea to wash down the lump. He simply nodded and stared down through his empty glass. His vision went wavy, and he blamed it on the glass distorting his sight. He blinked hard.

They sat in silence for several moments, listening to the sounds of the evening as crickets chirped, mosquitoes whined, and frogs and toads croaked. There must be a creek or marsh nearby. He wondered about cattails. He missed the tubers, although they'd be tough at that time of year.

Lightning bugs flickered in the yard. Ava loved them. She would have had a field day, running up and down the street, catching them. Jalen would catch a few, too, and pretend to be bored even as he darted off to catch one more.

"Tomorrow, I'll change the bandages again to make sure you're not getting an infection, and then you should be ready to continue your journey." Leona stood but remained gazing out into the yard. "I'm sorry I shot you, but I can't say I've been sorry for your company."

Noah cleared his throat. "I think I can speak for the others at the farm when I say that we'd be honored to have you join us if you'd like. The farmhouse is big. There's plenty of room."

She bowed her head, motionless, then sniffed. "I'm honored to be asked, don't get me wrong. But, while you say you speak for the others, what if you show up and I'm just another mouth to feed?"

Noah threw back his head and laughed. "You're kidding, right? Even if you didn't know how to can freaking pork, you'd be valuable for your medical knowledge. Hell, you'd be the most valuable person on the farm, survival-wise. The kids would love you."

"Kids?" Her voice took on a wistful note and she turned to face him. Her expression had lost all of the bravado she'd been showing before.

"Yes, the family I met when I came out of the woods. They have a boy, about fourteen, Jalen, and the sweetest little girl you ever saw. Her name is Ava." He couldn't help the pride in his voice. "They've really been fantastic through this whole thing. Jalen works hard but only complains because I think he thinks he's supposed to, you know? Like he thinks he should because he's a teenager, so he puts on a front. And Ava, she thinks this is a great adventure. Fortunately, she hasn't seen much of the… the carnage… out there. She's taken to the lifestyle like a pig to mud."

"How about if you go find out about your brother and his family, and then, if you still want me to join you, swing back this way. That would give me time to harvest a few things, pack, and whatnot."

Noah nodded. "I'm not going to change my mind, and I will come back. Everyone is going to love you."

TWENTY-FOUR

The next morning, Cassie went outside and almost tripped over jugs of water sitting on her back doorstep. Shocked, she retreated and grabbed her gun from the top of the fridge, which she'd put there only moments before. The kids were still sleeping in the hidden room, and she prayed they would stay that way for a few more minutes.

Peeking out from the door, gun at the ready, she looked around. "Hello?"

Did the guy who'd shot at us find our house somehow? She glanced down, noticing the other items besides the water. *Chips? Tuna?* Then a piece of paper fluttered, startling her at first, but after cautiously looking around, she snatched the note and brought it inside.

After reading it, she turned it over, looking for any other clues. "Ethan?" It didn't sound like something a grown man would write, but it could have been a trick.

She brought the water, chips, and packs of tuna in the house. The tuna and chips were still factory sealed, so she kept them, but she worried about the water as she returned to the stoop to inspect the jugs. *What if it's been poisoned or tainted some other way?* Cassie stuffed the note into her pocket then lifted a jug, unscrewed the cap, and sniffed. She shrugged and tipped her head to the side as she held the jug at eye level. It looked clean. Nothing was swimming around in it. She sniffed it again. There was no weird odor. After setting her gun down within easy reach, she tilted the jug, poured a little bit in her cupped hand, brought it to her mouth, and almost took a sip but decided against it. Even if the water was pure, the person who left it might have had the virus, and after handling the items, she could have it on her hands. She made a mental note to wash her hands with her precious stock of water as soon as she returned to the kitchen.

Holding the gun in one hand and the jug in the other, she walked around the back of the house and down the driveway, contemplating whether she should dare trust that it was really some kid named Ethan and not really the guy who'd tried to kill them.

She didn't spot anything out of the ordinary—the new ordinary, anyway. Standing on the edge of the street, she searched for signs of anyone, but nothing had changed except for the constant decomposition of the corpses. Those who had died in front lawns were at least mostly hidden by weeks of unmown grass and weeds, but those on the pavement had deflated to flattish bags of tissue, hair, and bones. When she had to take the kids with her, she always told them not to look. They did anyway, but they didn't ask many questions anymore.

Retreating back to the house, she left the jugs on the stoop and poured water from a pot she kept on the stove. Even if the stove didn't work, it had become her habit after the first few days when she lost power but still had water and gas. She'd been able to keep a warm pot for washing then. Now, the water had stopped flowing and no gas fueled the stove any longer, but the appliance served as a counter extension. Drying her hands on a towel, she went to her cup of pens on the counter. Rummaging around in her junk drawer, she found an old spiral notebook she kept to jot down recipe ideas. She flipped it open and began writing.

DEAR ETHAN,

Thank you so much for the water, tuna, and chips. As much as I appreciate the supplies, especially the water, I'm leery of accepting them. How can I be sure you are who you say you are? You could be a thirteen-year-old boy who is alone in the world, or you could be like the man who shot at us a few weeks ago. You could even be with him, for all I know. I need some kind of proof. At the very least, I need to see you with my own eyes.

I'm sure you can understand. I don't know if you have the virus or not. I don't know if my children or I have it either, although we haven't been near any living human since about at least a week before the pandemic apparently killed almost everyone. What I was able to read on the Internet, before I lost power, was that the virus was thought to spread very quickly and that people weren't sick for long before they died. I'm kind of hoping that anyone left alive now wouldn't be contagious, but I'm not a medical expert.

In a sign of trust and in thanks for what you have done, I will leave you a loaf of bread I just baked today. I don't have any butter or jam to spare, but maybe you have some of your own. When you get this note, if you want to make contact with me, leave me a reply and we can arrange to meet a safe distance apart.

Cassie

SHE TUCKED the note inside an envelope and wrote "Ethan" on the front. Then that struck her as silly. No one else was going to get it. It would either be Ethan or a man pretending to be a teenaged boy.

Cassie set the envelope aside and moved to the loaves of dough she'd left to rise earlier. She lightly poked a finger into all three of them. They were ready to bake, but she still had to get a fire going in the grill. That's what she'd been going to do when she'd nearly tripped over the supplies.

She left the loaves and went outside, using a round grill she'd found on a neighbor's back deck, and loaded it with charcoal. So far, she'd been able to get by with using a mix of charcoal and wood and had learned how to bank the fire in certain areas of the grill to get the kind of baking she wanted. Bread took a steady, consistent temperature, so she stacked briquettes around the inside perimeter of the grill, making it deep enough to keep it going for a few hours then started them burning with a lighter and a few wads of cotton smeared with petroleum jelly. Then she put the top on. When it came time to add the pans, she would add them in a triangle and do it as quickly as possible to build the heat. After they were in for a while, she would adjust the vents to control the temperature even more. She was quite proud of the loaves she'd produced through trial and error.

When the bread was finished, she left it to cool on the counter. The kids had awakened, and she fixed them breakfast, made sure they brushed their teeth, and let them play in the backyard with a soccer ball. They loved trying to get it past the other and shoot for goals that

Cassie had chalked out on the wooden fences on either side of the yard. If the ball went over a fence, it was a goal for the other player.

Cassie had also introduced them to jump rope, hopscotch, and four square, all games she'd played on the playground at school but that her kids hadn't ever had the chance to learn. She had to do something to keep them occupied. Even in the midst of the apocalypse, they were still kids and needed to play.

As they ran back and forth, laughing when they got by the other or stole the ball, Cassie sat on the stoop and watched. The sun shone, the weather wasn't too hot, and the sky was crystal clear. She still marveled at how much less hazy it was those days.

She unscrewed the top of a precious gallon of bleach she had and poured a few drops into each jug of water left by Ethan. After screwing the tops back on, she gave them a little shake then let them sit. They would be safe to drink in about an hour. Even though she worried about the water and how it had ended up on her stoop, she couldn't ignore it. They needed it desperately. They still had plenty of food, but with everything she'd been trying to do, finding water had been her most time-consuming task. She was sure there was plenty of it out there, but her house wasn't near a natural water source. That fact alone caused her stomach to twist. They couldn't stay in the house indefinitely. At some point, the homes near her would be picked clean, and she would have to widen her scavenging perimeter. That presented a whole host of new problems. *Do I take the kids every time? And what if I run into the man or another like him?*

Every time she contemplated the future, fear bubbled in her stomach, so she forced those thoughts aside. But she couldn't do that forever. The future was going to be the present sooner than she wanted, and she had no idea how they would make it through winter. Her car still ran, she made sure to start it every three days, and had, through trial and error, figured out how to siphon gasoline, but there was nowhere to go. If it had just been her, she would have headed somewhere far from the town, maybe to a lake or riverside or to the country, where she could find an empty house near a stream.

Smiling at Bella, who looked to see her reaction after scoring a goal on Milo, Cassie gave her a thumbs up. Milo grinned at Cassie, not in the least upset that his sister had scored on him. He just loved to play.

Cassie returned to her thoughts as the kids returned to their game. Alice's garden looked like it would produce a lot of vegetables. Already, the strawberries in the patch at the back had produced berries that were on the verge of ripeness. Cassie had tied bits of foil around them and found netting in Alice's garage that looked like its purpose was to protect the plants from birds. With the help of the kids, Cassie had covered the plants the week before. Her mouth watered at the thought of freshly picked strawberries. They definitely wouldn't leave until those were ripe. And a house down the block had potatoes planted. At least, Cassie thought they were potato plants, based on the books she'd taken from Alice's house. Potatoes would supply a lot of needed nutrients and would keep well into the winter. She dropped her head into her hands, her elbows propped on her knees. The prospect of a long, cold winter, even with enough food, with just the three of them made her shiver as if a dark cloud had crossed in front of the sun. She lifted her head, sighing, then tried to hide her despair when she caught Bella looking at her, her expression worried.

Cassie forced a smile. "Hey, who wants to play hopscotch?"

TWENTY-FIVE

Balancing the box on his hip with one hand, he steered with the other as he headed back to the house.

It wasn't until after he'd eaten dinner and was sitting in the backyard, listlessly throwing a stick for Dino, that he realized he'd never said when he would be back to get a reply.

Ethan glanced at the western sky. Soon, it would be dark. Then he could go. He wondered why he should even sneak anymore, since she knew he existed already. The more he thought about it, the more he realized it didn't really matter. He could check the mailbox and make sure nobody was near it more easily in the daylight than he could at night. Leaving Dino in the house and grabbing the box of pantry items, he headed around the corner.

When he reached the mailbox, he looked around. So far, the place looked just as abandoned as it had the day before. Not wanting to creep the mom out, he tamped down the urge to look in the backyard. There were no voices coming from there, and the house looked dark, but the windows were mostly boarded up except for a small window with thick blocks of glass, probably in a bathroom. The blocks were dark. He set the box of food down and drew a deep breath. He hadn't been so nervous since he'd passed a note to his crush, asking if she'd go to the Valentine's Day dance with him. He hoped the reply to last night's note was better than his crush's had been.

He plucked the door of the mailbox down and was bathed in the scent of fresh bread. Ethan closed his eyes and drew in the aroma. "Wow!" Peering inside, he spotted a loaf of bread wrapped in a clear plastic bag. Even encased, the scent made his mouth water. Taped to the loaf was an envelope with his name on it. Grinning, he tucked the loaf under his arm and tore open the envelope.

Ethan read it quickly, his grin fading. *Someone had shot at them? Who would do something like that?* He pivoted, searching the area. *Is the person with the gun watching me even now?* There was no movement.

He went around to the back of the house, debating whether or not it was too late to knock. It was still a little light out.

Screwing up his nerve, he knocked on the door and backed away. Seconds passed, and nobody came. He stepped up to knock again when he heard a shuffling on the other side, and he stepped away just before the door opened.

The mom, Cassie, as she'd signed on her note, stood on the other side of the screened door. The house was mostly dark, and he couldn't be sure, but he thought she might have a gun in the hand she held down by her side. He gulped. "Hi… I'm Ethan."

She studied him for several seconds. "Are you alone?"

He blinked and looked around. "Yeah. Of course." He spread his arms then let them fall. "I'm all alone." He scratched his elbow. "I'm sorry if I scared you or anything when I left the water. I didn't mean to. I thought it would help. That's all."

"It does."

Her response was so different from what he'd expected that he edged away even more. He lifted the loaf of bread. "Thanks for this. It smells really good."

She might have nodded, but he wasn't certain because her face was in shadows.

"Well, I guess I'll go." He felt stupid for getting his hopes up—for what, he wasn't even sure, but it definitely wasn't this.

Head down, he turned to leave but stopped. "I'll still bring you water as soon as I get more jugs and it rains again. I know it must be hard with little kids in the house. Sorry, again." He wasn't certain why he was apologizing, but the situation seemed to call for it. He must have done something to screw up.

"Ethan… wait!"

He paused his trudge down the driveway and turned back.

The screen door slammed, and Cassie ran around the side of the house. "Ethan, I'm sorry. You didn't do anything wrong. I was scared, but that wasn't your fault."

He scuffed a toe on the pavement and shrugged. "It's okay."

"I just had to be sure there was nobody else with you."

"There's never been anybody with me. Just a dog, but I left him where I'm staying."

Cassie pushed her hair back. "Where are you staying? Do you have food?"

He hesitated.

Before he could tell her, she said, "You don't have to tell me. I didn't mean to grill you. I only asked because I thought you might be hungry."

Ethan shook his head. "No. I've got food. And I've got this." He lifted the loaf of bread, but then could have kicked himself for saying he wasn't hungry. Not that he was, but he didn't want to leave. He hadn't spoken to another person in so long.

She nodded. "Yeah. Of course." She smacked her own forehead and said, "D'oh!" Then she laughed softly. "After what you left me, I guess I should be asking you how to get food these days."

Ethan shrugged and chuckled. "It's not too hard. A lot of stores are empty, but houses have a lot. You just have to be careful because of all the…" He made a face. He was unable to say "dead bodies."

"I know. I hate that. So many people… are gone now. Most of them, I guess—and I didn't think I'd say this, but I miss talking to people. I wondered if you might want to come in and have a snack? I have something, a treat I made for the kids." She half turned and motioned toward the house.

Ethan straightened, unable to stop the grin from stretching across his face. "I'd like that." Before he moved toward her, he remembered his biggest fear. "Um, as much as I'd like it, I'm scared you might get sick from me."

Cocking her head, Cassie studied him so long, he began to squirm. "I understand. It's a valid concern, and I have the same worry about infecting you. I was oblivious to the start of this virus, so I missed the warning signs, but I did manage to get to a few sites that explained it before the electricity cut off. It seemed like it didn't have a long incubation period, but it made people extremely social, and that's how so many were infected so quickly. Were you around your family when they got it?"

"I'm thirteen. I think. Not sure of the date, so maybe I'm fourteen by now, but anyway, where else would I have been?" He bit his lip, hoping she didn't take his comment for sarcasm.

"Right. What was I thinking? You seem older, even if you still look young. Sorry. Anyway, I can't be one-hundred-percent sure it's safe for either of us, but I wouldn't invite you in if I thought you would infect us."

Ethan hesitated a second longer. He wasn't worried about them infecting him. He'd already come to terms with catching it sooner or later. How he'd been so lucky already was a mystery. But he was so tired of being alone. "Okay."

They went in the house, and he stood in the dark kitchen until she pressed a battery-operated light on the wall near a table. "I found that still in the box in my closet. I try not to use it too much, though."

He peered at it. He'd seen infomercials about lights that stuck anywhere, but his parents hadn't ever used them. "I should look for those. I never thought of it." He could have used one in his travels.

The light gave the kitchen a weirdly bright look. He wasn't used to artificial light anymore and squinted. Then his mouth fell open. A chocolate cake sat on the counter. "Did you make that?"

"I did. I was hoping you'd come back. It's the treat I made, but I really made it for you."

"You made the cake for me?" He pointed to his chest.

She shrugged. "I was hoping—praying, really, that you were who you said you were in your note. I still worried you'd end up being the guy who shot at us." She motioned to a chair. "Have a seat."

He sat, keeping his hands on his lap. "Oh yeah. I read that in your note. I'm sorry that happened to you."

"Mommy!"

Ethan jumped. He'd forgotten about the kids.

"Hold on a second, Ethan. I have to let the kids know they can come out."

"Come out?"

"I should say up. They can come up." She darted a look towards a door that led towards some other room in the house. "Excuse me for a moment."

She disappeared, and he heard her going downstairs. A few minutes later, she returned with a child's hand in each of hers. "Here he is, just like I said. Milo and Bella, meet Ethan."

Bella's mouth dropped open. "A real boy!"

Ethan laughed. "Just like Pinocchio. Except my nose doesn't grow."

She giggled and Milo approached, stopping a few feet away. "Do you play soccer?"

Ethan nodded. "I do. I played on a travel team."

"What's that?"

Cassie laughed. "That was a team for really good players."

Was. The past tense hit him like a sucker punch.

"Can you play with me sometime?" Milo gave him a pleading look, his eyes wide.

Still trying to shake off the shock of the realization that everyone on his team was probably dead, Ethan hadn't even processed the question, let alone come up with an answer. Milo pressed his hands together in a praying gesture. "Please?"

"Sure. If it's okay with your mom."

The little boy turned his puppy-dog eyes on his mother, freeing Ethan from their hold.

He sighed, his shoulders slumping.

Cassie gave him a long look but then replied to Milo, "Of course. But it's too dark tonight."

"Do we get to have cake now?" Bella stood next to the counter, one finger already covered in frosting. She popped it into her mouth while her mom wasn't looking. She caught Ethan watching her, though, and grinned. He grinned back. He would never tell.

TWENTY-SIX

"At least you have your kids." Ethan ate a piece of cake. There were still several pieces left after the nighttime snack the night before, and Cassie had encouraged him to help himself. Her kids were too busy playing with Ethan's dog to want cake now. Besides, for them, cake wasn't a huge treat. While it had been less frequent after the first cupcakes had been eaten, she'd made treats a few times just to keep everyone's spirits up.

The night before, they had eaten cake, drunk juice boxes, and talked for over two hours. It had felt like a party. She'd invited him to stay the night, but he explained he had to get back to Dino. The kids had cried when he'd left. She didn't blame them. It wasn't just that he was the first person they'd seen in weeks, but he was a genuinely nice kid. His parents must have been really proud of him. His story had broken her heart, but she'd tried to hide her emotions because she sensed he'd barely been hanging on, himself. Any sign from her would have made it impossible for him to keep his emotions at bay. It was too soon for him to trust her enough to break down in front of her. He was a tough kid, but in a sweet way. He was a survivor.

He'd promised to return first thing, and she'd found a reason to be outside most of the morning. At first, when he'd pulled up in the delivery truck from a local garden center, she'd herded the children inside. When Ethan had hopped out, she almost died laughing. He was a least a few years too young for a license, but it didn't make much difference.

She leaned against the counter, eating a tiny slice of cake. It was getting a bit dry, but Ethan didn't seem to mind. He'd said he had plenty of food, but he was really thin. However, given how far he'd ridden his bicycle before reaching her town, she figured he'd probably burned off more than he consumed. Plus, he was clearly at the age where he would have a massive growth spurt.

"You're right. I do have my children, and a day doesn't go by that I don't say a prayer of thanks. Still, it's nice to talk to someone who's more like a grown-up."

He laughed. "I'm not a grown-up."

"Maybe you still have some growing to do, but it certainly sounds like you've done things most adults have never had to do."

Nodding, he shoved the last bit of cake in his mouth.

She turned and set her dirty plate in a shallow pan in the sink. When she had enough, she would pour water over them and wash with the water Ethan had brought with him. "What are your plans now?"

Shrugging, Ethan drew his fork through a few crumbs on his plate, not meeting her eyes. "I don't make plans."

She had always heard of living in the moment, but nobody over the age of ten ever really did—they couldn't. There had always been things in the near or far future to plan for, whether it was simply what to have for dinner. People made plans. Plans gave people hope for the future. She moved to the chair opposite him. "Well, we're going to start making plans right now. Okay?"

He lifted his eyes to her and held her gaze, and it was all she could do not to draw him into a hug. She couldn't stop from reaching out and taking one of his hands in hers, giving it a gentle squeeze. "We'll survive this, Ethan."

ETHAN STAYED until early afternoon then left, leaving Dino with them since they had all gone inside when it got too warm and had fallen asleep in a pile in the basement. Ethan returned to the house where he'd been staying to get all of the supplies he'd left there. He loaded his rain barrels, his bicycle, trailer, camping gear, and clothes. He felt like he was floating. The last time he'd felt so alive was before his family died.

As he arranged everything in the truck, he thought back to just before the virus hit. Mother's Day had been okay. He'd given his mom a cheap ring from a kiosk at the mall. He'd wanted something more expensive. His allowance hadn't allowed anything more, but his mom had exclaimed how beautiful it was. She'd put it on right then. As far as he knew, she hadn't taken it off. He should have checked to see if she still wore it when he buried her.

Rubbing his arm across his forehead, he paused to get a breath of air. It was hot inside the truck. He hopped down, closed the door, then moved to get his water bottle from where he'd left it on the stoop.

He tipped it, gulping the tepid water. He'd tried to keep it in the shade, but it was still warm. Pouring a little in his hand, he splashed his face. Talking about his family with Cassie had opened a floodgate of memories, and he couldn't seem to close the gate. For once, he didn't try. He let them flow and cherry-picked his favorite from the stream.

His last best memory was from Easter. It had been Ethan's job to hide eggs for his little sister, and seeing her toddle around, finding them and showing off her plastic eggs like she'd found the rarest jewels, was a memory he would hang on to for as long as he lived.

Tilting the bottle, he froze when he heard something. *A car? Could it be Cassie?* He'd described the house, and she said she thought she knew which one it was, but she wouldn't be coming over when he'd said he would be back soon.

Securing the lid back on the water, he tossed it in the yard and darted down the driveway. He ducked behind a bush when a truck drove slowly down his street. A man sat behind the wheel. Ethan's breath caught as he considered that it could have been the guy who had shot at Cassie. He watched, and when he saw the truck turn left down Cassie's street, Ethan swore. He had to warn her or something.

Instead of going down Cassie's street, Ethan raced around the other corner and sprinted to the house right behind Cassie's. There had been a low fence between the two, and he was sure he could climb it quickly. He cut across lawns dotted with thick grass and weeds, leaping over a few bodies, and it only took him a minute or so to get to the house. He wanted to catch his breath, but there was no time. He dashed through the backyard, ignoring the body of what must have been a dog. Putting both hands on the top rail, he vaulted the fence and raced to Cassie's back door. Pushing sweat-dampened hair from his eyes, he peered around the corner and down the driveway. The truck was parked right in front. It had to be the guy. *What is he doing? Why is he just sitting there?*

He ducked back and tapped lightly on Cassie's door. "*Cassie!*" he whisper-shouted.

The door opened. "You don't have to knock—what's wrong?"

"There's a man in a truck in front of your house."

Her eyes opened wide. "Get in." She stepped aside to let Ethan in, but he balked.

"No! I can stop him."

Cassie looked him up and down. "How?"

Ethan drew a deep breath. "I'll find a weapon. There must be something out here."

"I have a weapon. What I need is for you to take the kids down into the basement. There's a secret room there. They know how to get in."

When he hesitated, she gave him a look that brooked no argument, and Ethan nodded. "Be careful."

Cassie already had a gun in her hand, the same one Ethan had seen the night before. He'd forgotten about it. He rushed into the living room, picked up Bella, and had Milo hop onto his back. "Your mom wants you to show me the secret room." He gave a low whistle for Dino, who came to him. The dog raced down the stairs as though he'd lived in the home all his life.

"She told you about it?" Bella gave him a skeptical look as Ethan descended the stairs.

It was dark, but his eyes adjusted. "Yeah. She's going to check on something she saw outside and wants me to stay with you guys."

TWENTY-SEVEN

Finding his way around his brother's town wasn't as difficult as Noah had expected. When he saw landmarks, he remembered where to turn. The only issue was trying to remember the name of his brother's street. He cruised down several, weaving around wrecks and debris, surprised to see several tree limbs blocking roads. He supposed they'd fallen during a late-spring storm.

He came to the house and pulled up out front. He recognized his brother's car in front and frowned. From the layer of pollen covering it and one flat tire, it looked as though it hadn't moved since the apocalypse began. He contemplated whether to bother going to the door. He didn't want to see their bodies, especially after a few months.

Noah scanned the neighborhood. It looked no different from all of the other dead neighborhoods he'd driven through. He sighed. He'd come all this way.

His mouth dry, he took a drink from one of the jugs and twisted slightly to see the other side of the street. He winced as his wound pulled. Leona had redressed it and given him some antibacterial ointment and a change of dressings. He cracked the door, drew a deep breath, and exited the truck. Like every other yard, weeds had claimed possession of the land already.

He stepped onto the front stoop—the house looked like it was boarded up from inside. That was odd. Maybe it had been repossessed prior to the pandemic. Noah opened the screen door and knocked on the heavy front door behind it.

Even though he hadn't expected anyone to answer, he couldn't deny the pain and sorrow that hit him when nobody answered. He turned to leave, his chest tight and shoulders slumped. *Dammit. What if I'd have come right away? Maybe they'd still be alive.*

He didn't even have a damn picture of his brother or the kids. He did an about-face. He was there, and if nothing else, he could get photos. At least he'd have those to remember his brother and family by.

The front door was locked, so he decided to try the back. Maybe there was a key under a mat or something.

As he walked up the driveway, he glanced into the neighbor's backyard then stopped in his tracks. There was a garden, and it had clearly been tended recently. Tomato plants were staked and tied, and dead weeds had been tossed into a pile in the middle of the yard. He moved toward the yard. A faint path cut through the long grass. A few muddy footprints stained the top layer of flattened grass. Those had to be recent. Rain would have washed them away. Someone was alive. He started to turn but felt something hard prod his back.

"*Freeze!*"

Noah froze, as instructed.

"Why did you shoot at me and my kids the other day?"

Confused by the question, that the voice was female, and that it sounded familiar, he didn't respond as quickly as the woman liked, and she prodded him in the back, very close to where the bullet had wounded him. He hissed and twisted away.

"Don't move! And put your hands up!"

Noah raised his arms. He had his gun in his special holster, but the AC in the truck blew cold and he'd grabbed hoodie from the backseat of the cab. He'd forgotten about it. Lot of good it did him now.

"I'm sorry! If you quit poking me, I might be able to answer." Noah wished he could see his assailant.

"You didn't answer my question. You could have killed us! What kind of man shoots at children?" She prodded him again, but the cold anger in her voice made him bite back a hiss of pain.

"It wasn't me. I swear to God. I just drove in from the highway not fifteen minutes ago."

"Right. And you came straight to my house. Of all the houses in the town, you just happened to come to mine."

"No, I didn't just happen to. I came here because it used to be my brother's house. Dave and his family lived here."

"Your brother?"

The pressure in his back lessened. "Yeah. My brother. Do you live around here? Maybe you know him? Dave Boyle."

"Noah?"

Puzzled, he lowered his hands and tried to glance over his shoulder but couldn't see who was holding the gun. "How do you know my name?" Then it clicked. "*Cassie?*" He turned, his mouth dropping open. "Oh my God! You're alive!" Grinning, he reached to hug her, but she backed away.

"Whoa. Back off." She raised the gun, her brow furrowed.

Her hair was longer than he remembered, and she was even thinner, but he recognized his sister-in-law. "Don't you remember me? I'm Dave's brother." He thumped his chest. "I'm Noah."

She tilted her head, frowning. "You have a beard."

He fingered it. "Yeah. Actually grew it on my fishing trip before any of this happened." Every year, he grew a beard on his trip but shaved it when he went back to work. But no one had the time or inclination to shave during the apocalypse. He looked around. "Where's Dave?"

The gun wavered, and she finally lowered it. "I'm sorry, Noah. Dave is dead." She pointed listlessly with her left arm. "He died right over there in the neighbor's front yard. I should have buried him, but I never had a chance." She stared at a patch of weeds that was a little thicker than the rest of the lawn then turned to meet his eyes. "I'm so sorry."

The news shouldn't have been such a shock. He'd expected it, thinking his brother was dead for almost two months, but guessing and even assuming Dave was dead was a far cry from being told it as fact with the body decomposing mere steps away. Noah bent, bracing his hands on his knees. "Dave. Oh, *Dave*..."

He closed his eyes, awash in memories of his brother and how they had looked out for each other back then, each protecting the other the best they could from their dad. Scenes of fun and laughter, bittersweet in their innocence, gave way to later memories, when

Dave had battled his addictions. "I should have been here. I could have helped him."

"Noah, you couldn't help him. Ever since he started doing drugs again, Dave was different. This time, he never got the chance to go back to the old Dave, the brother you knew." She sighed. "Or the man I loved."

Noah straightened, rubbing the back of his hand across his eyes. "I knew he got out of prison. I hoped he'd spent the time getting his life figured out. Not that it matters anymore." Even if Dave had been the picture of virtue, it wouldn't have helped him escape the virus.

"No. It doesn't." Cassie watched him, her expression wary.

"Is something wrong?" He knew it was an idiotic question to ask in the midst of an apocalypse. Then it hit him. "The kids? Are they okay?" He spun, searching.

"They're fine, Noah."

This time, relief almost overwhelmed him. It was too much to hope for. He had his second chance to be a good uncle. They were his only kin. "Look, Cassie, I'm sorry about Dave. But it's a miracle you and the children survived. We can all go to the farm and—"

"Hey, hold on. I didn't say I'd go anywhere with you. I barely know you, Noah."

"But, I'm your brother-in-law. I was best man at your wedding."

"That was seven years ago, and I've seen you about five times since then. Other than that, our relationship has consisted of a few texts and Christmas and birthday cards. I sent you pictures of Bella and Milo, and if I was lucky, I'd get back a thumbs up." She posed with two thumbs up and a sarcastic smile.

Noah dipped his head. Guilty as charged. "I know. I wasn't much of an uncle before. I did send gifts, though." He hated the defensive note on the end of the sentence.

Cassie crossed her arms, the handgun still in one hand, but at least it was safely pointed away from him. "True. You sent Bella a doll every year."

Noah grinned and nodded. "Yeah. I did."

"She hates dolls. She loves stuffed animals. Dolls freak her out."

"Milo loves trains, though," Noah said hopefully. He clearly remembered seeing a video of his nephew pointing excitedly at the television as a large blue train chugged across the screen, screaming, *"Twain! Twain!"*

She rolled her eyes. "When he was two. It was a phase, but he moved on. Right now, he likes Hot Wheels and soccer." She dipped her head, toeing a dandelion that grew in the pavement cracks. "Also, you're not my brother-in-law, Noah. Not anymore. I divorced Dave when he got out of prison."

"Oh." He shook his head. "Sorry. I didn't know." His ignorance of something so important only proved her correct. He barely knew her or his niece and nephew. "But how are you getting by?"

Her chin rose. "We're surviving."

"Yeah, me too. It's crazy, isn't it? Have you seen other survivors?" Maybe the world wasn't as devastated as they thought. There could still have been pockets of civilization.

Her tough façade cracked. "It's so crazy. I've only seen two other people. One tried to kill me."

Noah stiffened. "Who? Where are they?"

"Cool your jets. It was days ago, and I haven't seen him since. I know your soldier instincts are to kill the enemy, but—"

"I may suck at being an uncle, but that doesn't mean I want anything to happen to Bella or Milo." He'd been overjoyed only moments before to find Cassie alive and learn the kids were okay. The joy was still there—nothing could take that away—but her words cut, mostly because they were true. He had just killed a man. Cassie was wrong about one thing, though. She'd said she barely knew him, but she did know him. She knew him too well. "Can I at least see the kids before I go? I'm not sure if I'll ever get to see them again."

Cassie's eyes widened. "What do you mean?"

He opened his arms. "Do you think I'll be able to pick up a phone and call you? Or maybe send a text?"

She waved a hand at him. "Stop. I get it. Noah, I don't know that I want to go anywhere with you. I dealt with your brother, and you're two peas that grew up in the same pod. Don't blame me if I'm leery of up and moving with you on a whim."

He widened his stance, arms crossed, mirroring her posture. "It's not exactly a whim. It's the end of the world."

"Cassie? Are you okay?"

Noah pivoted to find a shaggy-haired boy with a dog beside him, standing on the front stoop. The dog looked stiff, his eyes fixed on Noah. He darted a look at the dog before focusing on the boy again. "Who are you?"

"I'm fine, Ethan. This is Bella and Milo's uncle."

Noah relaxed. "Hi, Ethan."

Ethan's eyes opened wide, then his mouth curved into a smile. "You're their uncle?"

Noah nodded, returning the smile. It was impossible not to.

"Wow, that's amazing! Cassie, the kids have a living uncle! Isn't that insane?" He vaulted down the stairs and ran up to Cassie. He reminded Noah of an overly friendly puppy.

"I guess."

Ethan's smile faltered. "What's wrong?"

Cassie jabbed a finger in Noah's direction. "He's their uncle by blood, but he probably doesn't even know how old they are."

"She's right. I'm not certain." Noah had no room to call Cassie out for her rude comment.

Cassie gave him a smug smile. "Where were you when your asshole brother was shooting up opioids or trying to steal anything I didn't have nailed down so he could get more drugs? And where were you when he punched me?"

Noah's anger ignited. "Dave punched you?"

Ethan interrupted, "I don't get it, Cassie. Your kids have a living relative. Do you know how lucky they are?" His voice cracked with what sounded like sorrow, but his expression was angry. "I'd give anything to have a relative still alive. Even if it was a third cousin twice removed."

Cassie's eyebrows arched in surprise. "Ethan, you don't know the whole story. He wasn't there before—"

"Before doesn't matter anymore. There's only now. And your kids have an uncle right now."

Cassie stabbed her hands through her hair and blew out a breath. "Yeah. I guess you're right." She gave Noah a sidelong glance. "I'm sorry, Noah. I shouldn't have said those things."

Instantly, his anger evaporated. "You had every right to rake me over the coals, but as your friend, Ethan, has said, I'm their uncle, and I know haven't shown it like I should have, but I love those kids. You don't know how often I took out my phone and looked at their pictures. Anytime I was having a bad day, I'd watch the videos you sent me. I'm pretty sure I can recite everything they said in every one of them. That's why I thought Milo still loved trains. It's one of my favorite videos."

Her expression softened, her eyes shiny. "He was pretty damn cute in that one."

Noah grinned. "Right?" He grew serious. "I'm sorry if I came off like I was ordering you to come with me. Of course you don't have to. It looks like you're doing fine on your own."

"I'm not." She shook her head and tears spilled down her cheeks. "I have the kids hiding down in a hidden room I made. I was worried the guy who shot at me would come after us. I thought we'd hide there if we had to, but it was stupid. I don't think the fake wall would fool anyone."

"It's a good wall, Cassie. Milo had to show me where it was because I couldn't find it."

Cassie gave Ethan a soft smile and laughed. "You're too nice."

"Mommy? Who's that?"

Noah glanced at the doorway. He might have only had a handful of memories with the kids and a few pictures and videos, but the minute he saw his Bella and Milo, a feeling of wonder shot through him. Milo had grown to look like his dad but had Cassie's mischievous twinkle in his eye. He'd forgotten about Cassie's twinkle. And Bella. Her name fit her. She was beautiful but wary.

Cassie waved the kids over. "This is your Uncle Noah. He came to take us to a farm?" She raised an eyebrow in question.

He nodded. "But only if you want to go."

Milo bounced over to them. "Can I go too?"

Noah laughed. "It's a group invitation. You can all come."

Cassie looked at Ethan. "I won't go unless Ethan can go too."

Noah looked at the boy's eyes. His invitation had always included Ethan, if he'd wanted to go. Noah didn't know much about him except that he had no living relatives. That was enough—that and the way Cassie had stood firm for Ethan's inclusion. He must have been a helluva kid. "I wouldn't have it any other way."

TWENTY-EIGHT

Cassie handed Ethan the last sack of flour to take out to his truck. Her pantry was mostly bare now. Sugar had gone out earlier, along with several boxes of salt and a tin of pepper, a jar of peppercorns, and a peppermill. She was making one last pass in the house, a large box in hand. She lifted the spice grinder and cocked her head. It was electric, and she doubted they'd have any electricity, but it was small, so she tossed it in a box, anyway. Maybe the parts would be useful for something else. Setting the box on the floor, she bent backwards, holding the small of her back and wondering when she had acquired so much crap.

Dusting her hands off, she perused the shelves. All that remained was an empty jar of honey and an ancient jar of ginger that had lost all of its scent. Even after living off mostly what she'd had on hand, she'd still had a lot to pack. She'd forgotten how big her pantry actually was. It had been the selling point of the house for her, and now, it was empty. Every jar of spice, every herb, and every flavoring had been packed carefully away.

"I think I got all the pots, pans, and baking sheets, Cassie." Noah filled the door of the pantry. It made her nervous. After an awkward dinner of tuna and noodles last evening, Noah had bedded down in his truck. He'd said it was to be on guard for the man who had shot at her, but she thought he'd felt as uncomfortable as she had.

"Good. Did you find the cast-iron pans in the cabinet beside the sink?"

"Sure did. Those will be great when we cook over the fire pit. Did I tell you how I wanted to find an old wood-burning stove? I think I may know where one is. I'm going to swing by there on the way back. It'll be worth the detour if it's still there."

She shrugged. "I'm in no rush. How do you know about it?"

"I spoke to the chef who was restoring it."

"What if he's still alive and using it?" She shoved her bag full of plastic grocery bags into the box. She'd felt guilty about using the plastic bags since they were so bad for the environment, but they would serve many purposes while they lasted. She couldn't bear to leave them behind. She glanced at Noah, noting his pensive expression, and Cassie realized she'd sounded snarky and didn't mean to. "I mean, hopefully, he made it."

Noah must have let her tone slide because he only nodded and said, "That would be awesome if he was alive. I'd much rather have that be the case."

Chastened, she replied, "Of course. I mean, I knew you would."

"I'm going to take these last few boxes out to the truck. If you need me to carry anything else, just let me know."

His voice was so similar to her ex-husband's that some of her reactions were habit after years of dealing with Dave's issues, and it wasn't fair to pigeonhole Noah as though he was a carbon copy of his brother. Cassie moved into the kitchen, opening cabinets to double-check that she wasn't leaving anything important. Her mug of pens and pencils remained on the counter, and she grabbed that. She had a feeling that writing implements would be in great demand. For that matter, paper might be too. She opened her junk drawer and pulled out a spiral notebook, making a mental note to get the kids' construction paper.

Noah wasn't like Dave, and he never had been. Some of her resentment probably stemmed from the time she'd pointed out to Dave how Noah had managed to make something of his life even after being raised in the same house with the same cruel father. Dave had swung his fist at her. She'd ducked in time and had left the house. She hadn't seen him for almost a week, then, and when he returned, he had begged forgiveness. And she had given it, but some part of her had resented that it was Noah who had been able to go on with his life while her husband seemed to be stuck in rebellious adolescence for much of his adult life.

"I packed up all my stuffed animals and books, Mommy."

Cassie looked down at Bella, who had her Disney Princess suitcase in hand. "You have them all in there?"

She nodded. "And my blanket."

"Good thinking. We mustn't forget that." She bent her knees to lower herself to Bella's eye level. "You are being so brave and helpful, sweetheart. Thank you." She leaned forward and kissed the tip of her daughter's nose.

"What about me?" Milo, with all of his worldly goods stuffed into his pillowcase even with his pillow still in there, stood expectantly.

"You too. C'mere, sweet pea." She drew him into a hug. "Both of you have been the best kids ever." They really had been great. They'd seen a lot, even as she'd tried to shield them, but there had been no way to shield them from corpses rotting on the street or a man shooting at them for no reason.

"So are you driving the truck, or is Ethan?" Noah grinned as he entered the kitchen from the back door.

"We agreed he would, but we may end up taking turns." Cassie shook her head with a smile. "What a kid."

"What about your car?"

Cassie shrugged. "That's why Ethan is driving the truck. There's not enough room for all four of us in there, and I can't take all of my things with just my car."

"We have my truck too. Ethan or one of the kids could ride with me. We'd still manage to get us all in."

"Yes, I know, but I think I want my car, anyway. It's small and doesn't use a lot of gas. That could be important in the coming months."

"You're right." He smiled at the kids. "I guess I'll have plenty of time to get to know these two later."

Ethan and Noah moved the mattresses and bed frames out to the big truck. They'd decided to move the beds she had to the farmhouse because, while there was a lot of space there, there weren't enough beds for everyone. She also packed all the linens she had. Every item of clothing she and the kids owned and a few items of Dave's from before he'd gone to prison also made their way into a box. Someone could use them eventually. Even with everything they'd packed, the truck still had plenty of room.

Noah looked at it for a long moment, as if calculating.

Cassie looked from the half-full interior of the truck to Noah. "What?"

"I'm just wondering if there's enough space in here."

"That's everything I'm taking. There's plenty of room." Cassie scanned the boxes and beds. The mattresses took up the most space, but they leaned against one side of the truck, held there with boxes stacked against them. Bungee cords secured everything from sliding around.

"Oh, I know. I'm thinking about someone else. I promised I'd stop by on the way back to get her."

"Her? Who is she?" *Had Noah picked up a girlfriend already? In the middle of an apocalypse?* Dave had always claimed his brother could get any girl he wanted. She guessed maybe he'd spoken the truth for once. "And more importantly, how in the world did you meet her?"

Noah laughed. "It's a crazy story. She shot me."

"What? *Shot* you? As in, with a gun?"

He lifted the side of his shirt and revealed a white bandage taped around his left side. "Thankfully, it wasn't too serious. Still hurts like a bitch, though."

Cassie brought a hand to her mouth. "No wonder you jumped when I stuck the gun in your back. Sorry about that."

"It's okay. I'm getting used to women pointing guns at me."

"Why did she shoot you? What did you do?"

He spread his hand on his chest as he turned and sat on the back bumper of the truck. "What did I do? Why are you so certain I did something?"

There he was, sounding like Dave again. But unlike her ex, his tone held only mirth and gentle teasing. She started to say something about if he was anything like his brother, he would have known why but remembered how devastated he'd been the night before upon learning of his brother's death. She'd found him staring at a picture of Dave with the kids that she'd left on a shelf. The news was still fresh and raw to him. Instead, she gave a lame reply. "I just have a feeling."

"Okay, I had broken into her house. But in my defense, I thought nobody was alive in there. I was looking for food and supplies."

"And she shot you."

"Yes. She shot me."

"And now you want her to come and live with us on the farm." *Am I the only one who thinks that sounds like a crazy idea?*

Noah bent forward, laughing so hard that she worried about his wound when he clutched it suddenly, but he kept right on laughing.

ETHAN CARRIED the last box down from the upstairs and out to his truck. Sweat beaded his forehead, and dust clung to the sweat, creating muddy streaks whenever he tried to wipe the sweat away, but the last two days had been the best of his new life. He didn't think of his old life much anymore. He couldn't. It was too painful. There was the before and the blurry time when he'd wandered with Dino, with the past too painful to remember and the future too bleak to contemplate.

He felt like he had a future, though. He couldn't fathom what it would be like, but there was one, and he had a family—sort of—again. Milo and Bella already followed him around like a little brother and sister, and Dino loved to play with them. Cassie was awesome, and while he wasn't sure about Noah yet, he seemed like a decent guy.

His only worry was what would happen if they decided he was too much trouble and they didn't want him. He'd only known them for less than a handful of days, even though it seemed like a lot longer, especially for Cassie.

A few years before, Ethan had begun mowing neighbors' lawns and had done the best he could, but a few times he messed up and mowed over flowers or forgot to check for toys left on the lawn. He'd been new to working for pay and worried the neighbors would quit hiring him. His dad said one way to keep them calling was to make yourself indispensable. At the time, Ethan hadn't quite understood because he was just mowing lawns, but that lesson rushed back to him. If he worked so hard that they needed him—that he was indispensable—they would let him stay.

"Ethan, here's a bottle of juice and a few peanut-butter-and-jelly sandwiches for the road." Cassie handed him the juice and a paper bag.

"Thanks." He still couldn't believe he was going to be driving.

Noah approached, carrying a similar bag. He lifted it like a trophy. "I see you got your lunch too."

Ethan nodded.

"So, I'll be in the lead. I wish I could be in the back, but I'll have to show you both the way. You'll be in the middle, so you really just have to follow my tail. Cassie will be in the back. We're going to stay close together, and if you see Cassie flashing her lights, it means she needs us to stop. You can flash your lights, and I'll know you need to stop, too, okay?"

"Maybe I should be in the back?" It didn't seem right that Cassie should be in the back with two little kids. Something could happen to them.

Noah clapped a hand on his shoulder. "I know what you're thinking, but Cassie can handle herself. I filled up all the tanks as soon as it was light enough to see and even got an extra ten gallons, so we're good on fuel. We may even make it with one tank, but if not, there are plenty of cars along the way we can get gas from for now."

Ethan called Dino over, made sure he had a long drink from his bowl, then had him jump up in the truck. At least he would have the dog to keep him company.

TWENTY-NINE

Noah glanced in his side-view mirror. So far, the kid had been driving admirably. Granted, there was no traffic, but there were a lot of obstacles, and he was driving a partially filled truck. That changed how it handled when trying to maneuver around debris. Cassie stayed back just far enough to react to Ethan's maneuvers.

They had left around midmorning, and Noah hoped to get to Leona's by noon or so. As they left Cassie's city, he noted thick, black smoke on the other side of town. He wasn't sure if the fire had been started by a human, but he was glad Cassie wouldn't be there alone anymore. He hadn't told her, but while looking for gasoline that morning, he'd heard gunfire coming from the same direction as the smoke, and he wouldn't doubt that the fire and the gunshots were caused by the same person. Noah would bet any money the guy who had shot at Cassie had been angry that she was taking what he felt was his. There was always a subset of the population who hoarded and guarded everything, never sharing in times of need. He'd seen it during his tours in Afghanistan. Most of the families affected by the war there were good people, but there were the ones for whom money was their god. While money meant nothing anymore, goods did, and those people wanted everything.

At least on the farm, they hadn't seen any other people. From the house, they had a good view of the roads leading to the farm, and it would be difficult for anyone to sneak up on them. After the men in the forest, Noah had warned the kids not to wander off alone. The world might have seemed empty, but it wasn't. He'd left Dexter with one of his hunting rifles, and there had been a few guns left in the farmhouse with a fair amount of ammunition. The owner had obviously been a hunter, as the various trophies displayed on the walls attested to. Vivian had hunted with her father a few times, and Dexter had gone once with a friend. They weren't exactly a formidable pair, but hopefully, they wouldn't need to use the weapons at all.

He signaled his exit from the highway upon seeing the sign to Leona's town. Too bad he couldn't call her and warn her that he was coming. Noah pressed his wound. It was starting to itch, and he wondered if he could take the bandage off.

Noah located Leona's street and, taking no chances, started honking his horn as he turned down it. A few minutes later, Leona emerged from her home, her trusty gun in hand, but her wary expression turned into a smile as Noah parked in front of her house.

"Welcome back. I didn't expect you so soon." She approached Noah's window. "Is this your brother and his family coming up behind you?"

Noah's smile faded. "I didn't get good news about my brother. He died."

Leona dipped her head. "I'm so sorry, Noah."

"Thank you. Fortunately, his ex-wife and my niece and nephew made it through, and I found them. They're heading to the farm too."

"Excellent." She squinted at the truck behind Noah's. "Who's that behind the wheel? He looks kind of young to be driving."

"He is. His name is Ethan. He's alone in the world but came to Cassie's aid the other day. He's a good kid."

"Very good. Okay, I'm almost ready. I was hoping you'd come back and spent most of yesterday packing everything. Honestly, I'm not sure what I would have done if you hadn't returned." She laughed. "I probably would have gone off searching for your mythical farm."

Noah grinned. "It's hardly mythical, and I should have told you where it was just in case. You could have always gone there and joined up with Dexter and Vivian. They'd have welcomed you if you told them I sent you."

Cassie's door slammed, and she approached Noah's truck. "Hello. I'm Cassie." She nodded to Leona, who returned it.

"A pleasure to meet you. I'm Leona."

Cassie turned to Noah. "So, what's the plan?"

"Noah graciously extended me an invitation to move to the farm with him and the other lovely family living there." Leona looked to Noah for confirmation.

"Yes. The offer still stands."

"I have decided to accept, if it's okay with you as well, Cassie."

Cassie smiled, her face happier than Noah had seen since he'd found her yesterday.

"Of course, Leona. If Noah invited you, then you're fine in my book."

Noah lifted an eyebrow at Cassie, but she only paused for a moment to look at him before returning her attention to Leona. "The kids have to go to the bathroom. Is there a safe place to go? I don't want them wandering around if there might be something that they shouldn't see."

"If they go around to the back of my house, I have an outhouse I made out of a shed. It has a simple composting toilet in it. I even have toilet paper."

Cassie's eyebrows shot up, and she clapped her hands. "Very nice! I think I'll use the facilities myself." She laughed then. "I can't believe I'm excited to go use an outhouse, but after the last few months, it's a true luxury."

"We have them at the farm too," Noah said. It was the first thing they'd done when moving to the farm. They'd even rigged solar-powered ventilation fans. That was Noah's true pride and joy. He made a mental note to see about finding press-on lights to go in them for nighttime use.

"Great. Well, I'm going to get the kids."

Ethan lifted himself out of the cab of the truck, sitting on the window ledge, his feet on the driver's seat. "Should I back the truck up?" He pointed to Leona's driveway.

Leona patted Noah's arm through the window then moved to Ethan's truck. Noah hopped out of the cab. "Leona, I'd like you to meet Ethan."

"It's very good to meet you, young man. I hear you're coming with us to the farm."

"Yeah. Cassie said I could." He bit his lip, sending Noah a brief nod before sliding back into the truck cab. "So, I should back in so we can load up?"

Noah nodded. He sized up the driveway and the truck. "Do you want me to do it?" It was a fairly narrow driveway.

Ethan shook his head. "I need to learn."

Shrugging, Noah followed Leona to the house. "Show me what you need me to take."

"You really shouldn't be lifting anything just yet." Leona turned after walking through the doors. She hadn't been kidding. The entryway where Noah had been shot only days before was packed with boxes, plastic bins, and trash bags stuffed full of items. He wasn't sure what all was in them, but even though he'd only known Leona for a few days, he was certain she'd packed purposefully. He had been so impressed with her survival skills, he couldn't wait to get back to the farm with the group and introduce her to Vivian, Dexter, and the kids.

With all of their skills combined, they had a chance to really make a new life on the farm. "I'm fine, Leona. I just spent the morning loading the truck. I barely felt a twinge." It was a lie, but it wasn't too bad, and the more he moved, the better he felt.

"Okay, well, if you want to get started with this, or…" She hesitated. "I have an old exam table from my practice stored away in a shed out back, along with some other items. Could we load that first? I don't want to forget them."

"Absolutely."

Cassie appeared in the doorway, the kids at her side. "We're ready to help you load up."

"How's Ethan doing with getting the truck up the drive?" Noah moved around Cassie and saw Ethan put the truck in drive and move forward, straightening the tires before reversing. He jogged around the truck and motioned Ethan to keep going back, holding up his hand when the truck was within ten feet of the garage. "Perfect. Good job."

Ethan looked as though he was trying to hide a grin as he gave a nonchalant shrug. "Now what?"

They spent about an hour loading up Leona's items. Dino sniffed everything, and Leona spoiled him, giving him bits of food she said she hadn't had enough of to make worth saving. The dog loved it all, eating stale potato chips and old cereal with indiscriminate gusto.

In addition to the medical supplies, there was her bed, baskets of towels, blankets, and sheets, and boxes of stored food. Noah was shocked at how much she'd managed to stockpile, but she had started sooner than most people and had access to regular grocery stores. If only they had all seen the signs early enough, he thought, maybe they could have isolated better, and more people would have survived.

"Before we leave, I have a treat for you all." Leona went into her kitchen and returned with a large bowl of fresh strawberries and blueberries. There was even a bit of watermelon in it. "A fruit salad. The strawberries were the last. I picked them a few weeks ago and stored them in the coolest part of the basement, after a water and vinegar rinse. It helps keep them fresh a little longer. The rest, I preserved, so we'll have those later. The same with the blueberries. They're still in season, so we'll miss some as they ripen in the next few days, but these are perfect. The melon was the only one that had ripened already in my garden."

Noah's mouth watered at the sight of fresh fruit. They sat on Leona's front stoop, using old bowls that Leona was leaving behind.

"This is really good, Leona." Ethan tipped his bowl and drained the juice.

"I'm glad you enjoyed it. Would you like some more?"

Ethan shot Noah a look as if asking permission.

Confused, Noah simply shrugged.

After a brief hesitation, Ethan took a second helping.

The break lasted only about fifteen minutes. Noah set his bowl and spoon on the porch. It felt odd to just leave it, but chances were good that they would never be back. "Is everyone ready?" He looked at Leona. "Would you like to ride with me or one of the other two?"

She turned and looked at the others and said, "If you don't mind, and if it's okay, I'd love to ride with Cassie. It's been ages since I spoke to another woman. And the children have been a delight."

Cassie's mouth widened. "I'd love it, and so would the kids. I'm not sure if they will remain delightful, but if it gets to be too much, you can switch vehicles."

Noah took a sip from a can of V8 Leona had passed around to everyone. He had never cared for the drink before, but given all of the physical work, it hit the spot. They definitely had gotten all of their required vitamins and nutrients today. "Okay, we're ready to roll. Do you feel comfortable driving a full truck, Ethan?"

"I guess so. I've never had it this full before, but I'll be extra careful."

"I know you will. I was just asking because… well, never mind. No reason. You've been doing a great job." He smiled, trying to ease the kid's mind.

An hour or so later, the western sky darkened, and Noah frowned. The stretch of highway they were on was littered with wrecks, and it was slow going weaving around them. Their top speed had barely hit thirty miles per hour. The next exit was still miles north, and Noah contemplated whether they could they make it there before the storm hit.

THIRTY

Ethan gripped the wheel as the truck rocked from a sudden blast of wind. "Hang on, Dino." The dog cowered on the seat. "It's okay." He released his death grip on the wheel for a second to give Dino an encouraging few pats on the head.

A few seconds later, the first large splatters of rain hit the windshield. He fumbled for the wipers but couldn't find the button. He had never used them before and hadn't thought to look for them. He slowed to a crawl until one of his swipes at levers and buttons resulted in the wipers sweeping across the windshield. Able to see again, he hit the gas to catch up with Noah, who had opened a large gap between their vehicles. He checked to see if Cassie was behind him. Sometimes, she swung into other lanes and took an alternate path, staying even with him instead of being behind him. While the front window was clear between swipes, he couldn't see out of the side windows or mirrors. The rain was coming down too hard. The sound of it drumming on the roof of the cab filled his ears, and he found it hard to think.

Another blast hit the truck, causing it to swerve to the right. Ethan tried to fight the blast and yanked the wheel to the left. Suddenly, the truck spun, teetered, then slammed into something, coming to an instant stop. Dino yelped.

Ethan sat behind the wheel, stunned.

"Dino?" He turned to find the dog on the floor of the truck but already with his front paws on the seat, jumping up. He thrust his nose into Ethan's side. Still too shaken to respond, Ethan absently petted the animal.

He'd crashed the truck. They were going to hate him. He never should have yanked the steering wheel. He rested his head on it. He was such an idiot.

Dino whimpered and licked Ethan's face.

"Ethan! Are you okay?" Cassie pounded on his window.

He lifted his head. "I'm sorry. I crashed the truck."

"Unlock the doors."

Ethan hadn't realized they were locked but remembered hearing the click after he'd started the engine. They must have locked automatically. He tried to push the unlock button, but a sudden pain in his left arm made him yelp. "Ow!"

He had to cross over and push the button with his right hand. He cradled his left arm.

Cassie stood on the running board and reached in. "Oh my God, are you okay?" She reached for his head, turning it. "You're bleeding!"

Ethan blinked. "My head is okay."

Cassie turned and looked at the driver's side window. "You must have hit it on the window. Does your arm hurt?"

"Just a little. I'm so sorry, Cassie. Now what'll I do?"

She ignored his question and said, "Sit tight for a minute, okay, Ethan?" She stepped down, and he heard her voice as if coming from a distance.

"He's got a bruise and a little bleeding on his head. Also, his left arm is hurting him."

Leona appeared in the open door. "Hey there, Ethan. I'm just going to look you over before we get you out of here, okay?"

She had him track her finger with his eyes as she moved it from side to side and up and down. Then she felt his neck and head, asking him if things hurt. She looked in his ears, even going to the other side of the truck to look him over from that side, telling him not to turn his head yet. She even checked his mouth and nose, asking him if any of his teeth felt loose. He ran his tongue over them and was glad to find them all intact. His arm started to throb as the shock wore off, and he couldn't stifle a whimper when she gently examined it. She gave his belly a few prods, asking him about pain, but he felt fine except for a growing headache and his arm.

Cassie left for a few minutes, but Noah appeared during the exam and hopped into the passenger side of the cab. "Hang in there, Ethan." He touched Ethan's shoulder, giving it a light squeeze, as if afraid of hurting him.

It was Ethan's undoing. He blinked fast and hard as his vision blurred. "I'm so sorry, Noah. I promise I'll make it up to you all if you let me stay with you. Whatever's broken in the back, I'll replace somehow. I'll scour every house and store until—"

"Hold on there, Ethan. Nobody's kicking you out. Why would we do that?" Noah leaned forward, his hand resting on the nape of Ethan's neck.

"I wrecked the truck." He hiccupped and stared down into his lap, embarrassed at the tears that trickled from his eyes as well as getting in an accident.

Noah's hand fanned out on Ethan's neck, cradling the back of his head. "Listen to me, Ethan. The storm blew you halfway across the highway. I saw it in my mirror. Even an experienced truck driver would have had a hard time controlling his truck. You've been driving how long? A week or two?"

Ethan gave a strangled chuckle. "Not even. Five days? I think?"

Noah laughed, squeezing Ethan's neck before he let go and patted Dino. The dog's tail wagged and swept across Noah's face, making the man sputter.

Ethan laughed again. He looked out, surprised at the slash of sunlight cutting across the lanes. The rain had eased to a sprinkle. The storm had mostly passed.

"Here's what we're going to do. I spotted an abandoned U-Haul truck not far ahead, and I already tried to start it while Leona was checking you over. Shockingly, it started. It even had a mostly full gas tank. So, look, you saved me having to siphon gas today. The extra gas I brought with us can go in the other two vehicles. While the good doctor gets you patched up, Cassie and I are going to move everything over. It won't be hard. I'm going to drive it around and back it up to this one so we can slide everything right onto the other truck.

The little kids fell asleep, so we don't even have to keep them entertained."

"So, you're not mad at all?"

"I'd give you a hug if I didn't worry it would hurt you more. No. I'm not mad. Cassie's beside herself with worry, and Leona is getting stuff together to splint your arm. All we want is for you to be okay." He started to back out, giving Dino a good scratch behind his ears as he eased through the open door. Before shutting the door, he paused. "By the way, if she offers you pain pills, that will make the rest of the trip a piece of cake, so be sure to take them. They're like magic." He winked at Ethan and shut the door.

"I guess they do like me, Dino." Ethan rubbed his eyes with the heel of his hand. He had a family again. He wasn't alone anymore.

NOAH EASED the new truck in behind his truck, which Leona drove. Ethan rode with her, and just as Noah had suggested, he'd taken the pills Leona had offered. She'd insisted, and when Ethan was out, she had Noah help her set the kid's arm. Ethan's eyes had flown open, and he'd screamed but then fell back asleep as Leona wrapped his arm with an Ace bandage. She said she would give it a few days before she created a plaster cast for him. For the time being, he was as comfortable as possible.

The rest of the drive was uneventful, and they only stopped to let everyone use the bathroom. Cassie had passed bread slathered in jam to everyone to eat as they drove. Poor Ethan hadn't been able to eat his and had puked after trying. Leona said it wasn't unusual. It could be from the blow to his head, the pain pills, or both. But he was drinking water okay.

Noah forced himself not to go faster than was safe under the conditions. He was eager to get home. He longed to see the sunset over the slight rise to the west and hear the birds calling down by the stream before they bedded down for the night. He missed Ava and Jalen and had a dozen ideas he wanted to share with Dexter. He even missed Vivian and her sarcasm. He couldn't wait to see how she and Cassie got along, and how Ava would take to having two playmates and Jalen to having a boy near his own age to hang out with.

He turned onto their road and started honking the horn, grinning when he saw Dexter and Vivian both show up, rifles clutched across them. They clearly recognized Noah's truck but looked wary when Noah drove the U-Haul up.

Noah rolled his window down. "Hey guys, stand down. It's just me, my family, and a few new friends."

AUTHOR NOTE

I started writing this book in the spring of 2019. I'm a slow writer anyway, and this book was especially challenging. I never knew that when I was finishing the final chapters we would in the midst of a real life pandemic! For some writers, writing is an escape from the real world, but for me this story felt like real life taken to an extreme. It didn't help that my day job is as a respiratory therapist so I was/am dealing with it on the front lines to some extent. I kind of feel like I had no relief from pandemics.

Anyway, I hope you've enjoyed this book and if you have a moment, a review would be greatly appreciated! Receive my free short story collection when you sign up for my New Release & Newsletter list. Tell me where to send your free ebook

Find links to my books, including Infection: Book One of the Sympatico Syndrome Series. on my website:
M.P. McDonald

CONTACT ME

I love hearing from readers, so feel free to drop me an email telling me your thoughts about the book or series.

Email: mailto:mmcdonald64@gmail.com

Come and like my Facebook page! I hold contests and post updates and tidbits about the series. I love interacting with fans on the page:

M.P. McDonald Facebook

ACKNOWLEDGMENTS

I am so thankful for the fantastic editors at Red Adept Editing. I can't say enough about the insightful and timely edit provided by Kate, and the thorough proofreading job performed by Kat. Thank you both! And I'm grateful to Lynn at Red Adept for working with my crazy schedule so that I could complete this on time.

I would not have finished this book if it wasn't for the motivation author J.R. Tate gave me. If not for our renewed writing sessions in February of this year, I'd still be struggling through the middle of this book. She's a wonderful writer and not only did she inspire me, but half the motivation was getting to read her fantastic new book, Inception, as it was being written. If you're looking for something new to read, go check it out. J.R. Tate on Amazon.

And, finally, special thanks to my family for being amazing in this crazy time.

Printed in Great Britain
by Amazon

33770340R00126